C. Renee Freeman

A Fortune to Claim

From the author of
Love at the
Woolly Bookworm Shop

Copyright © 2025 C. Renee Freeman
All rights reserved.
ISBN: 979-8-9988382-2-4

This book is a work of the writer's imagination. Names, characters, places, and events have been created by the writer to present the story or are used fictitiously to enhance the story.

Resemblance to any place, event, or person (living or dead) is entirely coincidental.

No part of this book may be reproduced, or stored in a retrieval system, or transmitted in any form or by any means, electronic, mechanical, photocopying, recording, or otherwise, without express written permission of the publisher.

Library of Congress Control Number: 2018675309
Printed in the United States of America

.

A Fortune to Claim

This book is dedicated to all the caregivers in the world.

*You work tirelessly every day,
with little to no acknowledgment of what you do.*

On behalf of all the people who should say it…

Thank you!

A Fortune to Claim

Warning

This book contains a very brief reference to suicide. The central character also struggles with unresolved grief and other issues.

If you or someone you know is in crisis, please call **988** in the US to talk with someone who could help. Alternatively, please seek assistance from your doctor, a trained mental health professional, a member of the clergy, or even talk with a friend. You are not alone. Talk to someone!

ONE

WAS IT THE BLARING SOUND OF A CAR HORN THAT YANKED HER FROM THE DEPTHS OF SLEEP? Or perhaps it was the persistent chime of her cell phone that broke through the haze of her dreams?

No, it had to be the phone. The sound was too soft to match the annoying blast from the car.

Simone Grant's hand fumbled along the nightstand beside her bed as her fingers searched for the phone. They brushed past a half-empty water bottle and knocked a book onto the floor. Finally, she wrapped her fingers around the device.

As she slowly opened her eyes, she realized she was in an unfamiliar room. The walls were painted pale gray and adorned with black-and-white pictures of a cityscape that she did not recognize.

The phone that she clutched in her hands was the only familiar object. Raising it to her face, she scanned the blue glow of the screen and noticed the time: *7:30 A.M.* The crisp, digital numbers bounced repeatedly. With a few swift taps, she silenced the alarm.

She wished she could also silence the rising tide of questions about how she ended up there. This was not her home, a realization that sent a shiver down her spine. The very idea of waking up in a stranger's bed, without a single memory of how she got there, was utterly unthinkable. Sure, some people relished the thrill of a one-night stand, but that was never her style. She preferred the safety of familiarity.

Nothing particularly unusual had happened, yet the space around her was foreign. A thin sliver of light peeked through a gap in the heavy curtains draped over the window. The illumination was faint, casting a dim light that barely penetrated the room's darkness. The curtains themselves, a bold black houndstooth pattern, were thick and imposing. She didn't recognize the fabric, further amplifying her unease. She lifted herself from the pillow and tried to gather her thoughts.

The yellow cotton curtains in her room at home did not hang from a vaulted ceiling to a carpeted floor like the ones in this room. And the curtains in her familiar bedroom were so thin that the morning's light awakened her early every morning. Sleeping late there was impossible.

She spotted a pair of black leather armchairs beside the window. Nearby, a portable AC unit pumped out cold air. Its green digital display showed numbers in Celsius, not Fahrenheit. *Strange*, she thought to herself.

The bed was different, too. Its luxurious linens caressed her skin. The mattress cradled her body in the vast space that its king-size provided, and the pillows with their fine cotton covers were plump. This bed was totally unlike the one where she usually slept. Gone was the familiar bed - no threadbare sheets, lumpy mattress, and limp pillows.

She spread her hand across the smooth, cool sheets. There were no indentations where someone else had slept, so it was safe to assume that no one was or had been in the bed with her. Listening carefully, she did not hear anyone in the bathroom either.

Stories of people who were kidnapped usually did not end with the victims finding themselves alone in luxurious rooms. The whole situation was very peculiar. She rubbed her forehead as if the action might sweep away the cobwebs in her brain.

Then, the fog lifted from her brain. With a start, she remembered where she was: Edinburgh, Scotland.

She stretched her arms high above her head, savoring the exquisite experience of a good night's sleep. As her knuckles brushed the gray velvet of the headboard, rather than the solid wood of her familiar bed, its silkiness further reinforced the difference in place.

Indulging in the luxury of sleeping in late and enjoying the comforts of an elegant hotel were rare treats for someone who hadn't been on a vacation in years. She felt almost embarrassed by the pleasure she derived from the experience.

Simone swung her legs over the edge of the bed. The gray satin bedspread slipped away as she rose. She stumbled toward the window, squinting her eyes in anticipation of the harsh morning light.

"This is going to hurt," she mumbled as she reached for the curtains and pulled them apart. The morning sun would no doubt blind her with its light.

Only...there was no sunlight. A steady drizzle of rain splashed against the window's glass, tracing tiny trails down the smooth surface. White mist enveloped the tops of the buildings and blocked the sun's rays. The city was blanketed in a gloomy fog. It could have been any time of day.

The view from the window was the opposite of the backyard in her home in Oak Hill, North Carolina. She was accustomed to seeing tall trees, lush grass, and wild turkeys. Here, she faced the dingy yellow façade of a six-story building that stood outside her window. Its sandstone blocks were smudged with centuries of coal dust. The square bricks on the ground level resembled teeth, tidy rows perfectly fitted one against another. The other floors were supported by blocks of stone hand-carved into large, generic rectangles. If those blocks were teeth, they would have belonged to the buck-toothed cousins who lacked proper dental care. The building looked as grim as the weather.

The horn blasted again. This time, it was held longer to emphasize the driver's displeasure. She widened the opening in the curtains and peered down at the cobbled street below. The scene that was unfolding there made her giggle.

The driver of a red car leaned out the car's window

and repeatedly blasted the horn. He made rude gestures at a truck parked in the middle of the road. The truck's driver stood beside the vehicle, enthusiastically returning the gestures, before finally climbing into the truck and easing it out of the way. As the car passed the truck, its driver continued his barrage of foul language.

Some things are universal, Simone thought as she moved away from the window. How often was she blocked in downtown Asheville by delivery drivers who thought it was acceptable to park wherever they wanted? Flinging curses at the offended parties never altered the drivers' behavior, but it always felt good.

With the curtains drawn back, the room was sufficiently lightened for a closer inspection. Its mid-century modern aesthetic created a sleek, clean look. The color palette consisted mainly of shades of gray, black, and silver. A massive, flat-screen television hung above an inky black console. Its drawers provided a limited amount of storage. She wondered if people who favored this architectural style had a limited number of clothing pieces and thus did not require much storage space.

Beside the window, a small hammered steel table sat between two black leather armchairs. The table's circular top was connected to a chunky, square base by a cylindrical rod that was slim at the top and broad at the bottom. The table was placed in such a way that it was meant to conceal the portable AC unit, but it failed at the task. The room's chic aesthetic was almost ruined by the modern appliance that had obviously been added after its design.

The hotel room's decor was unlike the "thrift store

chic" style back home. Burdened with a mountain of student loan debt and a low-paying job as a waitress, Simone lacked the resources to have a proper design theme. The room of the house she shared with her friend Emma Robinson was smaller than the hotel room and not as lavishly furnished.

Shared – past tense. She sighed heavily. Now that Emma had passed away, what would she do? If the woman had not provided her with a place to live, renting an apartment of her own would have been impossible.

Her heart still ached whenever she thought about Emma. Not just a friend. Oh, no, something so much more. The woman became a surrogate mother in the turbulent aftermath of her biological mother's death. After everything that happened, attending and ultimately finishing college would have been impossible.

Abandoning her college education to tend to her grief-stricken and often drunk father seemed easier. "At your mama's funeral, I made a promise to her," Emma frequently told her. "You <u>will</u> get an education!"

Though she succeeded in getting a college degree, it felt like the only success in her life. Piles of rejection letters from uninterested publishers and literary agents offered a frustrating reminder that no one wanted her novels.

To make matters worse, the job search was disappointing. It had yielded only one positive result, an offer that she ultimately could not accept.

The sole consistent employment she managed to

find was as a waitress at a local restaurant. The position felt wildly beneath her qualifications. Every day, she swallowed her pride and donned a crisp white shirt and black apron. She took orders from customers who often barely noticed her. It was a far cry from what she had envisioned her life after graduation would be.

When she was at work, she couldn't shake the nagging feeling of underachievement. Her college diploma, framed and gathering dust at home, reminded her of dreams unfulfilled and aspirations that seemed out of reach.

It would have been easier to give up, yet Emma always pushed her to keep trying. "You are meant to be a writer," her friend said, "not a waitress."

Her friend repeatedly told her that resigning to the circumstances and giving up on her dreams was not a path worth following. Instead, she encouraged Simone to cling to the hope that something better lay ahead, waiting just beyond the horizon of her current reality.

Simone shook her head. She was on the trip of a lifetime.

"No tears," she reminded herself.

Isn't that what the will said?

"Well, it said other things, too," Simone noted as she headed for the bathroom.

TWO

SIMONE WATCHED THE NUMBERS ON THE SCREEN ABOVE HER AS THE ELEVATOR SLOWLY DESCENDED TO THE LOBBY. The doors slid open. She spotted her guide and inwardly cringed. If he wore flashing lights and paraded around naked, he still wouldn't be as conspicuous as he was then. Taking a deep breath, she exited the elevator and smiled tightly.

She approached the man with an extended hand. "Simone Grant." She felt a tiny callus on his thumb as he shook her hand. *That's odd*, she thought.

"Robert Gordon. A pleasure to meet you." He motioned toward the door. "Shall we begin?"

She ignored the snickers from the front desk staff and followed him. His outfit was not what she would have chosen. His employer, the Castles and Cairns Touring Company, must have thought his attire fit the stereotypical image of a Scottish Highlander whom some tourists wanted for a guide. Well, she intended to correct that false impression as soon as possible. Fulfilling Emma's final wishes certainly would not include eternal embarrassment over her guide's attire.

The tartan plaid of his kilt was a pattern of dark blue, black, and green shades. The garment extended to his knees, with a wide piece of cloth wrapped around his shoulder and held together with a silver pin resembling a clan's crest. An oversized linen shirt with billowy sleeves was not flattering.

The fat sporran, which appeared to be made from roadkill, didn't do him any favors. It hung limply at his waist as if it too was embarrassed by the display. The final touches were white socks that climbed to his knees and a pair of shiny, black leather shoes with silver buckles. Somewhere, Emma laughed hysterically.

To avoid continued scorn from the front desk staff, she waited until they were outside to speak with him. "Don't wear that outfit anymore," she hissed. "It's embarrassing for both of us."

The expression of relief on his face told her everything she needed to know. He remained polite, though, merely nodding and mumbling his assent.

As they climbed to the top of St. Giles' Street, Mr. Gordon talked about the history of Old Town Edinburgh. She struggled to pay attention. Jet lag and the lingering disbelief that she was in Scotland left her feeling disoriented and discombobulated.

"The itinerary listed several places – Edinburgh Castle, St. Giles' Cathedral, the usual tourist spots," he said. His tone was a little too gruff for someone who should be accustomed to dealing with sightseers. "We only have one day slated here, so we cannot see everything. Pick what's most important to you, and we will go there. Where do you want to start first?"

"If we climb to the top of the Royal Mile, we can visit Edinburgh Castle." The guide pointed across the street, to the right. "If we head over there, we can go to the National Museum of Scotland and Greyfriars' Cemetery."

Mr. Gordon waved his hand in front of them. "Or, we could pop into St. Giles' Cathedral on the way to the Palace of Holyroodhouse and the new Scottish Parliament building at the bottom of the hill." He donned the brown, waxed-canvas jacket that he clutched in his hands. The ensemble became slightly less noticeable. "It's a bit of a walk. If you choose that option, we can hire a car."

"Whatever you think is best," she said, turning her head from left to right and chewing her lower lip. She felt completely overwhelmed. "You're the guide."

"Very well. Let's visit St. Giles before we head to Holyroodhouse."

As they crossed the street, she tapped his arm. "I am capable of walking down the hill." Simone pointed to his feet. "Those shoes don't look comfortable. I'll understand if you aren't up for a long walk. We can call for a car."

"I appreciate your consideration, but I can manage," he said through gritted teeth. He seemed insulted. Had she offended him?

St. Giles' Cathedral was packed with tourists,

making it very difficult to listen. Should she ask him to raise his voice? It seemed odd to speak loudly in a church. The noise from the crowd destroyed the usual silence one normally enjoyed in a reverential setting. In the end, she did not ask him, mainly because she feared irritating the man even more than she already had.

Mr. Gordon noted various architectural features, particularly the stone angels playing bagpipes. He discussed the remarkable history of St. Giles' Cathedral, which was considered the mother church of Presbyterianism. He guided her toward John Knox's statue and told her about the preacher's religious reforms and austere views.

Throughout it all, Simone nodded but did not ask any questions. The whole experience was mind-boggling. For months, Emma and she talked about Scotland and all its magnificent sites. Never in a million years did she imagine standing in the church, much less starting a grand tour of the country.

As they left, she caught the annoyed expression on her guide's face. Her own dealings with the public taught her to always remain pleasant, regardless of how irritating the customers were. Apparently, her guide did not understand that fundamental fact. Or maybe he was just grumpy because of the ridiculous outfit. She decided to give him the benefit of the doubt and make an allowance for his unfriendly behavior. She held her tongue, even though she wanted to tell him how rude he was being.

The long walk to the Palace offered a break from the crowded, noisy Cathedral. Mr. Gordon continued to talk about the surroundings. As they passed the buildings and closes that lined the street, he tried to paint a picture of how the area would have looked in the 1600s. Simone was fascinated by his stories, but she felt rushed. Could they stop and take a breath for a moment? She wanted to appreciate the location.

Finally, she decided Emma would never forgive her if she didn't enjoy the trip. She paused several paces behind the man and stood in the middle of the sidewalk, staring at the sign for *The World's End* pub. The five-storied building sat on the corner of a cobbled street. The exterior of the ground floor was painted a distinctive blue. Above the door, the pub's title was displayed in gold letters against a black trim. The overall look set it apart from the other buildings on the same street.

"The Flodden Wall used to be here," Mr. Gordon explained, when he noticed that she wasn't following him. "It was part of the fort that protected the city during the 16th century. To Edinburgh's inhabitants of the time, the wall marked the end of their world."

She looked at the surface of the street. "It switches from cobblestones to asphalt here, too," she remarked. "I guess it was the end of the road back then."

"Can you imagine what it would have been like to have your world defined by a city's walls?" she asked. "Of course, if we never travel, it kinda is, isn't it?"

He offered his first smile. "A very astute observation, Ms. Grant."

They continued on the trek down the street. She could not resist touching the rough stone walls or staring at the old buildings. Instead of soaring skyscrapers, the tallest building seemed to be only six stories high. It was unlike the city centers usually seen in America. Plus, back in her hometown, the mostly wooden structures were a hundred years old at most, but these buildings were *centuries* old.

She stopped at the bottom of the hill in front of the new Scottish Parliament building. Its nouveau architectural style and untarnished exterior dramatically contrasted the surrounding buildings. Pointing to the metal embellishments affixed to the side of the building, she said, "Those cut-outs look like a child's drawing of a gun."

"I take it you're not a fan of post-modern architecture?"

"I suppose not."

"Then, you will appreciate Holyroodhouse. Parts of it were built in the 1600s."

"I read the gardens are lovely."

"Aye, they are. Queen Elizabeth II used to have parties there."

"Emma always loved flowers." She looked away when she said it, her eyes misty.

"My boss said Emma Robinson was your late auntie."

"Not by blood – and not really an auntie. More like a surrogate mother." Simone looked up at him. "She was my mother's friend. When Mom died, I moved in with Emma."

A loud group of people lumbered by them, briefly interrupting a conversation that had suddenly become very personal. "I am truly sorry about your mother,

Ms. Grant."

"You can call me 'Simone' if you like." She turned her back and resumed the walk. Over her shoulder, she said, "My mom died when I was 16, so it wasn't recent. Emma died a few months ago, though."

"Again, I am sorry for your losses…Simone." His tone softened. "And, please, call me 'Robert' if we are going to be less formal."

"Emma was supposed to take this tour. You got me instead." She turned to face him, a half-smile on her lips. "Aren't you lucky?"

Robert chuckled as he guided them toward the Palace's ticket area. Simone waited while he purchased their tickets, using the opportunity to observe the crowd. The other tourists spoke so many different languages that she had never heard in Oak Hill. "You aren't in North Carolina anymore," she whispered to herself.

They walked between the twin turrets and iron gate guarding the castle. Once in the courtyard, they stopped before a ruddy gray fountain. The fountain was a beautiful object that hinted at the ornate pieces they would find inside. Intricately carved stone lions and soldiers guarded the magnificent crown at its top. Robert commented that it was one of his favorite objects at the Palace.

He gestured toward the grand building in front of them. "The Palace has been home to Scottish and English royalty for centuries."

"The left side looks different from the right side."

"Aye, good eye. The left side is the original part of the castle and therefore much older."

"Why is everything so dirty?" She waved her hand at the sandstone walls covered in ancient grime. "Don't y'all have pressure washers over here?"

He laughed but stopped when he realized she was serious. "Old Town is a UNESCO world heritage site. There are strict regulations about any changes to our old buildings."

"Besides," he added, "the stone is hundreds of years old. It would turn to sand if we tried to clean it."

She accepted the explanation with a shrug and took a step forward.

"Do you want to take some pictures of the exterior?" he asked as he grabbed her arm. "I'll wait."

"I guess I should get it over with." She handed him a cell phone. "Can you take a picture of me in front of the fountain?"

He obliged. In the first picture, her smile felt forced. Then, she spotted the unicorn statue that proudly guarded its perch on the fountain. Remembering the mythical beast was the national animal of Scotland, she grinned broadly. Emma once told her that unicorns killed lions and that the lion was the national animal of England. Her friend would have laughed at the sight. Without asking, the guide snapped another photo at that moment.

"Thanks," she said when he returned the phone to her. With a few taps, she sent the first photo to the attorney. Slipping the phone into her pocket, she walked toward the Palace.

"Holyroodhouse is the official royal residence in Scotland," her guide said.

"I thought Balmoral was?"

"Balmoral is the private residence of the monarchy. The Palace of Holyroodhouse is the official state residence. They have official functions here."

"But, I thought they offered special visits to politicians and diplomats at Balmoral, too."

"They do."

Simone rolled her eyes. "I don't understand the British monarchy."

"Truth be told, neither do I."

He ushered her inside the Palace. Moving from room to room, Robert offered tidbits of history and explained who the figures depicted in the many paintings adorning the walls were. For the most part, she merely nodded at his comments and did not ask follow-up questions. Steeped in centuries of history, the elegant surroundings prompted a respectful silence.

The displays of the Crown's fine diamonds were impressive. Fashioned into splendid necklaces, earrings, and tiaras, the stones sparkled against a backdrop of rich red velvet. How much were they worth? Shaking her head, she estimated it was more than a waitress earned in many lifetimes.

The chambers of Mary, Queen of Scots, piqued her interest. The four-poster bed and heavy tapestries hanging on the walls were humbler than she expected for a queen. Simone giggled when Robert pointed to the spot where the woman's private secretary and rumored lover, David Rizzio, was murdered. He told her to look closely for the bloodstains on the hardwood floor. It was probably a gag the locals played on the tourists.

After walking through the Palace, she happily accepted his invitation to view the ruins of Holyrood Abbey and the adjoining garden. A refreshing walk outside was an excellent idea.

The East Doorway was the first spot they encountered. Its vaulted ceiling and stone arches soared high overhead. She stared open-mouthed at work produced before modern tools and computer-generated engineering existed.

He motioned for them to take a seat on a stone bench. "It is impressive, isn't it?"

"What's the story with this place?"

"The Abbey was founded in 1128. Legend has it that King David I hunted in the nearby woods. He was thrown from his horse when a hart startled the beast. Suddenly, a crucifix appeared. Its brilliant light scared the hart, saving the King's life. As an act of thanksgiving, he commanded that an abbey be built on this site."

"When did the Abbey lose its roof?"

"In the 1540s, English armies stripped the lead from the roof. Then, during the Scottish Reformation, looters did more damage. Things just got worse from there."

"Has there ever been an effort to restore it?"

"Aye. Over the years, many repairs have been suggested." He gestured toward the roofless part of the Abbey. "As you see, nothing was done. I am glad. I like the ruin as it is."

"Me too."

They meandered through the ruin of the Abbey. She touched the rough, hand-carved stones of the walls and read the writing on the tablets affixed to them. The tablets memorialized various people buried there. Centuries of history left her speechless.

A genuine smile popped onto her face when they moved toward the garden. The day was gray and gloomy, making the colors of the garden all the more vibrant. The lime-green color of the grass contrasted with the darker greens of the trees and shrubs. White, yellow, and pink flowers refused to let the rain dampen their beauty. With the garden's cheerful display, she decided that it was impossible for anyone to be glum.

She asked him to take a picture of her beside a statue of a fiddle player. This time, she did not send the image to the attorney. Instead, Simone looked at it, smiled, and tucked away the phone. No one said photos for her own amusement were forbidden.

They exited the garden and went to the café in the courtyard. While viewing the plants, her stomach had growled. She knew he heard it but was too polite to say anything. Unfortunately, her appetite had not adjusted yet to the time difference.

He selected a ham toastie while she settled on a blueberry scone and tea. They found a table with an umbrella that protected them from the drizzling rain.

Simone smeared a hefty dollop of clotted cream onto one side of the split scone and fresh jam on the other. The job done, she smooshed the two pieces together and took a big bite of her creation.

"Sorry," she mumbled, her mouth full of food. "I love scones and clotted cream."

"Oh, aye, I can tell." He chuckled as he took a bite of the sandwich.

"When I was a little girl, Emma and I had tea parties. She always made trays of little sandwiches, scones, jam, and clotted cream. It was fabulous."

"You told me she became a surrogate mother to you. Did she live near your childhood home?"

She hesitated for a moment. They had a long trip ahead. If she were silent the whole time, it would be a miserable experience. She figured it was a good idea to reveal a little bit about herself, solely to make the trip pleasant.

"Yes, in the same town," she finally replied. "As I said earlier, I moved in with Emma after my mom died."

"Do you still live with her?" He shook his head. "Sorry, I meant…."

"No worries. Yeah, I stayed in the house after she died. Oak Hill is the only place I have ever known."

"Is it a small town?"

"A few thousand people live there. Most folks live in Asheville, which is a city not that far from us. It's very popular with tourists." She swept her hand wide. "You know all about tourists here in Edinburgh, don't you?"

"I do." He paused. "I live in Leith to escape the worst of it."

"Where's that?"

"It is a neighborhood north of Edinburgh. It is a

historic port area. The Royal Yacht Britannia is there."

"Queen Elizabeth's former yacht?"

"Aye. It is a floating museum now. If you like, we can go there next."

Simone dabbed her mouth with a paper napkin. "No, I am tired. After we finish eating, I think I will return to the hotel."

He glanced at his watch and looked incredulous. "It is only 1 o'clock. Isn't it a bit early?"

She yawned. "Jet lag." For added emphasis, she stretched her arms high above her head. "We have a big road trip ahead of us. I want to be refreshed."

"Speaking of…." He removed a piece of paper from the awful sporran. "Your friend made the itinerary. Would you like to modify any part of it? Perhaps you are interested in seeing something else."

With a smirk, she retrieved the phone from her pocket and tapped it several times. She spun it around so he could see the same itinerary on the screen. "Let's stick to what Emma wanted. When do we leave tomorrow morning?"

"Is 8 a.m. too early?"

"Nope." She tossed the napkin onto the table. She pointed to his empty plate and asked, "Are you done?"

They walked back to the hotel in silence. Though she was curious about her surroundings, she was equally serious about being tired. Like a heavy blanket, a mixture of jet lag and depression fell over her. Simone found it challenging to concentrate.

When they arrived at the hotel, she thanked him and hurried inside.

THREE

SIMONE STAGGERED INTO HER BEDROOM AND COLLAPSED ON THE BED. She could feel the fatigue dragging her eyelids to a close. After taking a deep breath, she exhaled all the stress that had accumulated throughout the day. The room was dimly lit, with a few rays of afternoon light filtering through partially opened curtains. The portable AC unit pumped cool air into the room, creating the perfect atmosphere for a restful nap.

As she tucked a pillow under her head, she longed for a moment of peace. Outside, the muted sounds of urban life provided an unfamiliar soundtrack of car engines, conversations, and assorted noise, yet it wasn't so loud that she couldn't sleep.

No, the noise outside her room was not the reason why she remained awake. A million thoughts raced through her mind. She imagined how invigorated she would feel after a quick nap. She would be ready to face whatever challenges lay ahead with renewed energy and determination, if only she could quiet her brain. Or, at least that's what she told herself.

Guilt was a real problem. The trip to Scotland was something Emma desperately wanted to take. During days when the latest round of chemotherapy left her friend bedridden and nauseated, she held Simone's hand and talked about the sights she wanted to see. Discussing the Scottish adventure gave the woman a distraction from the cancerous pain that ravaged her body and slowly sucked the life out of it.

In the final months they had left together, the beauty and allure of Scotland dominated their conversations. They often lost themselves in discussions about its misty highlands and charming villages. Pictures they found online and in guidebooks tantalized them with vivid images of a beautiful, ancient country.

They steadfastly avoided any mention of the disease that ravaged Emma, refusing to consider the possibility of a bleak outcome. Instead, they immersed themselves in dreams of Scotland and clung to the hope of better days to come.

Of course, when Christmas arrived, buying gifts with a Scottish theme was only natural. It was best to maintain the fiction that Emma could take the trip. Simone fondly remembered their last Christmas together. She bought Emma a calendar of handsome, shirtless Scottish men in kilts. Her friend giggled like a schoolgirl at the pictures. "It is all about the bonnie Glens of Scotland, dear," she had quipped wickedly.

Sadly, their celebration was short-lived. It soon became apparent that the woman would not live long enough to take the trip. She made Simone promise to go in her place.

Naturally, it would have been impossible to go. The trip was unaffordable because of the expense and the income lost from time away from work. However, the lie comforted her friend, so Simone crossed her fingers and agreed.

"I am so happy you will see these places," Emma told her in those final days.

When Robert proposed changing the itinerary, it filled her with anger. How dare he? Experiencing Scotland exactly how Emma intended was her final chance to share something with the woman. It sounded weird when said out loud. In some strange way, she felt she was following in her friend's footsteps.

"Of course, you made sure I could take the trip," Simone mumbled into the overwhelming silence of her room.

AFTER EMMA PASSED AWAY, SIMONE DREADED WHAT WOULD COME NEXT. The house would need to be sold, and she would have to relocate. The thought of finding a new place to live weighed heavily on her, filling her with anxiety. How long would it take to find an affordable apartment that could feel even remotely like the home she had shared with Emma?

Finally, weeks after the woman's death, it happened. The phone rang, shattering the silence of the lonely house she couldn't leave. When she glanced at the screen, her heart sank. It was the attorney who managed Emma's estate. She had dreaded the call for so long. The idea of leaving a cherished home felt like tearing away a part of her very soul.

She was summoned to the attorney's office the next day. Simone took the offered seat in front of the woman's desk and braced herself for the difficult conversation to come. She knew she couldn't avoid the inevitable much longer.

The meeting with the attorney was shocking, but not in the way she had imagined. A friendly young woman not long out of law school, the attorney eagerly shook Simone's hand and introduced herself as Joanna. Not "Ms. Whitmire." *Joanna*. So much for formality.

Emma wanted her to take the long-discussed trip to Scotland. All trip expenses would be covered *if one specific condition was met*. As the attorney explained the provisions of Emma's will, Simone was shocked. All she had to do was send a daily picture from Scotland to the attorney. Without asking if she intended to take the trip, Joanna gave her an envelope containing a credit card and foreign currency to cover any incidental expenses.

"My assistant will email you the plane ticket and travel details," she had said as she escorted Simone from her office. "You will receive the other distribution if you prove that you took the trip."

"By sending you a picture?"

"Exactly," Joanna answered. "Have fun!"

The other distribution.

Her friend was a very shrewd woman. Life's usual expenses and outrageous student loan debt put

Simone in a real bind. Until a big publishing house gave her a substantial advance for her writing, or maybe she won the lottery, a waitress' salary hardly provided what she needed.

Aware of every potential hurdle, Emma tossed in an incentive. The grand Scottish adventure must be taken to receive the second part of the inheritance. Simone began mentally packing her bags when the attorney told her the amount. Who could turn down the offer? Emma knew it would be irresistible.

One million dollars. Simone could quit her job and pay off the student loans. The stack of rejection letters for her novels could be ignored for a while. The money gave her time to focus solely on her writing without the pressure of finding a good income. Leaving Oak Hill and starting over in a new city was also possible.

She had so many options. All she had to do was take an all-expenses-paid trip to Scotland.

When she said it like that, it seemed childish to complain. And yet….

"You should have taken this trip, not me," she said aloud.

She rolled over and stared at the ceiling. "The guide showed up in a kilt, Emma!" She laughed. "Sorry to disappoint - his name is Robert, not Glen."

It felt good to talk to her friend, so she continued. "He is handsome. It won't be hard to travel around Scotland with him."

Robert *was* handsome, now that she thought about it. Sure, his outfit was atrocious. But, the rest of him? He did not disappoint.

His dark brown hair was cut in the respectful fashion of a proper tour guide, not too long or too short; nothing offensive. Whiskers of black, brown, and silver dotted along a square jawline and climbed halfway up his face toward high cheekbones that any woman would covet. Was he trying to grow a beard? Or was Robert one of those guys who liked a bit of scruff, thinking it made him look cool?

Then, she recalled his outfit. His employer obviously wanted the man to resemble every tourist's fantasy of a Scot, kitted out in a kilt and sporran. Someone obsessed with a suave appearance would not be caught dead in that ensemble. She wondered how he would look in normal clothing.

Oh, his eyes, she recalled wistfully. She could not forget those eyes. Resembling two pools of melted milk chocolate, they softened his appearance. Whenever Simone met his gaze, she quickly looked away. It would be easy to lose self-control between those eyes and his rich, deep voice.

Mentally, she shook herself. The trip was not meant to be a romantic Highland fling. *Just take the trip and collect the money*, she commanded.

Simone imagined echoes of her friend's laughter at the thought. "Oh, shut up!" she grumbled, grabbing a pillow and covering her face.

FOUR

SIMONE PACED ANXIOUSLY IN FRONT OF THE HOTEL ROOM WINDOW. She had been packed and ready since dawn. The sights and sounds of Edinburgh lingered in her mind, a vivid tapestry of history and culture that had stirred a surprising yearning for adventure. Each step she had taken yesterday through cobblestone streets that previously lived only in her imagination had fueled her spirit and ignited a desire to discover everything Emma and she had talked about for months. What other hidden treasures awaited her just outside her door?

Amidst her excitement, a shadow cast over her. "The sooner I complete the trip, the sooner I get the money," she whispered to herself. This journey was not just about exploration; it was also about necessity. That reality could not be ignored.

The cell phone buzzed. It was Robert. He informed her that he waited downstairs in the lobby.

She took a quick peek into the bathroom, making sure she hadn't forgotten anything. Of course, she hadn't, but it always paid to be careful. Who knew how difficult it might be to replace things? Then, she grabbed her luggage and headed downstairs.

When she saw him, she was relieved that the kilt was gone. It was replaced with a pair of dark blue trousers that hugged his firm butt. A gray, short-sleeved t-shirt stretched almost to bursting at the seams across his broad shoulders and trim waist. His tourist-friendly ensemble yesterday hid his fit body. She tried not to stare. *Damn, he's fine*, she thought.

The bored front desk attendant took her keycard, not bothering to look up from the computer screen. Taking care of checking out allowed Simone time to rearrange her features from admiration to disinterest. She decided it would be a bad idea to swoon like a smitten teenager. She was there for the money, not a romance.

Fortunately, Robert did not seem to notice her gawking at his looks. He took the luggage and held the door open. Motioning toward the burgundy Range Rover parked in front of the hotel, he said, "The tour company makes sure we ride in style."

Simone approached the vehicle, her gaze fixed on the door on the right side. As she reached for the handle, she caught sight of the steering wheel in front of the seat. Shaking her head in disbelief at her blunder, she turned on her heel and walked around to the other side of the car. Meanwhile, Robert was busy loading luggage into the back of the car, too absorbed in the task to notice her mix-up.

She slipped onto the car's plush seat. The faint

scent of leather filled the air, mingling with a hint of cologne from the man who joined her. It created an intoxicating atmosphere. As the door clicked shut, she felt a flutter of excitement and an unfamiliar rush of anticipation that made her nerves tingle.

Determined to keep the moment light and carefree, she adopted a casual tone, as if jumping into cars with strangers was a routine affair. When he joined her in the vehicle, she turned toward him and asked, "So, what do you drive now?" After all, a person's choice of car revealed a lot about the personality behind it, and so far, the man remained a mystery to her.

"I don't have a car. I get where I need to go without one."

Her eyes widened, and she asked, "You do know *how* to drive, don't you?" She unbuckled her seatbelt, ready to bolt at a negative answer.

Robert laughed. "Put on your seatbelt, lass. I know how to drive." He clicked his seatbelt into place and started the Range Rover. "My first car was an old beater that used to belong to my Nan."

"It is tough to impress girls when you roll up in a car that's missing its bumper and whose doors have mismatched colours," he added with a wink. "Never mind the sticker on the back glass."

"What did it say?"

"Granny On Board."

She cackled, relieved that the man knew how to make a joke. His gruff demeanor the previous day would have been intolerable on a long road trip.

He whipped out a cell phone. "We go to Culross first." After tapping an app on his phone, he announced, "Says there are no issues with traffic, so that's good."

Simone was impressed that the man knew how to use a traffic monitoring app. After he produced a paper itinerary yesterday, she feared he was a Luddite.

As he eased the car into the street, he asked, "Do you have a car?"

"Yes. It's my mom's old car." Simone glanced at him. Was he really interested or just being polite? His interest seemed genuine, so she pressed on. "It's about a million years old. I had just turned 16 when she died. She already planned to give me the car because she wanted a new one."

He took a deep breath. Perhaps he, too, was unsure how much to reveal. "My grandfather died a few months ago."

"Oh, I am so sorry." She dared to touch his hand, the lightest and briefest of touches, before quickly pulling away. His skin was as warm as the blush that burned on her cheeks.

"Thank you, but I never met him. We got a phone call out of the blue, saying he had died."

"It is still a loss."

"Aye." He shrugged, an unusual gesture considering the subject. "Well, enough about that. Let me tell you about the history of where we are going."

Simone stared out the window as he told her about Culross. His voice became background noise as he launched into a lecture about the village's history. She nodded and pretended to pay attention, not wanting to dampen his enthusiasm.

The scenery outside the window was unlike anything she had ever seen. The city scene faded as they crossed a bridge and eased onto a narrow road that led them into the countryside. Giant wind turbines dotted the ridges. Instead of Oak Hill's tall, thickly forested mountains, barren hills gently rolled along the horizon. Golden fields of barley replaced Edinburgh's concrete cityscape. Occasionally, she spotted white stone cottages with black slate roofs and ancient castles tucked into dense forests. Dirty white sheep grazed lazily in fields. Low-slung, gray stone fences kept the animals in place.

The weather was better, too. The fog that blanketed Edinburgh had lifted, revealing sparkling sunshine and blue sky. The scene was mesmerizing. She spent the entire journey staring out the window.

When they arrived in the village, she understood the reason for its selection. Culross was positively charming. Stone buildings with red-tiled roofs lined the cobbled street facing the Firth of Forth. The river's water glistened in the morning's sunlight, its surface gently rippling from the light breeze in the air. Fluffy clouds that resembled balls of cotton peppered the blue sky. The previous day's rain and fog were a memory.

From her guide, she learned that Culross was considered a great example of a village in the 17th and 18th centuries. Many movies and TV shows had used the village as a stand-in location for ancient Scottish or Norse settings.

Robert maneuvered the Range Rover into a

parking spot. The engine hummed softly as he turned it off. Simone eagerly hopped out. She breathed in the fresh, invigorating air as she made her way toward the river. Its water sparkled like diamonds under the brilliant sunlight. The gentle lapping of the waves against the river's bank beckoned her closer. Lost in the beauty around her, she could have spent hours there.

"Come along," he beckoned, "if you want to follow the itinerary."

They walked toward Culross Palace, the main attraction in the village. Before going inside, Robert slipped into tour guide mode. While the structure shared the same style of terracotta tiled roof favored by other buildings on the street, its ochre-colored exterior set it apart from the bright whites, dull grays, and ruddy browns adorning the adjacent buildings.

"Culross Palace was built between 1597 and 1611 by a wealthy merchant named Sir George Bruce," Robert told her.

"Why is the color of the exterior a shade of dull yellow? The other buildings don't look like that."

"It was meant to be seen from the harbour. Sir Bruce was very proud."

They ascended the weathered stone steps that led into the first room of the house, ducking slightly as they passed through a low doorway. Inside, the room welcomed them with the sight of a sturdy wooden table. The air was filled with the scents from the timbered ceiling and the faint remnants of a fire that had recently burned in the grate.

As they meandered around the table, Simone's

gaze fell to its legs. Robert noticed her interest. He leaned closer and remarked, "Can you see the bite marks?" He pointed to the small, gnawed indentations that told a story of past inhabitants.

She ducked her head low as she inspected the table's wooden legs.

"The table has a detachable top. After the meal, it was removed, and the food scraps were tossed onto the floor. The bite marks might be from the family's dogs."

She shivered when she finished the inspection. "Or rats."

"Aye, but it sounds better to say it was the dogs." He chuckled and continued the story. "With the table cleared away, the family could have used the room to relax and spend time together. Remember, they didn't have the telly back then. They had to amuse themselves by reading aloud or…heaven forbid… having a conversation."

As they wandered from room to room, she took in the home's features with keen interest. It was astounding to imagine that all of it was built before the advent of modern tools and architectural design, yet the house had survived for centuries.

"Just look at those barrel ceilings," he remarked, pointing to the elegant arches overhead. "They were crafted by local carpenters, who also happened to be skilled shipbuilders."

When they entered one of the bedchambers, he gestured at the little panels in the bed frames. "They were there for ventilation because folks took *annual* baths and positively reeked."

Simone shuddered. "Gross."

He told her to take a close look at the fireplaces. She traced the circles etched into the wooden mantelpieces with the tip of her finger. "They were meant to entangle witches and drive them back up the chimneys," he whispered into her ear.

Simone was utterly captivated by his stories. His words wove a vivid tapestry of the past. The intricate details he shared brought its history to life, creating a setting more amazing than anything she could have imagined.

"We don't have anything this old back home," she exclaimed. Her eyes widened with wonder as she snapped pictures. She eagerly wanted to capture the rich history of the place.

He leaned closer to her as they entered one of the upper rooms. His breath tickled her neck, sending shivers down her spine. Suddenly, the room seemed very hot. Her cheeks flushed. She tugged at the collar of her jacket.

"This room once belonged to the lady of the house," he said, gesturing toward the ceiling above them. It was adorned with sixteen intricate allegorical paintings that came alive with color and detail.

Simone couldn't help but gasp in awe at the sight, her mouth ajar as she took in the artistry.

"Look closely at the inscriptions; they are written in Latin," he added, his voice filled with admiration of the scenes captured within the designs.

"I cannot believe they have survived for so long." She studied each image, amazed.

"Have a look at this one." He pointed to one of the panels. "Tell me what you see."

Though the colors had been dulled slightly by time, the image was still powerful. The panel showed a woman sitting under a tree. Behind her, a ship with billowing sails drifted in what was presumably the harbor in front of the house. She cradled a lyre in one arm. And, with the other hand, she clenched….

"Is that a dead cat?!"

Robert guffawed a bit too loudly. A nearby docent gave him a harsh look before she exited the room.

"Some people say it resembles one. It is actually a cluster of grapes."

She shook her head. "Looks like a dead cat to me."

They shuffled their way through the other rooms in the home and eventually went outside into the wild garden. Aside from the purple thistles that soared over their heads, Robert could not identify any plants. He apologized, saying, "Botany isn't my specialty."

"Emma would have loved it." Simone idly glided her hand over the untamed plants spilling onto the graveled path that snaked its way through the garden.

"Did your friend like to garden?"

She chuckled. "Emma couldn't keep a cactus alive." At the end of the path, she spotted a little shed made of gray, weathered wood. The building was open on one side. Its pointed roof protected two narrow seats attached to one of its walls.

Easing into a seat, she continued. "She would have loved the lack of pretense. Yesterday, the garden at Holyroodhouse was so well manicured, so formal."

"You cannot tell what anything is here." She pointed to a cluster of greenery that nearly covered the path. Its white, yellow, and blue flowers mixed with the purple thistles. "I doubt the Queen would have hosted parties here."

Robert squeezed into the seat beside her. With the tip of his finger, he traced the outlines of the red, yellow, and gold starburst pattern on the stained-glass window hanging to his left. "How could something so lovely end up here?"

Their shoulders brushed against each other in the confined space of the little shed. If she concentrated, she could hear his breathing. His cologne smelled like grapefruit, Mandarin orange, juniper, and musk. It was a subtle scent, yet impossible to ignore when he sat so close to her.

Simone studied him. He seemed more relaxed today than he had the day before, when his outfit had looked uncomfortable and attracted the attention of passersby. Did the change of clothing and casual country setting improve his mood? More importantly, why did she care? The primary objective of the trip was to fulfill the conditions for the million-dollar inheritance.

Shaking her head, she desperately wanted to clear her thoughts. Keeping her eyes on the prize was more important than how hot her guide looked. She removed the cell phone from her pocket and scrolled through the screens. "Our next stop is a village called Maiseach," she said, pointing to the itinerary.

"Aye, I suppose we should head that way." He rose from the seat. "We will spend two nights at a bed-and-breakfast inn there. The village is tiny. I think you'll like it, anyway. The inn sits beside a loch and is surrounded by mountains. It is very scenic."

She stood and took one last look at the garden. Although escaping the closeness of her guide's attractive body was welcomed, it also meant leaving such a beautiful place. Still, more adventure awaited. Maiseach sounded lovely, so she was excited to see the village.

The car park was a short walk from Culross Palace. He opened the car door for her when they reached the vehicle. "Black Linn Falls is near the village," he mentioned. "It is not on the itinerary to visit. If you are not too tired, maybe we could go there."

She nodded enthusiastically before slipping into the vehicle. As he closed the car's door, she spotted the smile on his face. Why did his grin make her happy? The trip was not about pleasing him.

He's a cutie, Emma's ghost whispered into her ear. *What's wrong with having a little fun?*

"Shut up, Emma," Simone demanded before he climbed into the car.

FIVE

SIMONE LOVED THE VILLAGE OF MAISEACH AS SOON AS SHE SAW IT. Set along the shores of Loch Tay, it looked exactly as she imagined a little Scottish village should. The village itself was small. It had a little inn with a restaurant inside, a pub most likely frequented by locals, a small marina for about a dozen boats, and an old Presbyterian church surrounded by a kirkyard packed with old gravestones.

Robert told her the church was built in the 1700s. The white structure perched on the edge of the loch's shore. It was nothing fancy, just a white church with a black slate roof. She admired his restraint. He probably could have told her the story behind such a simple building if asked. Sometimes, the best stories were hidden behind the most basic of façades.

There was undoubtedly no nightlife to be found in this serene setting, and that suited her perfectly. After the hustle and bustle of Edinburgh, Maiseach offered a tranquil retreat in the heart of the countryside. She envisioned city dwellers escaping to this charming village on weekends, immersing themselves in the breathtaking landscapes, hiking through majestic mountains, and wandering along the peaceful shores of the loch, where quaint communities probably beckoned with their rustic charm.

They arrived at the cozy little inn in the early afternoon, likely the only guests in the establishment. The village lay well off the typical tourist trail. It was a hidden gem that promised solitude and serenity. She could easily imagine the chaotic crowds that flooded Edinburgh in the summer, a cacophony of voices and activity that could drive anyone to madness. Here in Maiseach, she dreamed about stretching her legs and breathing in the fresh, crisp air without the worry of colliding with a stranger. It felt like a perfect sanctuary for a country soul like her, where the beauty of nature could be fully enjoyed.

Robert handed her the key to her room after handling the details of checking in. Simone assured him that she only needed five minutes to get ready for their trip to Black Linn Falls. His skeptical expression told her he didn't quite believe her. *Challenge accepted*, she mused, a grin creeping onto her lips.

She dashed into her room. She hurriedly flung her luggage beside the wardrobe, not bothering to open it. Unpacking would only slow her down. There would be plenty of time for that later; for now, she was focused on proving her guide wrong.

When she reappeared in the lobby, she checked the time on her phone. "Made it!" she exclaimed.

Only, Robert was nowhere to be found. The man missed her triumph.

Striding to the front desk, she waited patiently for the kindly looking woman sitting there to look up. "If you are looking for the handsome fella, he's in the restaurant," she said, pointing to the doorway behind her.

"Thank you," Simone said as she walked through the doorway. She found him standing by a window facing the loch, sipping a cup of tea. The stunned expression on his face when their eyes met was priceless. Nodding silently, he quickly gulped the last drops of tea from his cup and led her outside to their car.

"I hope you don't mind where we are staying." He glanced at her when he joined her in the car. "The itinerary was created for a much older woman."

"You guys didn't know Emma very well at all. She would have appreciated the quiet of the village, but she wasn't opposed to a little rowdiness. She liked to tell me stories about her adventures."

"Oh?"

Simone turned to him, a massive grin on her face. "Before Castro took over Cuba, Emma spent a wild summer in Havana. She danced on the tables at bars almost every night and made out with Hemingway on more than one occasion." She giggled. "I don't know if it was true. I really wouldn't be surprised if it were. Emma was that kind of person."

"She sounds like a real character."

"Oh, she was. Everyone loved her." Sighing, she added, "Emma would have enjoyed this trip."

"I am glad you decided to come in her place."

"The trip was her gift to me. Her estate is covering all the expenses."

"Well, let's make sure you have a wonderful trip as her one final gift."

A shadow passed over Simone's face. She bit her lip. *If he only knew the whole story,* she thought.

BLACK LINN FALLS WERE NOT FAR FROM THE INN. As Robert parked the car, Simone eased to the edge of the seat and unclipped her seatbelt. Her eyes shined with excitement. She had been silent for the rest of the drive. His comment was a grim reminder of the incentive for coming to Scotland. Now, her sense of adventure was renewed. She was eager to explore.

"I normally hike in the less touristy area of the forest," he explained as they exited the car. "The established path through the woods will be easier for us."

She swallowed a sarcastic comment. The man acted as if she was a hundred years old.

He guided her toward a dirt path that took them to the Falls. The tang of pine needles, fallen leaves, and rich earth hung heavy in the air. The decaying forest debris muffled their footsteps. The only sound came from the River Braan, its waters flowing to the left of the path.

The path narrowed as they crossed through the stone arch at its beginning, forcing Simone to take the lead and set a leisurely pace. She strolled with no haste, something that probably bothered her companion. She did not care. The trip was meant to be enjoyed, not rushed.

The giant trees towering above them were an incredible sight. Sunlight cast shifting patterns of light and shadow on the path. Captivated, she spun in a circle. "It doesn't look like this in my backyard."

"You have trees, don't you?"

"Yes, but none of them are this tall."

"The Douglas firs here are among the tallest trees in Britain." He pointed to the snarled roots and jagged rocks on the path. "Mind your step. It would be awful to trip on something and break your leg."

The path widened, allowing them to walk side by side again. The sound of rushing water filled the air. It grew louder as they continued their walk through the woods.

"Is that sound coming from the waterfall?" Simone asked.

"Aye. We are not far from it." He waved for her to follow him toward the gray granite boulders lining the river's banks. "Come see the river first."

The embankment was steep. One false move and a person would quickly tumble into the water. Simone clutched his arm as she leaned forward. The bubbling river's current was more vigorous from the previous day's rain. Moss-covered boulders along the riverbed looked like an ancient giant had carelessly tossed them there. She snapped several photos, eager for a reminder of the place's beauty.

She impulsively kissed Robert's cheek as he helped

her climb up the embankment. "Thank you so much for bringing me here."

A slow blush crept up the man's cheeks. He rubbed the place where her lips touched his skin. "You haven't seen the best part yet."

"I know. I just wanted to say it now in case I forgot." Realizing she had created an awkward situation, she hastily said, "Let's keep walking. I want to see the waterfall."

"Aye. Ossian's Hall isn't far."

"What's that?"

He grinned, urging her onward. "You'll see."

As they approached the waterfall, the path widened, and the roar of the water grew louder. The thick forest enveloped them in its protective green grip, blocking the sunlight overhead. They encountered more tourists there, too, so she suspected they had grown closer to the Falls. Eager to see the waterfall, Simone quickened her pace.

"Not yet," he said. He motioned for her to take the narrow path to the left. Its gray-black dirt was muddy from the rain. They paused momentarily to let two fellow hikers pass by before continuing onward.

They stood underneath a stone bridge that crossed the river. The Falls remained hidden from view, much to her disappointment. From the vantage point, Robert and Simone could see the foamy pools of water swirling in the river below. They spotted other admirers on the bridge above them.

"When can I see it?" she asked impatiently after taking several pictures of the bridge and river. She shivered slightly. The air next to the water was cool, although her excitement also contributed to the trembling.

Her enthusiasm seemed to please him immensely. His smile wide, he took her hand and walked away from the bridge, leading her along the same path they had previously traveled. "Mind the rocks," he advised.

Simone tightly clutched his hand. The rocks along the path were slick, causing her to slip several times. She tried to ignore how warm and soft his hand felt in hers. Holding his hand seemed natural. *Stop it!* she told herself. *You aren't here for romance.*

The path was too short. He released her hand at its end and turned toward a round, gray building with a conical roof. It stood only one story high. The structure was too small for a home, so she wondered its purpose. Its massive stone door was open. She looked up at Robert. "What is it?"

"It's a folly called Ossian's Hall. The Duke of Atholl built it in the 18th century. Do you know what a folly is?"

Simone shook her head.

"Follies were a total conceit showing you were rich enough to build something that had no real purpose other than to entertain guests."

"Some rich people have more money than sense. Times haven't changed."

Robert chuckled at her observation.

They stepped inside the building. They entered an antechamber with a tile floor and a mural of green foliage on its walls. She spotted the real attraction straight ahead and rushed through the room without studying the painting.

An arched wall of glass doors opened onto a half-moon-shaped balcony with a black iron railing. Gasping in awe, she walked onto the balcony and lightly placed her hands on the cold railing that was wet from the spray of the water.

Robert joined her, standing close. He swept his hand wide as he raised his voice to be heard above the thunderous falls below them. "I am sure the duke used to impress his guests with the view," he shouted.

Although this waterfall wasn't the most spectacular she had ever seen, it possessed a rugged charm that enchanted her. The water cascaded down the jagged, black rocks, its frothy white spray catching the light and creating a faint rainbow. White mist hovered over the water.

The emerald hues of the trees that bracketed the river contrasted beautifully with the dark stone. She wondered how the area would look in autumn. The leaves on the trees probably turned to shades of bright yellow, warm orange, and fiery red.

The roar of the rushing water filled her ears, mingling with the chirping of distant birds and the whisper of the wind. The atmosphere was both wild and serene.

A smile spread across her face as she snapped photos of the scene. Her head twisted from left to right as she surveyed the area. What a gift the experience was! In her mind, she thanked Emma.

Robert leaned close to her ear, his breath tickling her skin. "Do you want me to take a picture of you?"

"Oh, yeah, I almost forgot." She handed the phone to him. "The attorney told me I have to send a picture every day if I want the expenses to be covered."

Reluctantly, Simone turned her back to the waterfall and leaned against the railing. Her smile was so big that her eyes were nearly closed.

Robert snapped two pictures and returned the phone to her. She inspected them before selecting one and sending it to the attorney.

"Thanks for reminding me." She returned the phone to her pocket and turned back to look at the waterfall. "It is so beautiful."

"Aye, it is."

Robert and Simone moved away from the balcony so the noisy group behind them could take their place. He bade her to follow him as he exited the building.

"If you are up for it, the hermit's house is not far from here." He pointed toward a trail to the right of the folly. "Some people see the Falls and turn back. They miss the best part of the area. I warn you, though, the area might not be very crowded."

"Are you worried about being alone with me?"

"I don't want to make you uncomfortable. We only met yesterday, and here I am, already taking you to a secluded spot."

Simone headed toward the path. "Did your boss give you a lecture about sexual harassment?"

"Aye. We live in a litigious society. I was warned to be on my best behavior."

She felt an urge to respond with a flirty comment, but instead, she directed her gaze to the winding path ahead. The trail narrowed into a single-file dirt footpath that was flanked by towering trees whose leaves rustled in the breeze.

After a few minutes of walking, they arrived at a clearing where the path opened again and revealed more space to move around. To their left, an old, weathered wooden bench stood beneath the shade of a nearby tree. With a smile, he waved for her to come over and join him on the bench.

"In loving memory of Mairead and David McKenzie," Simone read aloud the words carved into the bench's wood. She extended her left hand and traced the carving with her fingertips. "Do you know who they were?"

"No. I like to imagine it. I picture a couple who brought their wee bairns here until the children eventually outgrew the place."

"The couple kept coming back, year after year," Simone guessed as she joined him. She tilted back her head and gazed at the trees. The canopy was thinner, allowing glimpses of the powder-blue sky above them.

Robert's gaze followed hers. "And they loved this spot, so their children put the bench here to honor their parents."

Simone hugged herself. "It is nice to imagine a love story like that, isn't it?"

"Aye."

"If it is too personal, tell me. I was just wondering. Are you married, Robert?"

"No – and I don't have a girlfriend."

"I don't have anyone special either." Shrugging, she added, "I have never been able to find 'the One.' Emma did, briefly."

"Oh, aye?"

"He died in a car accident a few months after they married. She said he was her true love, so she never remarried."

Robert lowered his head. "How very sad."

"I know the saying is *'it's better to have loved and lost than never to have loved at all,'* but damn, wouldn't that just suck?" Simone shook her head. "It's hard enough to find someone and then to lose them so soon. It's just terrible."

"What is 'soon'? Some people might say a lifetime would be an insufficient amount of time together."

They sat in silence for several moments until he spoke. He sighed heavily, saying, "My grandfather left the family without warning. It hurt my father deeper than he will admit."

"You said your grandfather died recently, didn't you?"

"Aye. After hearing the news, Mum said Dad went to the pub. The man never drank a drop until that day. Came home reekin' of whisky."

"When Mum told me the news, I thought she meant my grandmother's current husband. Technically, I guess that man would be my stepgranddad." Robert shook his head. "We never spoke about my dad's biological father. My step-granddad is the only man I have ever known as a grandfather."

"I finally learned of my biological grandfather's existence. Then, I immediately learned that he was gone, just like that." He snapped his fingers. "I know a thing or two about 'too soon.' I have so many questions that may never be answered."

"I felt the same way after my mother died. It happened so suddenly." Simone's voice quivered. "She had so much more to teach me."

Robert dared to place his arm around her shoulders. She did not flinch. The gesture brought comfort to her. Yes, they barely knew each other, yet something about him made her feel better. She never spoke about her mother to anyone except Emma. He listened to her but did not seem to pity her, just like her late friend.

"You told me you went to live with your friend after your mother passed. Is your father dead, too?"

Simone stood abruptly. It felt like someone had tossed a bucket of icy water down her back. Suddenly, his arm around her shoulders was not so comforting.

"Didn't you say there was more to see up ahead?"

"Aye, there is." Robert slowly rose from the bench. "Let's carry on then."

SIX

AS THEY MADE THEIR WAY BACK TO MAISIEACH, SIMONE GAZED OUT THE CAR'S WINDOW, HER ARMS TIGHTLY CROSSED OVER HER CHEST. The landscape passed by in a blur - towering mountains, gentle streams, and the remnants of mist from the previous day's rain - yet she remained disconnected from it all. Robert tried to break the tension with small talk, asking her what she thought of Black Linn Falls and the beauty of the countryside. Her responses were short, reduced to mere one-word answers. Eventually, he surrendered to the palpable awkwardness that hung between them and stopped any attempt at small talk.

Freed from the pressure of conversation, her mind spiraled to darker thoughts. Her father's shadow hung over her like a dark cloud. He was a seemingly inescapable presence that suffocated her spirit. She had grown accustomed to his sudden, unannounced appearances back home, but now, in the midst of her grand Scottish adventure, his specter felt even more intrusive and unsettling.

She attempted to enjoy the scenery flashing past, but each time she did, her father's image pushed through. The thought of him obscured the beauty around her. The joy she had felt while standing at the waterfall vanished in the suffocating weight of memories and was replaced by a tangled mess of emotions. She felt trapped in a web spun from sorrowful memories that refused to release her.

"Not this time," she whispered. "Leave me in peace."

"Excuse me?" Robert said. "Did you say something?"

"I asked how far away we were from the village."

"Another five minutes."

"Good," Simone said as she gazed out the window.

THEY CROSSED THE THRESHOLD OF THE INN, THE WARM GLOW OF THE FLICKERING FIREPLACE IN THE LOBBY BARELY REGISTERING IN SIMONE'S MIND. An overwhelming sense of urgency compelled her feet to move faster, so she quickly made her way to her room. Her heart pounded against her chest. Anxiety flooded her body.

Simone reached her room and shut the door, thankful for the solitude. The air was still and quiet. She leaned against the cool wooden door and took a moment to collect herself. Thoughts raced through her mind, tangled and chaotic. She desperately craved a break from the world outside.

Even the image of her guide, with his charming smile and attentive demeanor, felt too overwhelming right now. He had offered her companionship and adventure. In this moment, though, all she wanted was to be alone.

Her luggage remained in the same spot, its contents unpacked. She stared at the bags but couldn't bring herself to open them and put the items in their designated places. Although the activity would have provided her with a badly needed occupation and hopefully a distraction from the chaos in her mind, the task seemed too daunting.

Inhaling and exhaling methodically, Simone tried to slow her racing heart and quell the anxiety bubbling to the surface. Reminding herself that she was in Scotland, far away from Oak Hill and the man who plagued her thoughts, did not help either. After several moments, the walls of the room seemed to collapse on top of her, suffocating her. The space would not provide the respite she craved. She needed fresh air.

Simone grabbed her jacket and the key to her room, fleeing for the shores of the loch. She hoped the quiet comfort of its peaceful setting would be a balm for the jagged wounds of her soul.

Standing on its shore, she closed her eyes and inhaled the crisp, clean air. She savored the change from city to country. Edinburgh was lovely, but at her core, she always preferred a country environment.

The glassy surface of the clear water reflected the gray sky and the densely forested mountains. Occasionally, a car passed on the road that hugged its shores, the engine's low hum interrupting the setting's quiet atmosphere. Otherwise, the serenity of the moment was preserved.

The air was also cooler here, away from the city's paved surfaces. Wearing a jacket was a smart idea. Standing beside the lovely loch might be less pleasurable without it.

The mist clung to the slopes of the mountains like a heavy blanket, shrouding the landscape in a ghostly gray. The sunlight struggled to penetrate the layer of vapor. The eerie stillness of the scene made it feel like twilight, although it could have been any time of day. The setting was totally unlike the sunny scene at Black Linn Falls.

She bent, picking up one of the smooth stones littered along the shore. Its ruddy surface was pitted and rougher than she expected. The rock's flatness made it perfect for skipping along the water, if only she knew how.

Skipping stones across water was a skill often learned on family camping trips. Didn't families usually have happy memories of those trips? Fathers patiently taught their children life lessons like how to build a fire, skip stones, or catch fish. Sweet tales always painted a picture of perfect families gathered around crackling campfires. They made s'mores, cooked hot dogs on sticks, and told spooky ghost stories before tucking into sleeping bags underneath starry skies.

Well, that certainly wasn't her childhood

experience. The only camping trip they took was a complete disaster. She and her mother missed running water and indoor plumbing. Her father longed for an icy cold beer. Everyone had been too busy complaining about the lack of modern amenities to enjoy their time together. After only a few hours at the campground, they packed their things and headed home. She shuddered at the memory.

Her examination of the rock was interrupted by Robert's sudden appearance. He wore the same jacket from the day before. His hands were stuffed into its pockets. He removed one of them, producing a silver flask.

Unscrewing the cap, he handed the flask to her. "You cannot travel all this way without sampling a fine Scottish whisky."

Simone accepted the flask and took a healthy swig. The fiery liquid seared her throat and lit a fire in her stomach. Coughing slightly, she returned the flask.

Robert took a sip before placing the cap on the flask and tucking it into his coat. He seemed unfazed by the liquid's power.

"I am sorry if I upset you earlier when I asked about your father."

"It's fine." From the corner of her eye, she caught the expression on his face. He wanted to know more but didn't want to pry. With a sigh, she added, "He is not dead. I moved in with Emma because raising a teenager would have been hard for him. Besides, it wasn't long afterward that I moved away to college."

"You came back to Oak Hill after college, didn't you? And you lived with Emma? You didn't live to your father?"

"She was always traveling and needed someone to look after her house. Living there made sense."

Robert gazed at the loch, saying nothing. His face was expressionless.

Simone wondered if he had told his boss what happened. A private tour through Scotland was probably expensive, so happy clients were important. The company wouldn't want negative attention. Did his boss tell him to smooth things over with her? Was that why he stood there, not because he was genuinely concerned?

Regardless of his motivation for being there, she felt further explanation was necessary. "I don't like talking about my father. I hope you don't think I was angry with you for bringing up the subject."

"I did not mean to pry." He withdrew the flask, unscrewed the cap, and took a long drink. He offered her the flask. "It might bring you some comfort."

She waved it away.

"Are you hungry? The inn has a nice restaurant."

Simone carelessly tossed the rock into the loch, watching as it broke the surface with a gentle splash. She took a step back from the water's edge.

"No," she said, shaking her head as she turned away from the tranquil scene. "It's been a long day. I think I'll head back and turn in early."

He stared at her and then slowly nodded as if he had reached some conclusion about her. "Aye, well, rest. We'll leave at 8 in the morning."

Nodding, she stepped away, half-expecting him to

stop her.

Are you disappointed he didn't? Emma's ghost whispered into her ear.

"Shut up." Simone sighed wearily at the ghost's relentless badgering. As she walked toward the inn, she hoped the voices of her past would be silent and give her a few moments of peace.

SEVEN

SIMONE FLOPPED ONTO THE BED, UTTERLY DRAINED. Who would have thought that a vacation could be so exhausting? She had no frame of reference since the trip was her first real vacation in years. Were trips supposed to be as tiring as this one?

As promised, they had set off early that morning. Robert navigated the winding roads of the countryside with ease. Roofless stone cottages along the side of the roads marked the location of long-dormant farms. Their weathered walls whispered tales of another era. Ancient stone circles emerged at nearly every turn, shrouded in mystery and thick with the murmurs of magic.

At long last, they had arrived at a fairytale-like castle. Its tall turrets jutted towards the sky, and an air of enchantment surrounded the building. Simone half-expected knights in shining armor to ride out on huge white horses, with swords drawn and brilliantly-colored banners flapping in the wind.

The three-story, rectangular castle fit the stereotypical image. Each corner was anchored by circular towers with black slate conical roofs. Long walkways between each tower were topped with a crenulated roof. The scene conjured images of tin soldiers guarding the fortress, ready to protect the castle from any enemy who dared to storm its walls.

On the ground floor, they toured a handful of rooms open for tourists – a reception room with armaments hung on the yellow walls, a grand salon where dances were once held, and a dining room with a long table set for twenty people. Portraits of notable family members lined the walls of all of the rooms, their grim visages staring down in disapproval of the tourists who gawked at the quiet grandeur of the castle.

Ten bedrooms were on the second floor, yet only three were open to the public. Like the reception room, their walls were painted yellow. Ornate, gilded wood frames enclosed paintings portraying pastoral scenes and religious stories. The portraits hung in each room, the images covering every inch of available space on the wall.

Every room was packed with an array of furniture, forcing the sightseers to tour the spaces in single file. Imposing wardrobes, intricately designed writing desks, grandiose fireplaces, and oversized beds filled every corner. No inch of space was untouched. The effect of the design showed the opulence of another time.

As she had seen in other buildings they visited, the

curtains on the four-poster beds carried hidden messages. If the curtains were especially fine, they allowed the castle's owner to quietly display his wealth. In this particular castle, the bed's curtains were made from thick tapestry embroidered with gold thread. The images on the curtains told tales of the clan's exploits over the centuries. The fabric was faded and worn in spots, but the quality was apparent. Robert whispered that they were originals from the 1700s.

One of the guest bedrooms held an interesting place in history. Bonnie Prince Charlie spent the night there on his flight after the disastrous battle at Culloden. A painting depicting the dashing version of the prince hung on a wall for all to admire. Through a story from her guide, Simone learned that the disgraced prince had lived the rest of his life in Italy and didn't look nearly as fetching in his old age as he did in the portrait.

They spent most of their time in that room, where Robert lectured about the '45 Rising. She felt proud when she noticed several tourists hovering in the doorway. They listened attentively to him. Was it typical for guides to possess such an extensive knowledge of Scottish history? The man seemed to be very well educated on the topic. He quoted the names, dates, and places of each notable event with no effort. She made a mental note to offer compliments to his boss.

When she wanted to see more of the castle, he explained that the clan chieftain and his family still lived there. Only certain rooms were available for viewing. The rest were used by the family as private living quarters. Pointing to the water stains on the ceiling, he said, "They open part of the castle to visitors so they have funds for its upkeep."

The kitchen was located in the basement. Simone's steps echoed on flagstone floors that had been scrubbed clean of any soot or food crumbs from its days of use. The walls were painted white. She guessed the color brightened what would have been a very dark and dreary space.

Plastic versions of food were displayed on the tables, ovens, and cupboards that would have been used by the servants of the time. Little placards written in beautiful calligraphy told the uses of the kitchen's equipment and described how the servants would have lived and worked in the space.

They enjoyed lunch at a small café adjacent to the kitchen. Robert and she both ordered ham toasties. When Simone snapped a picture of her lunch and tried to send it to the attorney, the image could not be sent. Her guide pointed to the walls. "They are easily ten feet thick down here," he said. "I doubt you can get a signal. Wait until we are outside."

She furrowed her brow and placed her phone in her pocket without saying anything. Instead, she focused on enjoying the sandwich.

When they finished eating, they popped into the gift shop next door. It was packed with the usual items available at any tourist spot, from t-shirts with the castle's image emblazoned across the front to Scottish-themed tchotchkes. Hidden amongst the souvenirs, she found a table displaying locally-made crafts whose quality far exceeded the cheap trinkets. She bought a miniature watercolor painting of the castle, a lovely reminder of her visit.

As they exited the castle and made their way to the car, Robert asked if she was tired. "No, I am fine," she said. "Why do you ask?"

He opened the car door for her. "You'll see," he said mysteriously.

He took her to a nearby forest for a hike that was vastly different from the one they had enjoyed on the well-maintained trails at Black Linn Falls. The area felt like a secret haven where only a handful of local hikers took advantage of its beauty. A narrow dirt path meandered through a dense wood where trees soared high above. The thick canopies filtered the sunlight into soft, dappled patches on the forest floor. In certain spots, undergrowth spilled over the edges of the path. They carefully pushed aside the tangled branches and foliage to continue their adventure deeper into the wilderness.

They walked for about a mile before reaching a waterfall. Simone stumbled a few times and was grateful for Robert's assistance. He always rushed to her side, pulling her upright before she hit the ground. It was hard to ignore the feel of his strong arms wrapped around her waist, but she tried. As she repeatedly told herself, romance was not on the agenda.

The area surrounding the waterfall was cleared of all vegetation. She and Robert crossed a rustic wooden bridge, its sturdy planks creaking underfoot, as they drew closer to the waterfall. Standing just inches from the edge of a foaming pool at its base, they could feel the mist rising from the crashing water.

This waterfall was easily three stories high. The roar of the water harmonized with the gentle rustle of leaves from trees that surrounded them. The sunlight danced on the water's surface and created sparkling rainbows in the mist as it had at Black Linn Falls. As she took in the scene, her worries suddenly melted away.

Simone had closed her eyes and felt the cool mist upon her cheeks. It was refreshing after the heat from Edinburgh's concrete jungle. For a brief moment, the reason for the trip disappeared from her thoughts. She became just another tourist.

Of course, the serene feeling faded quickly. *Never forget why you are here,* she reminded herself. She opened her eyes and checked the signal on the cell phone. Seeing that it was strong, she asked Robert to take a picture of her. She immediately sent it to the attorney.

Though she could have lingered longer, it was getting late. They returned to the car and headed back to the inn. The drive probably wasn't remarkable for Robert. It was to her. The two-lane road wove through a countryside that was unlike anything back home. Mountains soared high above them, their raw faces peppered with granite boulders and random patches of green. Every few feet, thin lines of water cut tiny trails down the mountainside and trickled into crystal-clear streams at the bottom.

Quaint stone cottages nestled along the rocky banks of the streams, their chimneys releasing wisps of smoke into the air. Summer in the Highlands was much cooler than the humid air of the American South or even the heat in Edinburgh. The climate difference was jolting at times. Sitting by a crackling fire probably chased away the slight chill in the air. It sounded like heaven.

Occasionally, she spotted fluffy, shaggy sheep wandering through the emerald fields. Leisurely Highland cows ambled by the roadside, a meal of green grass dangling from their mouths. The familiar landscape of Oak Hill seemed a world away from the picturesque scenes unfolding outside the car's window.

When Robert parked the car, he had asked her to dine with him. Simone reluctantly agreed, promising to meet him in the lobby at the agreed-upon time. She did not believe that she could decline another dinner invitation.

Now, as she lay stretched upon the comfortable bed, the exertions from sightseeing and lingering effects of jet lag caught up with her. The memories of the day's adventure were terrific, but fatigue turned getting up from the bed into a difficult task. If only she had time for a nap.

Come on, lazy bones, Simone thought as she pulled herself upright and headed for the bathroom. Maybe a hot shower would help.

DINNER WITH HER TOUR GUIDE WASN'T TECHNICALLY A DATE, WAS IT? Simone paced, a mix of excitement and apprehension swirling within her. The bedside lamp illuminated the room, giving her enough light to pick an outfit. She glanced at the clothes spread upon the bed and felt increasingly uninspired.

What should she wear? She rifled through the pile

of clothes on the bed, pulling out a dress she had brought "just in case." While the itinerary did not indicate that fine dining was an option, being prepared for any eventuality was always practical. Maybe the dress she brought would work. The garment was casual, yet slightly elegant. She could add a scarf and make it a little dressier, couldn't she?

Thoughts raced through her mind as she imagined the evening ahead. It had been so long since she felt this kind of thrill. The idea of dining with someone handsome and intriguing made her heart race. Would they share laughter over the meal? Would their conversation flow effortlessly, or would she struggle to find the right words?

As she placed the dress against her body, she couldn't shake the questions: was this just a simple dinner between a guide and a traveler? Or was there something more to it? Most importantly, did she want there to be?

She glanced at her phone and cursed when she saw the time. Spending thirty minutes on her outfit selection was a poor use of time, especially when her options were limited to whatever was available in her suitcase. She needed to hop into the shower now, or she would be late.

After a quick shower, she applied makeup and styled her hair into something more attractive than usual. She desperately attempted to improve her appearance from rumbled tourist to...*what exactly??*

The dress would have to do, something she realized as she slipped it over her body. She tried to improve its appearance by adding a blue silk scarf and donning a pair of black kitten heels. With a little luck, the outfit would look effortlessly elegant. Or at least that's what she hoped.

You look like a desperate woman looking for a good time, Emma's voice rang loudly.

"Shut up!" she hissed as she left her room and headed for the lobby.

On the way, she spotted a mirror hanging on a wall in the hallway and stopped to inspect her appearance. The black wrap dress was as basic as they came. The garment revealed just the right amount of cleavage, so the style might be unimportant. She adjusted the scarf to cover the spot where it dipped the lowest, trying to preserve a little bit of modesty. *There is no sense in giving away the goods*, she thought.

Still, was it flattering? She chewed her lower lip. All her life, she fretted over her figure. The pencil-thin girls of high school made her feel self-conscious about it. Though she looked fine, those extra pounds on her frame made her self-conscious.

Shaking her head, she ended the inner monologue about her weight and shifted her focus to her face. She tilted her head from side to side, looking for makeup smears. Smoky gray eyeshadow complemented her hazel eyes. A sweep of pink blush brought color to her pale face. She thought the red lipstick gave her thin lips a lovely pout.

She fluffed her long, light brown hair, allowing it to cascade over her shoulders, and carefully rechecked her makeup in the mirror. Taking a deep breath to steady her nerves, she squared her shoulders and made her way toward the lobby. "It's probably not a big deal to him," she said. "Just breathe."

Robert paced in front of the reception desk. When she approached him, her knees nearly buckled at the sight. The man's hair was still damp from a shower. The dark navy color of his trousers contrasted nicely with a neatly pressed, burgundy-colored shirt that was open ever so slightly. The opening revealed a bit of brown chest hair, but in a good way. Simple loafers rounded out the look.

She was careful to avert her eyes lest he see how much she appreciated the effort. Perhaps it *was* a date. Immediately, she chided herself for being so giddy. Romance was not the purpose of the trip.

He bade her to follow him into the inn's restaurant. The hostess seated them at a table beside a window facing the loch. The sun had already slipped behind the mountains, so the ordinarily crystal-clear waters were now an eerie black.

They were alone. Simone wondered aloud if other guests were staying at the inn.

"Doubtful," Robert answered. "The place is usually empty during the week. It doesn't get busy until the weekend."

"How do you know?"

"Maiseach is a favorite place of mine. I come here as often as I can."

"I suppose you have taken a lot of tourists here."

Robert stared at her for several moments, confused.

"In your role as a guide." Simone offered.

"Oh, I see." He set aside the menu. "You are my first client. I meant that I like to come here on my own."

"You know a lot about the places we have been." She leaned forward and whispered, "How long did it take to memorize the script?"

"Well, I hope I don't need to," he said, laughing heartily. "It would be a shame if I needed to study."

"How do you mean?"

"I am a history teacher."

Simone's mouth dropped open. "Why are you doing this then? Did you lose your teaching job?"

"No. I needed to make some money over the summer while school was out. The owner of the company is an old friend."

She wanted to ask why he needed to make money but thought the question might be rude. If the U.K. were anything like America, teachers were not paid nearly enough to support themselves. Maybe a summer job provided extra cash to get through the school year. It didn't feel appropriate to ask, so she held her tongue.

The waitress glided over to their table, her ponytail bouncing lightly with every step. She flashed a confident smile as she wrote down their selections on a notepad - hearty venison stew for the main course and a decadent sticky toffee pudding for dessert.

"You're in for a treat," she said, punctuating her words with a pop of her gum. "Our pudding is something you won't want to miss. Everyone loves it."

The waitress returned shortly with the bottle of wine they had also ordered. She poured each of them a glass before leaving the bottle at the table and walking away.

Robert took a sip of the wine, staring at the glass as if contemplating what to say next. With a flick of his hand, he finally made up his mind and said, "I needed extra money for a gravestone. My grandfather does not have a proper one."

"Why wouldn't your father do it?" Simone raised her hand to her mouth at the error. "Sorry, you don't have to answer that question. I shouldn't have asked it."

"It's fine. I don't mind." He leaned back in his chair and gazed out the window before turning those gorgeous, chocolatey brown eyes back to her. "I don't think my dad has ever forgiven my grandfather for abandoning the family. I cannot ask my dad to do it."

He added. "The man is kin. It is the least I can do."

Simone was intrigued by the circumstances. She hoped he would not be offended if she probed further. "Aren't you curious why he left?"

"Oh, aye. I tried to learn what I could, but it hasn't been much. He lived a solitary life after he left."

He played with the stem of the wine glass. She wondered if the subject was closed. Discussing family was never easy, something she was well aware of. She would not fault him for it.

"One of my grandfather's old friends lives in Inverness." Biting his lower lip, he asked, "Would you mind if I popped by to see him one evening when we are there? I'll make sure you're settled at the inn before I leave. It shouldn't be a bother."

"I don't mind at all. You should go."

His shoulders lowered as if her ready acceptance eased his mind. She tried to ignore the warm feeling it gave her. *Focus*, she reminded herself.

The waitress brought their meal, providing a brief respite from the serious personal talk. She placed white plates containing piles of venison, potatoes, and carrots that all swam in brown gravy. Steam rose above the hot dishes. Robert lowered his head and inhaled the aroma, a slight smile forming on his lips.

Ignoring the food, she hoped it was not rude to continue their conversation. His revelation interested her. Simone was curious, so she did not hold her tongue for long. "How did the man know your grandfather?"

"They worked on the same boat," Robert answered between bites. "My grandfather was a fisherman."

He placed the fork on the plate and looked at her. Her heart skipped a beat as his eyes peered into hers. "He is buried in Oban, a town on the western coast."

The intensity of his look was not from budding feelings for her. No, he wanted to ask her something but was afraid to bring up the subject. She lowered her eyes to hide her disappointment. *Why does it even bother you?* she asked herself. *You aren't here for that, remember?*

"We are going to Oban in a few days, aren't we?" she asked. At his nod, she said, "Then, we should stop at the cemetery where your grandfather is buried. It would be a shame to skip a visit."

He refilled her empty wine glass. "Thank you,

Simone," he said, grinning. "It's a huge favor. I wouldn't have mentioned it, but I can tell you have a kind heart."

Taken aback, she asked, "What gave you that impression?"

"This trip," he answered. "You must have meant a lot to your friend, or she wouldn't have sent you on such an expensive excursion."

He lowered his voice. "I can only imagine the cost. I wonder why she didn't just give you the money instead of spending it on an extravagant trip." He held up his hand. "No offense."

Simone nearly choked on the food. Coughing slightly, she gulped wine. "Emma really wanted to take the trip. When she couldn't make it, I guess she decided that sending me was a thank-you for taking care of her."

The waitress approached their table to collect their empty plates. Her presence was a welcome interruption. Simone was relieved. She still grappled with the size of the inheritance and wasn't ready to divulge all of the details. The revelation might change his opinion of her, which surprisingly mattered at the moment. Every time he looked her way, a flurry of butterflies leapt excitedly in her stomach.

She found it challenging to find the right words to continue their conversation, so she tried an easier tactic. Most people liked talking about themselves. Since it seemed like the safest topic, she gestured towards his hands. "How does a history teacher get a callus?" she asked. "Or, is teaching a contact sport here in the U.K.?"

He chuckled as he examined his hands. "I suppose they are a wee bit rough." He placed his palms on the table and spread his fingers. "The school where I teach has a nice woodworking shop. The instructor lets me make furniture there when the students leave."

"What do you like to make?"

"I took up woodworking a couple of years ago, so I don't have a preference yet. I am still learning."

"Well, then, what do you make now? Do you enjoy it?"

"Oh, aye, I enjoy it very much. I made a dining table and a couple of side tables for my flat. They aren't fancy pieces."

"I am sure they are lovely."

He raised his glass in salute. "As I said, you have a kind heart."

The waitress returned with dessert. Simone studied the dish. When she ordered 'pudding,' she expected something completely different. A warm mound of dark brown cake bathed in a caramel sauce on the plate before her. For good measure, a scoop of vanilla ice cream rested beside the cake and was already melting from the dish's heat.

Plunging her spoon into the cake, she carefully carved a piece and slid it into the sauce and ice cream. The resulting bite coated her tongue in the best way as she placed it in her mouth. Moaning, she mumbled, "Where have you been all my life?"

"Told ya," the waitress said when she overheard the comment. She refilled their wine glasses and carried away the empty bottle.

They remained silent for several moments as they appreciated the decadent, warm dessert. Eating their newfound piece of heaven was a near-religious experience. Ruining the moment with conversation would be sacrilegious.

When the last bit of rich caramel sauce was consumed, she eased back in her chair and sighed with pleasure. Whoever claimed British food was dull had never eaten sticky toffee pudding. She had found a new favorite dessert.

"You know a bit about me. Now it's your turn." Robert propped his elbows on the table and tented his fingers in front of his face. "What do you do for a living?"

"I am a waitress." His expectant stare told her she wasn't getting away with the bare minimum of information. She took a deep breath. "Not by choice. I studied creative writing in college."

"Ahh, so waiting tables is not what you always wanted to do with your life?" Robert paused as the waitress cleared away their plates. His cheeks were flushed. Was he embarrassed because the woman might have heard him?

"I wanted to be a writer."

"Have you written anything I might have read?"

She shook her head and frowned. "No one will publish my work." Tossing her hands into the air, she added, "I wrote a couple of novels, a few short stories. I sent them to literary agents and publishers. So far, no luck."

Simone hesitated. Being so vulnerable with another person should have felt weird. With Robert, it didn't. He seemed to be genuinely interested in her. Talking with him was easy. He wasn't judging her. He wasn't lecturing her on the frivolity of pursuing her writing dreams. Only her mother and Emma had ever made her feel so comfortable.

In her mind, she took a tentative step toward the wall around her heart. Robert was a charming man now that they were away from Edinburgh. He shared deeply personal parts of his life. Perhaps she could, too, just a little bit.

"Emma traveled a lot and needed someone to watch over the house. That was always the official excuse I used. The truth is, living with her made economic sense. A waitress' salary didn't give me enough money to rent a place while I pursued my dream of becoming a published writer."

"So, you aren't a waitress after all. You are a writer."

"I haven't been published," she said, trying to ignore the proximity of his hands to her own. "How does that make me a writer?"

"Being published has nothing to do with it. Lots of famous writers took years to get their books published. Would you say someone like Jane Austen or Sir Walter Scott wasn't a writer, just because their books were not immediately published?"

"Well, no, but...."

"Do you think of yourself as a writer?"

"Yes."

"Then, you are." He smiled. "We're both stuck in 'real' jobs, even though we want to do something creative."

Simone had never thought of it that way. Shaking her head, she tried to regain control of the conversation. Talking so much about herself was uncomfortable. "Don't you like being a teacher?" she asked.

He ran his hands through his hair. "Don't get me wrong. It's great." He hesitated, briefly looking out the window as he found his words. When he turned his gaze to hers, the look took her breath away. *Damn, girl, get a grip*, she chided herself.

"I feel so alive when I make furniture," he said. "It's as if I was always meant to create things, not talk about stuff that happened hundreds of years ago."

"Emma always encouraged me to follow my dreams. She never wanted me to settle."

"She sounds like a very special person." Robert stretched his hand across the table and gently held hers. Simone did not pull away. "What happened to her?"

"Cancer," she replied, her voice barely a whisper. She struggled to swallow the lump in her throat. "She died six months ago, though the doctors had already told us several months before that she didn't have much time. In those final months, she was in a lot of pain. To distract her, I asked questions about the places she wanted to see here. It was a good diversion."

"I am happy you are here."

Impulsively, she squeezed his hand. "I am, too."

The waitress picked that particular moment to bring the bill. Simone could have strangled the woman.

Robert released Simone's hand and quickly took care of paying the bill. She used the opportunity to settle her nerves. It had been a long time since she held hands with a handsome man. The feel of his warm flesh pressed against hers stirred all sorts of naughty feelings. *You aren't here for that,* she reminded herself.

"You know, the loch is lovely this time of night," the waitress said as she tucked the bill into the pocket of her apron. She winked at Simone. "You should take a stroll, love."

"Excellent idea." Robert stood, offering her his hand. "Shall we?"

"Yes."

SIMONE NO LONGER FELT THE URGE TO STRANGLE THE WAITRESS. The woman had spoken the truth. Surrounded by the breathtaking beauty of the loch, she felt all of the tension fade away. It was impossible to feel anything but awe at the scene's beauty. Once again, Scotland's majesty left her speechless.

During the day, the loch's waters reflected the sky and the mountains. At night, the moon's gentle beams reflected on the surface of the water, making it look like a piece of silver satin. Each ripple of the water shimmered in its brilliant light. If Nessie's sister rested there, she slept in splendor.

Millions of stars twinkled like little diamonds strewn across the black velvet of the night sky. If she stretched out her hand, could she touch one? Logically, it wasn't possible, but she felt she could do it.

Calling the scene 'magical' seemed trite. She could not think of another word, though. At home, she never had time to enjoy the simple pleasure of the night sky's beauty. Oak Hill was far away from the light pollution of a major city. She could have experienced something similar to what she saw now if she had stepped outside.

But she didn't. It made her a little sad. Did she miss the beauty before her in the daily grind of her life? Days filled with Emma's medical appointments, tedious chores, countless trips to the pharmacy, and a plethora of other responsibilities left little time for herself. What had she lost all those years?

She turned to her companion. He stood in silence beside her, staring at the sky. Its beauty equally transfixed the man. Robert was her guide on this gift of a road trip. It didn't hurt that he was also incredibly handsome. Tonight, she learned how charming he could be, too.

She didn't intend to have a fling.

What if she did?

Assuming she completed the trip (and she had no reason to think she wouldn't), she would be a millionaire upon returning to Oak Hill. Her life would change in the blink of an eye. Why not grab the opportunity in front of her? Why not do something entirely out of character? Emma would have, wouldn't she?

She took a deep breath and moved closer to Robert.

He must have sensed her nearness. He turned to her.

Simone's heart raced in her chest, each beat echoing in her ears like a drum. She stood just inches away from him and could feel the warmth radiating from his body. Inhaling deeply, she caught the unmistakable scent of his cologne, a blend of grapefruit, Mandarin orange, juniper, and musk. It was a subtle scent, yet impossible to ignore when she stood so close to him.

She felt her breath catch in her throat as the intoxicating aroma filled her senses. A shiver ran down her spine, and she trembled, caught in the thrill of the moment. Tumbling into bed with someone who she didn't know very well was unusual for her. She wanted the experience, though, with him. To forget about her past and stop worrying about the future was an enticing prospect, even if only for one night.

"Oh, lass, you are cold." Robert took a step back. "Perhaps we should return to the inn."

"I'm fine." She eased closer to him and attempted a seductive look, though he likely could not see her face in the darkness of the night.

"No, I insist. Besides, you probably need time to pack. We leave for Aisling in the morning."

Simone's shoulders sagged. The night's dark shadows concealed the disappointment etched across her face. Reluctantly, she trailed behind him toward the glowing lights from the inn. The warmth they would find inside definitely could not chase away the chill in her heart.

Her anticipation was replaced by a reluctant acceptance of his refusal. She questioned how the night might have been different as she followed him inside. The original intent would have been sweet, but Robert seemed clueless.

He escorted her to her room. She tried to convey her feelings into what she believed was a tempting look. In the bright light of the hallway, surely the man could see her face. Unfortunately, Robert did not notice. With a casual wave, he bade her goodnight and left her alone at the door to her hotel room.

"As seduction attempts go, that was a complete disaster," she muttered to herself.

Amen, sister! Emma's voice called to her.

"Oh, shut up!" Simone exclaimed aloud.

EIGHT

THE FOLLOWING MORNING, SIMONE AWOKE WITH A SENSE OF DREAD CREEPING INTO HER CHEST. She resolved to pretend that the previous night's attempted seduction had never happened. Blaming it on a few too many glasses of wine, she dismissed the incident as just a fleeting mistake, a momentary lapse in judgment that would soon be forgotten.

A mischievous thought lingered, whispering in her ear: Maybe this was her chance to let loose and finally embrace a little adventure. Emma's ghost danced on the edges of her mind. The woman wouldn't have thought twice about drawing the man into an affair. Simone felt the spirit's presence and tried to ignore the intrusive thoughts that followed.

She reasoned with the ghost that it was always best to avoid reckless behavior. After all, indulging in something so wildly out of character was unthinkable.

No, it was better to focus on the real purpose of the trip. Besides, she was already having lots of fun on her first vacation in years. She didn't really need a passionate encounter with her sexy guide to improve the trip. Or so she told herself.

When Simone met Robert in the lobby, she plastered on a smile and engaged in light conversation about the day's weather. It was a safe and mundane topic. He seemed blissfully unaware of what had transpired the previous evening, much to her relief. Judging from his relaxed demeanor, he had not noticed her advances, and she had no intention to revisit the topic.

The pair stepped outside the inn and discovered a surprisingly sunny day. He briefly looked at the sky before loading their luggage into the car. "It's a fine morning," he remarked cheerfully, and she nodded in agreement. Indeed, it was. The powder blue sky was clear, with no threat of rain.

She decided that romantic advances must be a common occurrence in Robert's world. She forced herself to believe that he hardly noticed any attention directed his way. Climbing into the car, Simone took a deep breath and buried the feelings swirling within her. She was determined to shake off the echoes of the previous night.

As she adjusted the seatbelt, he hopped into the car. "Ready for the next adventure?" he asked.

Nodding, she whipped out the phone and stifled a groan when she retrieved the itinerary. "We are going to a whisky distillery."

"Aye. They give you free samples at the end of the

tour."

Simone looked to the sky in exasperation. *This was Emma's doing,* she thought.

SIMONE STUMBLED INTO THE LOBBY OF THE HOTEL IN AISLING. Her feet somehow moved one in front of the other from sheer muscle memory. The haze over her brain made it difficult to think about where she walked or what she thought about…well…*anything.* Thankfully, Robert seemed to know where they were headed, or she would have ended up in a ditch somewhere.

She had never drunk so much in her entire life. Staying sober was an impossible task from the start. Robert and the guide working at the distillery were old friends. With a wink, the man offered them a behind-the-scenes tour. It spelled trouble.

They had visited areas usually off limits to visitors. The highlight was private access to a massive room, its floor covered in barley. Windows open to the outside allowed fresh Highland air to perfume the barley. The theory was that the air gave the whisky a taste unique to the distillery. Simone declined an invitation to dive into the mounds of fruity-smelling grain. Her companions seemed shocked at her refusal. Robert later told her that it would have been a great honor.

The tour had ended in a dimly lit room stacked to the ceiling with rows of dusty oak barrels. The guide offered them very liberal whisky samples, some straight from the cask. Robert did not indulge since he was driving. Of course, it didn't stop his friend from plying her with glass after glass of the fiery spirit.

By the fifth drink, she feared Robert would have to peel her off the floor. Fortunately, he had recognized the desperate look on her face and practically carried her to the car.

Slumped in the backseat of the Range Rover, Simone dozed on the drive to Aisling. While she typically would have pressed her face to the car window, viewing the Scottish countryside was the last thing she wanted to do at the moment. She was thankful that Robert drove the vehicle slowly along the road's winding route. Perhaps he feared the consequences of fast driving on her queasy stomach.

Robert handled all the tasks of checking into the hotel. He left their luggage in the car, a good thing. She wasn't even sure she could form a complete sentence, much less recognize which bag was hers.

He grabbed their room keys and took her arm. She tried to focus on what he was saying as they made their way down a long, dark corridor. Something about her room being in the hotel, and his was across the street? And, something about bringing the luggage later?? None of it made sense to her alcohol-addled brain.

With some effort, he opened the door to her room. Simone spotted the bed and pushed past him, flopping onto it. Within moments, the world turned to black.

SIMONE AWOKE FROM A FITFUL SLUMBER SEVERAL HOURS LATER. The brown tweed curtains on the windows were partially open, revealing the fading light of the day. How long had she been asleep?

She groaned. The bed was twin sized and appeared to have its original mattress from decades ago. It felt as if metal springs pushed through the mattress and into her skin. Every muscle in her body ached, and her head pounded with every beat of her heart. She wasn't sure if her condition was from the mattress or the drinking. Regardless of the cause, the feeling wasn't pleasant.

She shoved aside the heavy tweed blanket draped across her body. How did *that* get there? Then, the memories of Robert helping her to her room rushed back to her. At once, she felt both shame and relief. Drinking so much was not typical behavior, yet her guide had not taken advantage of the situation.

She took another look at the blanket. Did he put the blanket on her? *How sweet*, she thought.

Easing herself upright, she leaned across the bed and switched on a yellow lamp. It was the only decoration on the nightstand. The sight that greeted her made her cringe. "Oh, my goodness!"

The curtains blocked some of the light from the windows. The thick grime that coated the glass blocked the rest. Smudges of black mold grew along the windows' frame. A slender, red line ran along the outer edge of one window. She shuddered to think what *that* substance might be.

Like the emerald green carpet on the floor, the pink bedspread was threadbare and stained in places. The dark brown furniture that had been crammed into the tiny room was cheap, dented, and scratched. The dust on the nightstand's surface was so thick that she could probably write her name.

Stumbling to the bathroom, she discovered a small, plastic shower that could accommodate one person...one *very small, very short* person. Strips of duct tape were arranged in neat rows along the bottom of the shower's pan. Had it leaked at some point, and *that* was the fix? A glass door encircled the shower. A slender crack in the glass ran vertically from the top to the bottom and was encrusted with mildew and soap scum.

She dared to look inside the shower. Black mold grew in one corner, threatening to crawl up the walls. An odd-looking square box hung below the showerhead. *What the hell is that?* she wondered.

Shaking her head, she hoped the toilet was clean enough to use. She lifted the lid and was relieved to see sparkling white porcelain. Nature called, regardless of the room's condition. The toilet was the cleanest thing she had seen so far.

After attending to her necessities, she flushed the toilet. The water barely left the bowl, its pressure abysmal.

"You're just being a pampered American," she said to herself. "Be thankful you have a bathroom."

She moved to the sink and stopped abruptly. The square basin looked like something from the 1950s. It had two silver taps with a nob beside each of them. Staring at the taps, she was puzzled. "What am I supposed to do?" she asked aloud.

Blazing hot water spewed from the first tap after

she turned the knob beside it. Cold water flowed from the opposite tap when she turned the other knob. "How do I get <u>warm</u> water?" she asked. This time, her voice was shrill.

She washed her hands as best as she could by alternately moving them between the scalding hot and icy cold water. It wasn't the most pleasant experience, but what else could she have done?

"Enough!" she exclaimed as she headed for the bedroom. The tour was probably expensive. Staying in a room as disgusting as this asked too much. She didn't care how spoiled it was to complain.

Retrieving her phone from her purse, Simone called Robert. "There is no way I am staying here," she said when he answered. She explained the room's conditions, finishing with a vivid description of the sink. She gave him a moment to stop laughing. "What? Your room cannot possibly be nicer than mine. I'm coming over."

NINE

SIMONE STOOD FROZEN IN THE CENTER OF ROBERT'S HOTEL ROOM, HER MOUTH DROPPED OPEN IN DISBELIEF. She took a moment to absorb the sheer luxury of his surroundings. Her eyes swept across the space as if trying to catalog every detail. She tried to comprehend the difference to her own cramped hotel room, which was far less inviting. This room was a world apart, a sanctuary of comfort and elegance that left her both envious and awestruck. "Are you freakin' kidding me??!!" she exclaimed loudly.

Robert tried not to laugh. He failed.

She walked around the room—or should she say *rooms*? The area was practically an apartment. Its spaciousness was a dramatic contrast to the dingy room where she was supposed to stay. Obviously, his room had been recently renovated. Hers looked as if it was in its original state from a hundred years ago, with the addition of electricity and plumbing being the only "modern" updates.

A petite kitchen space to the right of the doorway offered the essentials for a short stay. A stainless-steel sink had been set into a small maple cabinet. The adjacent marble countertop provided space for an electric kettle and a basket of tea bags. Open shelves above the sink displayed a collection of mugs, glasses, and plates. A table and two chairs served as a dining space.

A plush beige sofa sat in front of the fireplace on the opposite side of the room. A crackling fire burned in its grate. Above its rustic mantel hung the largest TV she had ever seen, where a football match was being played on the screen. The sound quality was so good that she felt like she was sitting in the stadium.

The sheer curtains hanging over the floor-length windows softly filtered the light. She was rewarded with a view of the bucolic countryside when she pulled back the curtain. A field covered in blue and white wildflowers butted against towering granite mountains. "There's probably a flock of happy little sheep out there somewhere," she mumbled as she dropped the curtain and continued her inspection.

The other walls in the room looked like the original brick from the building's bygone use. The ruddy-colored brick lent a warm feeling to the room.

Looking down, she noticed the wide planks of the gleaming hardwood floors. "I bet they are original, too," she muttered. No awful green carpet there. Tartan plaid patterned rugs were scattered about the room, the muted greens, blues, and blacks blending well with the other decorations.

She spotted an open door to a darkened room in the back of the space. She abandoned her suitcase and walked toward the room, her curiosity overcoming all manners. Tugging the string on the overhead ceiling fan, she was nearly blinded by the light that flooded the room. She gasped at the king-sized bed fitted with a black houndstooth bedspread. Its dark gray headboard didn't have dust on the wood. Equally clean, black walnut nightstands framed the bed. Brass lamps with pristine white shades adorned each nightstand, providing gentle illumination for bedtime reading. A large TV hung on the wall opposite the bed.

Seeing another door to her left, she flipped on a light there and entered the spacious ensuite bathroom. No duel taps here. The bathroom's overall design was fresh and modern. Two brushed-gold handles and one tap stood atop a gleaming white porcelain sink and matching marble countertop. The vibrant blue of the cabinet on which it rested had two drawers for storage and an open area at the bottom for a stack of fluffy, freshly laundered towels.

The shower's blue-gray glass tiles climbed the wall to the ceiling in a chevron pattern. By contrast, the bottom of the shower looked like river rock with its gray, black, and beige stones. A rainfall-style showerhead dangled from the ceiling. The shower's glass door was sparkling clean and, most noticeably, did not have any cracks in the glass.

She returned to the living room, where Robert stood with a sheepish grin. Flinging her hands into the air, she said, "Well…."

"The hotel bought the property last year," he

explained. "They converted it into hotel rooms. I assumed they renovated the original rooms, too."

"Yeah, well, you assumed wrong." She shook her head. "This place is so much nicer than mine. My room is disgusting."

Robert stepped toward the bedroom, dragging her suitcase behind him. "You stay here. I'll stay in your room."

Simone shook her head. "No," she said. "I cannot do that to you."

"I insist. You aren't happy with your room. Besides, it is only one night." He took another step toward the bedroom. "I just need a moment to pack."

She grabbed his arm as he passed. "No, Robert, I cannot ask you to stay there. Let's check with the front desk. Maybe I can switch to a better room."

"The hotel only has six rooms. It is fully booked."

"Really? I didn't realize Aisling was so popular."

"Aye. It is within five miles of several excellent whisky distilleries and close to Cairngorms. Everyone loves to come here for the libations and hiking."

"Well, then, I guess we're stuck." She looked around the room, envious. It was beautiful.

"It's not a bother, lass. You should stay here. I'll stay in your room."

While she feared the cooties that lurked in the dark corners of her room, she also didn't want to inconvenience the man. "Let's compromise then. I'll sleep on the sofa. It is way nicer than that horrible bed in my room."

Robert gave her an exasperated look. "I cannot let

a client sleep on the sofa."

"Fine," she said through gritted teeth. "Then, you sleep on the sofa, and I'll take the bed. But you *are* staying here. Neither one of us is going back over there."

She snatched the handle of her suitcase and wheeled it into the bedroom. "I'm going to take a shower," she said. "I gotta wash off the cooties from that awful room."

Even through the closed bedroom door, Simone heard Robert's laughter.

TEN

SIMONE WIPED THE CONDENSATION FROM THE MIRROR. She probably spent longer in the shower than she should have, but she rationalized that she was on vacation. Moving at a slower pace was expected. After all, there was no reason to fear being late for work or missing a personal commitment. That's what vacations were, right? An opportunity to escape one's day-to-day life?

Additionally, the bathroom was luxurious and designed for enjoyment. The showerhead was not the generic one she had back home. It hung above her, not in front of her. Hot water simulated gentle rainfall. Every muscle in her body relaxed as the water cascaded over her body. The steam from the hot water cleared the cobwebs from her brain, eased her aching head, and awakened her mind. The experience was fabulous.

The chrome towel warmer mounted on the

opposite wall was another luxury. The fluffy, soft towel was already warm when she hopped out of the shower. She wrapped it around her body, reveling in the pure luxury. "I need one of those in my next home."

The reality of her new situation rushed to the forefront of her thoughts. *One million dollars.* The inheritance gave her so many fabulous opportunities, more than she ever dreamt for herself. The money allowed her to pause for a little longer. She didn't have to figure out her next step, at least not right away. Instead, she could live off the money and write her novels without worrying about the need for an income. She could focus entirely on herself.

She had to complete the trip. It was the most important thing at the moment.

More important than impressing the handsome guide.

Examining her bare face, she decided it wouldn't hurt to put on some mascara.

And maybe some concealer.

And a little blush on her cheeks.

"Well, while I'm at it, I should fix my hair, too," she said as she switched on the hair dryer.

WHEN SIMONE FINALLY STEPPED OUT OF THE BEDROOM AN HOUR LATER, SHE FOUND ROBERT SITTING AT THE DINING TABLE. He was completely engrossed in his task as he carefully selected each stem from a loose bundle of wildflowers spread upon the table and placed them into a vase. The vibrant colors of the wildflowers popped against the backdrop of the brown paper in which they were previously wrapped.

He arranged the blossoms in a glass vase, taking care to study each flower's placement when he added it to the arrangement. The wildflowers – an assortment of daisies, cornflowers, and lavender - oozed a delightful fragrance that mingled with the faint aroma of his cologne. The scene felt relaxed and homey, filling her with an unexpected joy as she watched him work.

She kept her feelings to herself as she walked toward the table. "The flowers are lovely," she said instead.

"When I told the folks at the front desk about the condition of your room, they felt terrible." He pointed to a pink box on the table. "They sent us the flowers and a box of pastries."

She opened the box and found an assortment of scones – plain, blueberry, and red currant. She grabbed a napkin and selected a plain scone. To her disappointment, there were no containers of clotted cream or jam. "They are delicious," she mumbled, her mouth full of scone.

"Here," he said as he stopped his task and rose from the chair. He retrieved a bottle of an orange beverage from the mini-fridge beside the cabinet. Before he gave her the drink, he grabbed a glass from the shelf and filled it to the brim with the drink's orange liquid. "You'll need this after all the whisky you drank."

She twisted the bottle so she could read the label.

"Irn-Bru?"

"It cures what ails you."

Her tongue felt as if it was wrapped in a thick layer of cotton, leaving her too parched to protest. She lifted the glass and slowly sipped the fizzy drink. The cold, syrupy sweet liquid cascaded down her throat. It was refreshing and invigorating. The drink washed away the dryness that clung to her mouth. "I do feel better," she remarked, a faint smile on her lips.

She strode to the window, with the glass in hand and a scone wrapped in a napkin. While she was asleep, it had rained. A light mist floated along the craggy points of the mountains. Here and there, she spotted tiny waterfalls and patches of vibrant green grass amongst the granite boulders. The view was superior to the one she had in the other room, which offered a glimpse of an alleyway packed with overflowing trash bins.

She nibbled on the scone. It crumbled slightly in her fingers. The dry pastry tasted somewhat lackluster without clotted cream or jam to complement it. She quickly dismissed any impulse to voice her disappointment. The staff had gone out of their way to provide fresh flowers and homemade scones, unexpected treats that they certainly weren't obligated to offer.

As she returned her attention to the view, she was certain Emma would have liked it. The countryside was so peaceful. Oak Hill was serene, too. The woman enjoyed visiting active places but didn't want to live there. Maybe that's why her friend lived in a small North Carolina town. Seeing the busyness of another place without actually living there was exciting, but returning home to peace and quiet was greatly desired.

Simone felt Robert's eyes on her. He stared at her, a slight smile on his face. "What?" she asked.

"Nothing." He shook himself as if to snap out of a trance. "I was supposed to take you for a tour at a local castle, but it's too late. Would you like to stroll through the village instead?"

He glanced at his watch. "We have about an hour before the shops close. We could grab a bite to eat after our walk. The pub serves decent fish and chips. Of course, it's not as good as what we will find in Oban, but I think you'll like it."

She finished the scone and downed the remnants of the drink. Placing the empty glass in the sink, Simone said, "I'll grab my jacket."

AISLING WAS A CHARMING VILLAGE. In addition to the hotel and its sister property across the street, the village had a restaurant, a pub, and a handful of shops selling a variety of items, from souvenirs to food and other essentials. Its three cobblestone streets sat beside a field of colorful wildflowers and butted against the craggy mountains Simone had come to expect in Scotland.

On the outskirts of the village, an ancient church tucked itself into the surrounding pine forest. Its gray stones and black slate roof reminded her of the boulders lining the mountainside. Judging from the size of the rectangular building, it probably held twenty people at most. The arched, stained-glass windows honored various saints, with one notable exception. That particular window glorified the masons and other laborers who built the church in the 1700s.

The church doors were locked, so they strolled through the adjacent kirkyard. Gray gravestones stood silently in tidy rows surrounding the building. Some dates on the stones went as far back as the church's inception. Simone wondered if the tall Celtic crosses on top of some of the graves marked the last resting place of important local figures. The mystery of each person was intriguing. Would Robert know their stories if she asked?

Realizing he might launch into an hours-long lecture, she decided to refrain. Her growling stomach agreed. Instead, she focused on the recently departed. "Have you picked out the marker for your grandfather's grave?" she asked, hoping it wasn't a sensitive subject.

Robert slowly strolled closer to her. "Aye. Since he was a fisherman, I thought he might like something nautical," he replied. "A friend of mine is an artist. He is carving a boat into a lovely piece of granite. We'll use the stone for the grave."

"That sounds nice." She continued walking past each gravestone, occasionally examining the intricate carvings of mythical creatures or Celtic knotwork on the stones. Some of the gravestones were so old that the lettering was difficult to read, their blackened etchings worn thin from centuries of exposure to the elements.

"He said it will be ready at the end of the summer. By then, I should have the money to pay for it." He traced the outline of a cross etched into one of the gravestones. "What did you use for your friend Emma's grave?"

"She was cremated." Simone chuckled at the memory of the conversation. As with most things, her friend had a firm opinion on the subject. "Emma refused to be stuck in a coffin and buried in one spot. She told me to wait until there was a windy day. Then, scatter her ashes into the wind. That way, she could travel the world forever."

"Have you done it?"

"Yeah, I didn't have to wait long. It's always windy in Oak Hill."

He stopped in front of two gravestones and motioned for Simone to join him. "Well, I'll be damned," he said, incredulous. "Will you look at that? A Campbell and a MacDonald, married to each other and buried side by side."

"Why is it so extraordinary?"

His mouth ajar and eyes wide, he spoke to her as if he were telling something to a child. "Campbells and MacDonalds have been mortal enemies for centuries."

"Why?"

He mumbled something under his breath. Judging from the expression on his face, it wasn't flattering.

"Hey, I'm an American," she said defensively. "Scottish history isn't taught in schools over there."

He looked as if he had something very negative to say but held his tongue. Instead, he patiently explained, "All clans have long histories of fighting against one another. However, the Campbells and the

MacDonalds have a particularly brutal event to thank for a large part of their rivalry. Have you heard of the Massacre of Glen Coe?"

"No."

"In 1692, the MacDonalds hosted a troop of government soldiers who happened to be led by Captain Robert Campbell. The orders were to remain in the village while they awaited further instruction. They stayed for several days, all the while enjoying the clan's hospitality."

"It turns out that the MacDonald clan's chieftain was late declaring his oath to the new monarchs, William and Mary. The King decided to make an example of the Glen Coe MacDonalds, so he ordered the troops to slaughter their hosts." He pointed to the mountains. "Some of the clans' people fled into the hills."

"Not to sound callous, but fleeing into the hills sounds like something a person could survive," Simone interjected. "Surely, they found safety in another village."

"It was winter. Many died from exposure to the cold."

"Oh, dear." She pointed to the dates on the gravestones. "This couple lived in the 20th century. It doesn't matter anymore, does it?"

"To some, aye, it does." He sighed. "Many historians will point out that only a handful of Campbells were in the troop, so they should not shoulder the full blame."

"Why have they?" she asked.

"I guess it was more about the symbolism of the act. You see, it was a violation of our traditions. The Campbells are known loyalists to the Crown. Everyone assumes they had no problem following the King's orders and hate them as a result."

She gave him a blank look. The whole situation was beyond her understanding.

Robert continued the stroll, shaking his head and mumbling, "Unbelievable."

Simone wasn't sure if he referred to her lack of knowledge or the union of the two souls buried in the kirkyard. She decided it was best not to ask.

ELEVEN

THEIR LEISURELY STROLL THROUGH THE VILLAGE CONCLUDED WITH A DELIGHTFUL MEAL AT THE LOCAL PUB. Simone had never tasted fish and chips, a dish she picked because it seemed like quintessential Scottish cuisine. She was pleasantly surprised by the great taste of the crispy, golden-battered fish that flaked apart at the first touch of her fork. The fries – a.k.a. chips – were heavily salted, just as she liked them. It was a culinary experience to remember, even with Robert's repeated comparisons to the fare at his favorite chippy in Oban.

Local musicians played rousing songs with their fiddles, bodhráns, and guitars as she and Robert savored their pints. The lively tunes stirred some dormant part of her blood. The Grant family had roots in the area. She felt it deep in her blood that evening. Involuntarily, her foot tapped in time to the music.

Caught up in the moment, some of the patrons danced to the tunes. One of the men tried to coax her into joining, but she declined the invitation. She preferred to enjoy the music and atmosphere rather than take to the floor herself.

Fortunately, the music wasn't so loud that conversation was impossible. She and Robert laughed as they discussed the visit to the distillery, an adventure made infamous by the aftereffects. He entertained her with tales from his classroom while Simone painted a vivid picture of life in Oak Hill. She compared the peaceful surroundings at home to those in Aisling and Maiseach. "If you love those villages, you would like Oak Hill," she commented.

A sense of ease washed over her as she spoke. She felt herself relax, embraced by the warmth of the pub and the camaraderie of their exchange. It was a rare feeling. The last few years had been full of sorrow.

Unfortunately, the mood quickly vanished upon their return to the hotel room. It shifted from playful and light-hearted to tense and guarded. One look at his downcast eyes and rigid posture told her he, too, was uncomfortable sharing a room.

She adopted a cheerful tone rather than addressing the proverbial elephant in the room. After giving him time to use the bathroom for a bedtime routine, she bid him goodnight and closed the door to the bedroom. Once there, she climbed into the large bed and pulled the duvet to her chin. Thoughts raced through her mind, their volume high. "Just go to sleep," she whispered to herself.

It was a difficult task. Emma was alive the last time she shared space with another human being. The steady beep of her friend's medical devices often lulled her to sleep. In the stillness of her current room, there was no such noise to distract her. Sleep proved elusive.

The person in the other room was very much alive and healthy. If she listened carefully, she could hear him repeatedly fluffing the pillows and tossing and turning. The sofa was probably too small for a man as tall as him. She doubted it offered much support for sleeping either.

She flipped onto her back. Her eyes squeezed shut; she counted backward from a hundred. That didn't work. Then, she tried pulling in long, deep breaths before releasing them and listening to the slowing beat of her heart. Focus. Relax.

Robert coughed, interrupting her mediation.

She rolled her eyes. *This is ridiculous!* she thought. He probably would not appreciate the offer she was about to make. Would he get the wrong idea? She decided it didn't matter. Listening to him toss and turn would not help either of them.

Flinging aside the covers, she stomped to the bedroom door and flung it open. "Why don't you sleep in the bed with me?"

He snapped to his feet. "Excuse me?"

"There are lots of pillows." She waved her hand at the bed. "We can put them in the middle of the bed. We'd never know the other person was there."

Robert folded his arms over his chest. Frowning, he said, "I do not think it is appropriate for us to share a bed." He gestured toward the sofa. "I am not even keen to stay in the same hotel room with you."

Simone groaned. "I doubt you will get a good night's sleep on the sofa – and I am not crazy about the idea of a tired person driving me around on the twisty Highland roads." She pointed to the bed. "You'll be more comfortable here."

He shook his head. "No, I won't."

"Why not?"

He strode toward her and stared down at her, his face serious. "I was hired to be your guide on a road trip through Scotland," he said. "I am not your gigolo."

"Don't flatter yourself. I'm just trying to be nice."

"Is that what you Americans call it?" He snorted. "Around here, we call it something else."

"Listen, asshole, I am not trying to seduce you. If you want to sleep on that lumpy sofa, go for it. I thought you might prefer to sleep in a real bed."

She turned on her heel and headed toward the bedroom.

Robert followed her closely. "Oh, you aren't trying to seduce me *this time?*"

She spun to face him. *So, he had noticed.* Her cheeks burned as she recalled her behavior.

"If I only wanted *that*, I could have had it when you were drunk." He grabbed her arm. "Call me old fashioned, but I don't want to be a tourist's Scottish fling."

She jerked away her arm. "Get out!"

"Gladly." He slammed the bedroom door on his exit.

SIMONE CLICKED THE SEATBELT INTO PLACE. The sound echoed in her throbbing head and threatened to split it in two. She closed her eyes and leaned her forehead against the car window, savoring the glass' coolness. The chill provided a momentary escape from the pain.

The events of the previous night haunted her. After their argument, sleep was impossible. Anxiety coiled tightly in her stomach. She tossed and turned in bed, the sheets tangling around her, until a wave of nausea surged through her. The bile crept up her throat, forcing her to rush to the bathroom just in time to empty the contents of her stomach into the toilet bowl.

Robert hastily followed her into the bathroom. He held back her hair and massaged her tense shoulders, murmuring words of comfort. When the vomiting finally subsided, he helped her rise from the bathroom floor and guided her to the sink. She splashed cold water on her face. At his insistence, she brushed her teeth. The action helped her feel like a human again.

He had led her back to bed, where he cradled her in his arms. His comforting presence drowned out the echoes of their fight and soothed her frazzled nerves. She felt a sense of security in his arms, unlike anything she had experienced in a long time. Simone eventually drifted off to sleep.

She awoke alone the following morning. No words were exchanged as they gathered their things and prepared for the journey. Breakfast, too, was a silent affair. The tenderness they shared in the wee hours of the night was a bittersweet memory.

"Drink this," Robert said, handing her a bottle of Irn-Bru when he climbed into the car. "It will help."

She accepted the drink without comment. The man had not led her astray yet regarding queasy stomach cures. There was no point in challenging him now. As instructed, she took a big swig. The refreshing liquid gave her instant relief as it spread down her throat and into her stomach.

He and Simone rode in silence on the journey from Aisling to Inverness. He drove slowly on the two-lane road, taking great care with the curves. She was grateful. Her stomach remained unsettled from the previous evening.

Instead of admiring the fine Scottish scenery, she kept her eyes shut and pressed her head against the window's glass. The trip would be over soon, or at least she hoped. At that moment, it was no longer fun. *The things we do for money,* she grimly thought.

The steady hum of the tires against the asphalt was the only sound. Last night's relaxed conversation at the pub was forgotten. It had been replaced with a silence between them that was awkward and annoying. Something needed to be said.

"Thank you for taking care of me last night." She took another swig of the drink, suspecting her skin was probably orange by now. How many Irn-Brus had she drunk in the last 24 hours? Her blood sugar level must have been a million points after consuming so much sugar.

He shrugged but said nothing. Was he still angry?

"I don't think of you as a fling." She wished he would speak. He kept his eyes on the road, looking uninterested in what she had to say. "I wasn't trying to seduce you last night. I only wanted you to be comfortable."

Robert pulled the car off the road and into a layby. As he switched off the engine, he twisted in his seat and said, "Simone, you are my client. It would be inappropriate to engage in any behavior that…."

She hastily placed the bottle in the drink holder and turned toward him. "I truly apologize for making you uncomfortable. I crossed a line." She briefly closed her eyes, aware of the consequences of her next words. The thought of his acceptance made her slightly nauseous, but she had to say it. "I understand if you want to call your boss and end the tour."

"The attention would have been considered as inappropriate if it was unwanted."

Her mouth dropped open. *Wait, what??* she screamed in her head.

"You are a fabulous woman. Of course, I am flattered." He cleared his throat and idly traced the outlines of the steering wheel, suddenly shy and unable to look at her. "My last relationship ended about a year ago. I wanted to settle down and start a family. She didn't."

"Since then, I haven't dated anyone." He gazed into her eyes. "Truth is, I have been scared. Then, you made me want to give it another try."

He grabbed the door's handle and shoved it open. "There's nothing wrong with you. It's me. I don't want to be someone's fling."

He exited the car and walked several steps away.

Simone was stunned. She watched him pacing in front of the car and repeatedly running his hands through his hair. He mumbled something impossible to hear. What should she do?

Her cell phone buzzed in her pocket, offering a momentary reprieve. "Hello?" she answered.

"Hi! It's Joanna!"

"Oh, hi, how are you?"

"I'm fine." She paused. "You didn't send a picture yesterday. I've been worried about you. Is everything ok?"

"Yes, it is. Sorry. I forgot." Simone hesitated but had to ask. The day couldn't get any worse, could it? She could almost feel the money slipping through her fingers. "Does this mean the inheritance is in jeopardy?"

"Of course not! You can be forgiven for missing one picture." The attorney shuffled papers in the background. "You're traveling to Inverness today, aren't you? Your inn is along the banks of the River Ness. Send me a pic of it, would you?"

Simone wished she and Joanna were friends. She wanted to tell someone what had happened and ask for advice. The situation with Robert had taken a strange turn. What did he mean? How should she respond? Unfortunately, their relationship was professional at best. Emma had been her only real friend.

She kept her mouth shut about the dilemma with Robert, focusing instead on meeting the requirements for the inheritance. She wasn't sure what was unique about the inn, but she agreed to send a picture. With the promise secured, Joanna ended the conversation.

Simone tucked the phone into her pocket. Her companion continued to pace in front of the car and looked more anguished by the second. She should do something, say something... *but what?*

Taking a deep breath, she hopped out of the car and walked toward him. Heartache was a familiar pain. How many times had her heart been broken? It started with the sudden death of her mother and continued with her father's thoughtless behavior in its aftermath. Pain followed her to college, where romances ended in tears, and then into her adult life, where hopes of publishing her work were dashed with each rejection letter. Oh, yes, she knew the pain well and felt terrible for causing it.

Robert moved toward her, an urgent look in his eyes. "I would regret it for the rest of my life if I did not ask," he said as he closed the distance between them. "May I kiss you?"

She nodded mutely, edging closer to him. Kissing him had been on her mind, too. The other night, a lot more than that was possible, too, but now was not the time to rehash it.

When he wrapped his arms around her, time seemed to stop. She placed her hand on his muscular chest, feeling his body heat radiate through the thin fabric of his shirt. The scent of his cologne tingled her senses. Her eyes fluttered to a close as she pressed her body against him and lost herself in the haven of the embrace.

Bending low, Robert gently placed his soft, warm lips upon hers. She parted her lips and slipped her tongue into his mouth, a bold move but something that was irresistible. Simone tasted the honey from his cup of tea.

Lifting her hand to his cheek, she was surprised that his scruffy beard felt much softer than anticipated. What other surprises awaited her? The racy thought flitted unbidden through her brain. His arms tightened around her as the kiss deepened.

Her bones felt like liquid. If he had not been holding her, she would have crumpled into a heap at his feet. How long had it been since someone kissed her like that? Pushing aside the thought, she forced herself to surrender to the moment. The past could be contemplated later. Right now, she stood on the side of a Scottish road, kissing a handsome man.

They would have remained locked in the embrace if the passing car's horn had not startled them. With reluctance, she peeled away her lips from his. "Wow," she said, breathless.

He looked equally flustered. Rubbing her back, Robert gazed into her eyes for several moments. "I don't want to let you go," he whispered. Truthfully, she didn't want him to let go.

Finally, he released her with a heavy sigh. "I supposed we should head for Inverness."

Taking her hand, he guided her back to the car. The feeling of their entwined hands felt perfect, as if they held hands all the time. She dared to savor the feeling, knowing in her mind that it might be fleeting. Those moments always were.

He opened the door for her and helped her to climb inside the vehicle. She watched as he walked around the front of the car, a little smile on his face. Once inside, he sat behind the steering wheel for several moments before starting the vehicle. Obviously, he wanted to say something. So did she. The moment required a comment.

Simone sat frozen as the sweetness of the moment enveloped her. Each beat of her heart echoed in her ears, overwhelming her senses and drowning out any semblance of coherent thought. Words eluded her. She wanted to articulate the sheer thrill of the experience, but the surprise of it all left her speechless.

Peeking at Robert, he, too, wore an expression of surprise and bewilderment. She was relieved she wasn't the only person discombobulated by the experience.

It had been a long time since her last relationship, if she could even call it that. Two dates in, everything ended. The man acted like a nice guy, but he was a total jerk once he discovered she was over 30. He didn't call or text after that. The jerk was only interested in much younger women, even though he had to be over 40 himself.

Sadly, Oak Hill wasn't exactly teeming with eligible suitors. Romantic prospects were very few. Most of the men were already married or well into their senior years. People who were Simone's age tended to have settled lives with their spouses and children. Their single years were long behind them.

Unconsciously, she touched her fingers to her lips. Was it a dream to think they were still warm from his flesh pressed against hers? Robert reawakened a part of her heart that she had closed long ago. Her focus had been on survival for so long. With the money, she could finally relax.

She didn't travel to Scotland in search of romance. Her journey had a singular purpose: to fulfill Emma's wish. This wish was the key to unlocking the million-dollar inheritance that awaited her back home. As she wandered through the gorgeous Scottish landscape, her mind should remain focused on the goal. Each step brought her closer to the fortune that could change everything.

The kiss rocked her world, though. She repeatedly said that romance was not the goal, but the feeling of his arms wrapped around her and his lips moving against hers made her question why it wasn't something to seek.

She glanced at him. Should she tell him about the rest of the inheritance? He thought the trip was a gift, which it was, but he didn't know about the second part. Would it change his feelings toward her? The knowledge might fuel his worries that she only wanted to have a little fun and then return home, solo, to her newfound riches. A fling was the last thing she wanted, but what exactly *did* she want? She wasn't quite sure.

"When we get to Inverness, I'll see you settled at the inn," he said, interrupting her musings. "My grandfather's friend wants to meet this evening."

Simone nodded but said nothing. Why didn't he ask her to go with him? She wrinkled her eyebrows and looked at him. He seemed utterly oblivious to her feelings.

With horror, she realized the moment may have had little meaning to him. The glimmer of hope for something more than a kiss faded, leaving her feeling empty and foolish. It wasn't supposed to be the start of anything. He just wanted the kiss. Now that he had it, he didn't want or need anything else from her.

She felt like an idiot. Here she was, ready to tell him about the money and potentially jump into a relationship. What was she thinking? It was only a kiss to him; nothing more.

Her face reddened with embarrassment. She didn't want him to see how upset she was. Turning her head, Simone stared out the window as they traveled to Inverness. She fought back the tears that filled her eyes. Opening her heart to him was a mistake. It always led to heartache. Why hadn't she learned that lesson?

TWELVE

AS THEY DREW CLOSER TO INVERNESS, SIMONE STILL HELD OUT A FAINT HOPE THAT ROBERT WOULD MENTION THE KISS THEY HAD SHARED. Instead, he seemed eager to give a lecture on the city's importance in Scottish history. He explained how it was considered the unofficial capital of the Highlands and mentioned that they would be staying in the quaint Old Town section. She merely nodded and forced a smile to mask her disappointment as she pretended to absorb his words. Inside, however, she yearned for more than just history lessons, though it chafed her pride to admit it.

When they arrived at the inn, she was pleased to see that it looked well maintained, at least from the exterior. Their inn was a Victorian townhouse that was built along the east bank of the River Ness. The three-story building was made of gray stone like so many of the other structures on the street. The ground floor was dedicated to a small restaurant, a reception area, and, from what she could tell, a few guest rooms in the rear of the building.

To her dismay, her room was on the second floor and could only be accessed via a winding, carpeted stairway. Lack of lifts was a common theme in buildings constructed hundreds of years ago. She reminded herself that lifts, or *elevators* as fellow Americans called them, were a privilege, not a right.

True to his word, Robert made sure she was settled at the inn before he left. He carried her luggage to her room and deposited it there. Handing her a list of good restaurants close to the inn, the man asked if she had everything she needed, told her he would see her in the morning, and left.

She stared at the closed door for several moments, irritated that he had departed so abruptly. Then, she chastised herself for forgetting that it was only a kiss, nothing more. Hoping for a grand romance was foolish. After all, she came on the trip seeking a fortune, not love. Squaring her shoulders, she resolved to enjoy her evening and put aside any worries about his thoughts.

She was pleased to find that the room was cozy and, most importantly, clean when she surveyed it. The room was not as updated as the one they shared in Aisling. Leaving her alone there was not nearly as devastating as it would have been in their previous lodging, though. With a shudder, she recalled how horrid the original room in Aisling was.

The overall furnishings leaned toward practical rather than chic. Thick brown wool curtains hung over the only window in the room, and a matching wool blanket was draped across the end of the twin-sized bed. The mahogany wardrobe on the opposite wall filled the room's available space, leaving a narrow path to the door.

The bathroom was small, too. A massive shower took up nearly the entire room. The white porcelain sink had the same double-tap setup as her original room at the hotel in Aisling. *What the hell was it with that style of faucet?* she wondered.

She tossed her suitcase onto the bed with a thud. Sorting through the garments inside, she selected what would be needed for their time in Inverness and carefully hung each garment in the wardrobe. The task took far less time than she preferred.

Restlessly, she began to pace the hardwood floor. Her footsteps broke the silence, and the sound made her even more anxious. It was too early for bedtime. An odd sense of loneliness settled over her in Robert's absence.

Eager for something to occupy her mind, she grabbed her phone and scrolled through the texts. A couple of people back in Oak Hill promised to check on her father while she was away. They all reported that he was doing well, providing little detail. Her own texts to the man had gone unanswered, which was not unusual. He never seemed to place communication with her as a task that was high on his to-do list.

She flung her hands into the air. Spending the evening in the room would drive her mad. She grabbed the room's skeleton key from the bedside table and twirled it absently. Should she venture out for dinner? Or, perhaps a stroll through the charming streets would help clear her mind? Not having Robert by her side to discuss their plans felt strange.

With a huff, she grabbed her jacket and raced to the door. She didn't need him to tell her what to do every second of the day. "I've done fine without him all this time," she said as she locked the door.

Upon exiting the inn, she took a picture of the place and sent it to the attorney. Forgetting the previous day's picture was a careless mistake she had no plans to repeat. Fulfilling the obligations of the inheritance and collecting the money upon her return was more important than ever. She chided herself for a momentary hiccup in the plan.

The River Ness flowed in front of the inn, its waters glistening in the waning light of the day. A paved, tree-lined path stretched along its banks. She crossed the street and sat on one of the many benches that lined the trail. It seemed like a better place to sort out what to do than sitting in her room.

From her vantage point, she had a lovely view of the opposite side of the river. Inverness Cathedral stood on its west bank. The church's red sandstone looked pink in the sunlight. Rows of green trees surrounded the church, their leaves brightened by the sun.

Old buildings in varying hues of gray clustered around the church. Simone was amused by how quickly she grew accustomed to seeing aged architecture. Stone buildings that were easily hundreds of years old were commonplace now. How strange that the relatively young structures in Oak Hill seemed like a distant memory.

Turning to the right, she noticed a burly man

taking pictures of the church. He eventually sat on a nearby bench and scrolled through the screens on his phone. Did his flaming red hair mark him as a local? *Oh, the Scottish stereotypes,* she thought with amusement.

A pregnant woman waddled toward him and joined him on the bench. They spoke for several minutes. Then, the conversation seemed to shift from friendly to hostile. She gesticulated wildly while the man nodded and seemed to accept whatever criticism the woman gave.

Simone envied the woman. She wished she could have been so expressive with Robert. He had hurt her feelings without realizing it. She wanted him to know but wasn't sure how to explain it or if he would even care to hear the words.

She stood, deciding to walk in the opposite direction. She passed two- and three-story Victorian townhomes converted into bed-and-breakfast inns to accommodate weary travelers. Their names were quintessentially Scottish—the Jacobite, the Thistle, the Bonnie Lass. She smiled at the wooden signs in front of each one, appreciating the absence of neon.

She found a lovely garden at the end of the street. It honored those lost in World War I. On one side of the garden, the names of the fallen were etched into a thick marble slab, its rose color soft in the sun's diffused light. A Celtic cross made of red sandstone towered high above her.

On the opposite side, red, purple, yellow, and white flowers nestled in snug beds between patches of vibrant green grass. A red brick path looped through the garden and ended before a black plaque.

Simone carefully read the gold letters of the inscription on the plaque. The place was called Cavell Gardens. A nurse named Edith Louise Cavell assisted 130 people in their escape from Belgium. She was captured and executed in October 1915. The garden memorialized her bravery and that of the souls lost in the First World War.

She snapped several photos of the garden as she strolled through it again. In all of the conversations Emma and she had about Scotland, Cavell Gardens was not mentioned. She felt deep regret that she could not tell her friend about the peaceful place. Emma would have loved the beautiful memorial garden.

Would Robert find the garden interesting? The desire to share the beauty of the garden with him was intense, despite her current feelings about the man. She tucked her phone securely into her jacket pocket as she returned to the inn.

A plan began to take shape in her mind. Simone decided to casually mention the garden, hoping the description would interest Robert and, in turn, compel him to open up about his experience with his grandfather's friend. A slight smile tugged at the corners of her lips as she envisioned the conversation unfolding, pleased with her clever approach. Tricking him was not something that made her proud, but she ruefully decided it was a necessity.

TO HER DISAPPOINTMENT, ROBERT WAS NOT AT THE INN. Simone first knocked on the door to his room but received no answer. She headed downstairs, where she peeked into the empty restaurant. He was nowhere to be found. Could he still be visiting with his grandfather's friend?

Just as she was about to give up on her search, she glanced outside and spotted Robert sitting alone on a bench across the street. He seemed deeply engrossed in a book. Simone debated leaving him to his reading, but curiosity got the better of her.

She carefully arranged her features into what she believed was a casual expression. Her heart raced slightly from excitement and nerves as she strode toward him.

"I discovered a garden at the end of the street," she said, trying hard to sound nonchalant. "It's called Cavell Gardens. The paths are lined with flowers and greenery. It's gorgeous. Have you had the chance to see it?"

"Aye. I should have told you about the garden." He continued to read the journal, not bothering to look up at her. "It is very nice."

She slid her hands into the pockets of her jacket. She felt the familiar shape of her phone nestled inside. A flicker of temptation passed through her as she contemplated sharing the pictures with him. But doubt crept in when she caught his distant, preoccupied expression. She decided against it.

"I am surprised you are here," she said.

He nodded but did not speak.

"I thought you might stay longer with your grandfather's friend."

He seemed annoyed by the interruption. "It was a

short visit." He briefly looking up at her before returning his attention to the journal.

Simone pointedly looked at the space beside him. When the man did not take the hint, she huffed and sat anyway. "Was it a good visit?"

"Aye. He gave me a journal that my grandfather wanted the family to have." He waved the book in his hands. "I have been reading it."

She wanted to grab the book and fling it into the river. The man seemed completely oblivious to the tension that she felt so plainly.

Realizing that only someone truly desperate would choose to linger where they so clearly weren't wanted, she decided to leave. With a heavy sigh, she pushed away from the bench and rose to her feet. "Well, I suppose I'll leave you to it then," she said, forcing a lightness into her voice that she didn't feel. "See you bright and early tomorrow."

"Aye, 8:00 a.m. sharp!" He had already turned his attention back to the journal, her presence dismissed.

Well, that didn't go as planned! Emma's ghost exclaimed.

"Tell me about it," Simone grumbled as she crossed the street and stomped back into the inn.

THIRTEEN

SIMONE STOOD ALONE ON THE PAVED PATH, STARING AT THE LONELY EXPANSE OF CULLODEN MOOR. In April 1746, the Jacobites made their last stand there. Tired, hungry men fought in terrible conditions against a well-fed and well-rested British army. Whole generations of families were cut down. A way of life ended.

She scanned the tall, golden grass waving in the cool breeze. In the distance, she saw gently rolling mountains and wondered if dying soldiers looked to the hills, some spying their distant homelands. If she concentrated hard enough, she could almost transport herself to that sad day in 1746.

Almost. The endless chatter from a nearby band of teenagers shattered any reverence for the place. The group was always close at heel, eager to snap selfies or loudly discuss who liked whom. Their weary teacher tried to wrangle the kids as best as possible, but there were too many of them. Finally, she pointed them toward the battlefield and headed for the café in the museum.

Maybe she'll find Robert, she thought. His services were not needed today. The carefully curated exhibits inside the museum told the whole story of the battle, and docents were on hand to answer any questions she might have.

In addition to the exhibits, an immersive theater played a film that re-enacted scenes from the battle. The brutal scenes filled her with dread since she knew the battlefield was the next destination. Out of the corner of her eye, she saw Robert flinch with the firing of the Redcoats' guns. The film was hard to watch especially when one was as well-versed in history as he was.

They stumbled out of the theater together. Though she would have preferred that he accompany her, he pointed to the glass doors leading outside. His work was done for him, so he told her to stay on the battlefield's path. Then, he headed back to the café.

As he walked away, she spied the journal in his hand. He undoubtedly wanted to tuck away in a corner of the café with a cup of tea while he read his grandfather's words. She should be happy for him. Really. But, why wasn't she?

You know damn well why, Emma's ghost fussed in her ear.

For one brief moment, the money waiting for her after the trip's completion was forgotten. Wasn't it the reason she came to Scotland? A bright future awaited her. She could do whatever she wanted, free from debt and flush with cash. And, yet, she hesitated.

As Emma's ghost said, she knew why. Long dormant feelings stirred in her heart the moment his lips touched hers. His arms around her gave a sense of peace and security she had not felt since her mother was alive. All the anxieties that plagued her thoughts disappeared. There had only been that moment, nothing else. It was just the two of them, kissing on the side of a Scottish road.

She wanted to hold on to the calm. It felt terrific to stop the constant whirlwind of thoughts in her brain, to just stop thinking about *everything*. Sadly, the serenity slipped away in the blink of an eye. His behavior since the kiss confirmed her fears. Opening her heart always led to disappointment.

The basic fact was they lived different lives. He was a history teacher in Edinburgh, thousands of miles from Oak Hill. She was a writer – yes, she could finally proclaim it – who lived in America. Thanks to her friend's benevolence, the world was at her feet. She didn't need to be with Robert. Did she *want* to?

She closed her eyes and inhaled the cool air. There had to be a way to make it work. Travel was now within her means. Jetting back and forth to Scotland wasn't a crazy idea. A long-distance relationship was possible.

Of course, if she left Oak Hill, it would mean leaving her father. Who would take care of him in her absence? The man needed her, didn't he? Simone feared the answer to that question as much as she did her own feelings.

The sound of heavy footfalls pulled her away from her thoughts. She opened her eyes to see Robert striding toward her, journal in hand. He was the last person she wanted to see right then. She needed time to sort out her feelings.

"I'm ready to go back to Inverness," she lied. She attempted to pass him, but he grabbed her arm.

"Why? We haven't been here that long."

She jerked her arm out of his grasp. "What's your deal?" she said, louder than she meant.

Her outburst caught the attention of the teenagers who gathered a few feet away. One of the bolder lads made an unfriendly gesture at Robert before retreating to the crowd's safety. Simone tried not to smirk. At this point, she wanted to flash the same gesture.

"What is it?" he asked, returning her attention to him. "What have I done?"

"You haven't done *anything*. That's the problem!"

He gave her a confused look.

She raised her hands to her face. "Oh, my goodness! You have no idea, do you?" At the shake of his head, she exclaimed in disbelief, "Absolutely maddening!"

Simone took a few steps away, needing some distance between them. "It is hot and cold with you, Robert. One minute, you are lecturing me about the inappropriateness of sharing a room. Then, you take care of me when I am sick. And THEN, you kiss me on the side of the road and talk about how I have made you want to date again."

She paused to draw her breath. "And THEN, you act as if nothing happened. You leave me in Inverness while you visit your grandfather's friend. You don't tell me what happened." She pointed to the journal. "You don't even tell me what's in the journal."

She closed the distance between them, her face inches from his. "So, *what's your deal?*"

Robert moved several steps away from her and paced, his agitation evident. Running his hand through his hair, he finally returned to her side. He opened and closed his mouth several times as if struggling to speak.

Simone felt the heat creeping up her neck. "Consider your words very, very carefully," she warned.

"When we arrived in Inverness, I felt my grandfather's presence. I don't know how to explain it. It was as if my grandfather wanted me to be there." He lifted the journal. "This book was his gift to our family."

"Did you find answers to your questions?"

"Aye." He offered the journal to her. "Please read it."

"No."

"No? Why not? You said you wanted to know."

"I wanted *you* to tell me. Not because you felt you had to. Because you *wanted* to."

"That's what I am doing now, Simone."

"What do you want?"

He flung his hands into the air. "We are having two different conversations," he said. "What are *you* talking about?"

"What are we doing?" she asked, suddenly drained. "I honestly don't know what you want from me. Are you looking for a relationship? Do you only want to be friends?" She lowered her voice. "Did the kiss mean anything at all?"

"It meant something. It's just..."

"What?"

"I am supposed to show you our bonnie country." His shoulders dropped. "That was the assignment. I never expected I would meet such a wonderful woman."

"For the rest of my life, I would regret it if I hadn't kissed you," he said, pulling her close. "I meant that when I said it. Yes, I'm being selfish, but that's how I feel."

Simone pushed away from him. "Is that all you want, Robert?"

"No, it isn't, but we cannot ignore the truth."

"Which is?"

"You will depart for America in a few days, and I will stay in Scotland. You will return to your life. Then, I will return to mine."

She stared at him, unable to argue. After all, the same thought ran through her mind. "I'm ready to go back to Inverness," she repeated.

This time, Robert did not stop her.

THE FULL MOON'S SLENDER FINGER OF LIGHT POKED THROUGH THE OPENING IN

THE WINDOW'S CURTAIN. The silver orb ascended into the indigo sky, gliding past sparkling stars. Its ancient magic was alive, ready to open hearts and minds. Simone felt it deep inside her bones, a mystical feeling she couldn't quite explain.

She looked down at the garden behind the inn. The trees cast long shadows over a little patch of grass, creating mysterious spaces where all manner of sins could be committed. A stone bench rested beneath one of the trees. It marked the perfect spot for a late-night kiss...or perhaps more.

Beyond the courtyard, row upon row of townhomes slept in the stillness of the night. Their darkened windows resembled eyes shut tight after a long day. What scenes had the homes witnessed over the centuries? What secrets did they hide?

Sleep came for them, but not her. Her mind refused to rest. Instead, it repeated the scene at the battlefield. So many things were not said that should have been. The outcome could have been very different, yet Simone's past prevented her from telling him exactly what she wanted. After endless hours of fretting about it, her heart trembled at the thought of revealing her feelings to him.

She twisted the curtain in her hands, its wool making her skin itch. Shaking her head, she released the curtain and shook it to remove any wrinkles. It wasn't the poor curtain's fault that she was restless this evening.

Looking at the ceiling, she said aloud, "What have you done, Emma? You didn't have to send me to Scotland. You could have given me the money outright."

She lowered her head and waited for an answer.

Simone's life had not been easy. When her mother died, she was forced to grow up. The carefree teenager who worried about wearing the right clothes or dating the right guy disappeared overnight. Her father needed her. Lost in a drunken fog of grief, the man was incapable of caring for himself, let alone his child.

"If you hadn't been there to push me, I would have abandoned college," she said, still awaiting a response. "You supported me when no one else did."

You were there for me, too, the ghost whispered.

Simone sniffed loudly, willing herself not to cry. For three agonizing years, she stuck by her friend's side while Emma battled cancer. It was brutal. Endless visits to the doctor. Several stays in the hospital. Three terrible rounds of chemotherapy. They managed to beat it back for a few months. Just when they thought the enemy was retreating, cancer roared back and ultimately won the war.

"Now, I'm alone," she said. "Sure, I'll be a millionaire when I return to America, but money means nothing without you here by my side."

You have him, came the reply.

Simone knew exactly who 'him' was. Not her father. Never that man. A tiny tear escaped her eye and trickled down her cheek. It was the only tear she would surrender. She must remain strong, as she always did.

She leaned against the invisible hand caressing her cheek. *My sweet angel,* Emma's ghost whispered, *it's time to take care of yourself. Open your heart, and you will find happiness.*

Swallowing hard, she grabbed the room's key and flung open the door. Her hand shook as she closed and locked it. Her feet carried her down the hallway, her body moving on its own. Her conscious mind was no longer in control. She found herself in front of the door to Robert's room before she realized what was happening.

She placed her hand on its surface. The wood was worn smooth from decades of use. Looking down, she noticed the brass lock. The door probably wouldn't open without a skeleton key.

Or a knock.

She lightly rapped on the door. She heard no answer, so she knocked harder.

Again, no one answered. She stepped away from the door and turned back to her room. Coming to him was a foolish idea.

The click of the lock stopped her. The door slowly opened.

"Hello?" Robert's sleepy voice asked.

He leaned one arm against the door jam and blinked at the bright light streaming into his dark room. "Simone," he said, rubbing the sleep from his eyes. "Is everything ok?"

Her heart pounded as she stared at him. *What am I doing?* The phrase repeated itself in her brain. The words, thankfully, did not reach her mouth.

"Yes," she answered, her voice sounding strange to her ears. "I couldn't sleep."

He widened the opening of the door and stepped

aside. "Come in."

Her feet propelled her into the room. He closed the door behind her, plunging the room into darkness. She heard him fumbling with a lamp. When he switched it on, its yellow light revealed a surprising sight. She forgot the original purpose for coming to him.

"Son of a bitch!" she exclaimed.

He chuckled. His room was twice the size of hers. The double bed took up a great deal of space, but there was still plenty of room for a nightstand on each side of the bed, a large wardrobe, and a small desk. Without thinking, she rushed to the bathroom and flipped the light switch. Light flooded the space.

As she suspected, the commodious bathroom sink had only one tap. "Son of a bitch!" she exclaimed again.

A gleaming white tub with shiny brass claw feet stood atop sparkling marble tiles. Beside it, a shower that could easily accommodate two people offered another bathing option.

"I guess the guides are given the best rooms," he said, guffawing loudly.

"Apparently." She shook her head. "Unbelievable."

"If you want to switch rooms, we can."

"No, no," she said, stepping out of the spacious bathroom and switching off the light. "My room is fine. I am just surprised; that's all."

Robert grasped the wooden chair and slid it away from the desk. He gestured for her to sit. As she did so, he settled himself on the edge of the bed, its springs creaking softly beneath him. The room's dim light created an intimate yet still tense atmosphere.

He studied her for a moment, an eyebrow raised. "I doubt you came here in the middle of the night just to compare rooms," he remarked, with a hint of curiosity in his voice.

Simone perched on the edge of the chair. The room's fancy fixtures were a momentary diversion. Why *was* she there?

She cleared her throat and scanned the room, avoiding his eyes. "I couldn't sleep."

"Aye, you already told me."

"Oh." She looked down at her clenched hands.

He reached across the space between them and gently opened her hands. As he massaged the palms of her hands, he asked, "What troubles you, lass?"

"There's something I need to tell you." She forced herself to peer into those lovely eyes that reminded her of pools of melted chocolate. Her heart skipped a beat. *Oh, goodness,* she thought, suddenly unsure of herself.

Swallowing hard, she tried to ignore the feel of his warm fingertips and focus on what she wanted to say. "Ever since my mother died, everyone else came first."

"Including Emma?" he asked, his hands moving up her arms.

She nodded. "I never told her this story." She closed her eyes, reliving the day. "About three years ago, I was offered a dream job in New York City. I was so excited. I raced home to tell Emma the news. When I walked through the door, I knew something was wrong. The last time she had that look on her face, my mother died."

"Emma's doctor told her that she had cancer." Simone opened her watery eyes. "Naturally, I couldn't leave her, so I turned down the job."

"When you return to America, will you search for a similar job?"

"I have different dreams now." She joined him on the bed. "Robert, could we forget everything wrong about this situation? For a few moments, at least."

"Aye," Robert answered. He swept one hand up her back and wrapped it into her hair. "I would like that very much."

Years later, Simone would look back on what happened next as the most amazing experience of her life. The moment felt like a union of souls more than bodies. Calling it *sex* seemed vulgar. The physical act became spiritual as they poured their hearts into every caress and every kiss.

Like two souls thirsty for blessed relief, they surrendered to the passion that had built between them since they met. Time seemed to stop. It was only the two of them together. All worries and doubts about the future faded away.

They collapsed into each other's arms when they reached the inevitable climax. No words were said. Nothing needed to be just then. The morning would arrive soon enough with its harsh reality. Then, sleep tiptoed into the room and carried them away to sweet rest.

FOURTEEN

SIMONE AWOKE WITH A START THE NEXT MORNING. The light streaming through the window meant she had overslept. She bolted upright. Was Robert waiting for her in the lobby? Her heart pounded as she flung aside the bed covers and dashed around the room, collecting her clothes from the floor. She had never been so messy in her life. Why had she overslept? Did she have time to pack her things?

Then, she heard laughter coming from the direction of the bed. Robert watched her, a massive grin on his face. "It's usually the man who tries to leave before the lady wakes up, not vice versa."

In a rush, she recalled the events of the previous evening. She blushed. It was unusual of her to hop into bed with a stranger, but did he qualify as one? They had already been together for a few days. She couldn't exactly call him a stranger.

Don't overanalyze, Emma's voice whispered in her ear. *Enjoy the moment.*

Carrying her clothes, she returned to the bed and sat beside him. She fumbled with the frayed edge of her pajama bottoms. Simone had never been the one doing the leaving. What was the protocol?

He slid closer to her. "What are you doing?" he asked, pressing her hand against his lips. "You are welcome to stay longer."

"It must be late." She couldn't look him in the eyes. Trying to divert attention, she pointed to the window. Golden sunlight streamed through the glass. "Don't we depart for Oban today?"

He rubbed his eyes, trying to wake up. "Aye, but I thought things might have changed after last night."

Simone looked down at their interlaced hands. Something had changed in her heart, yet she was afraid. She wasn't sure if she was ready. Everyone else who ever occupied a place there let her down. She would be crushed if he joined the list.

"Didn't you say your grandfather is buried in Oban?" She decided to guide the conversation to safer territory. It was too early – and she was too naked – to discuss feelings about what had happened between them.

Reaching for her, he tried to pull her back into the bed. She resisted. He cocked his eyebrow but said nothing.

Robert sighed heavily as he pushed aside the bed covers and sat upright. "Aye, he is. I suppose we should hit the road soon." He glanced at the wad of clothes in her hands. "How quickly can you be ready?"

She stood and hurriedly began dressing. It did not take long since she came to the room the previous evening in her pajamas. Locating her slippers and her room's key, she raced to the door. "Give me 30 minutes," she said, her hand on the doorknob. "I'll meet you in the hallway."

Simone opened the door and fled before he replied.

SIMONE TOOK THE FASTEST SHOWER IN HER LIFE. After quickly applying blush and mascara, she pulled her damp hair into a loose ponytail. It didn't take long to pack the few items into her luggage and head for the door. She had every intention of keeping her promise to be ready quickly.

She shoved her luggage into the hallway. Robert was walking toward her with his bags. Perhaps he didn't expect her to be ready and intended to wait in her room. That seemed like an awfully intimate experience.

With a blush, she vividly recalled their genuinely intimate experience the previous night. Waiting while she packed was not comparable, of course. She still was not quite ready to speak with him, and, if he had lingered in her tiny room, conversation would have been unavoidable. The drive to Oban promised to be very awkward.

She made a show of locking the door and fiddling with her suitcase. When he reached her side, there was no help for it. She had to speak with him. Forcing a smile, she stupidly asked, "Ready to go?"

Of course, he's ready to go. His bags are packed, and he is standing right there. If ghosts had eyes, Emma's were no doubt rolling at the moment.

"Not now," Simone whispered to the woman's ghost.

"Excuse me?" Robert said as he made his way towards the staircase that led to the lobby.

"Nothing."

Thankfully, Robert needed to tend to the details of checking out. The activity gave her an excuse to leave him and the luggage at the front desk. As she stepped outside, she inhaled the cool, crisp air and noticed the damp pavement. She had not heard the rain last night. Her face turned red when she recalled why.

Are you gonna stop worrying about how he will react to your feelings? Emma's ghost asked. *You like the man. Tell him. He may surprise you, and say that he likes you too.*

Simone sighed in exasperation. Though dead, the woman apparently would not leave her in peace today.

The truth was, she was scared. Everything Robert said about them living separate lives, thousands of miles away from each other, was true. They were thrown together on a road trip through Scotland. When it ended, would their relationship end, too? Would last night become a lovely memory, something to recall with fondness as the years went by?

While she was not a relationship expert, she felt sure it didn't have to end. The way he looked at her, the way he touched her, the things he whispered to her in the quiet moments of the night…all signs pointed to ardent affection. He wanted more from her if she was willing to give it.

Simone jumped when he appeared at her side. "I am a bit peckish," he said. "There's a nice café not too far from here. Why don't we put our luggage in the car and grab breakfast before we head out?"

She nodded. While he loaded the bags into the car, she walked across the street and sat on one of the benches. The gentle murmur of the River Ness as it glided by and birds singing in the trees above her created the perfect soundtrack for serenity. Closing her eyes, she took a deep breath. She needed a settled mind before the unavoidable conversation over breakfast.

"Lass, do you mind if I sit beside you?" a voice interrupted her quiet meditation.

She opened her eyes. As the man took a seat, she immediately recognized him. He was the flame-haired man. "You were here yesterday, taking pictures, weren't you?"

"Aye, I was." He smiled warmly. "I have taken a keen interest in photography."

She swept her hand to encompass their surroundings. "You have fine scenery for it."

"Oh, aye, I do. Scotland is a bonnie country." He gave her a quizzical look. "I do not mean to be rude, but you don't sound Scottish. You sound a lot like my wife."

Simone chuckled. "I am from America. North Carolina, to be specific."

"Oh, aye? My wife is from North Carolina."

"Small world."

He jerked his thumb over his shoulder. "Is your man from North Carolina, too?"

"Oh, no, he's Scottish, like you."

Something about the stranger put her at ease. Confiding in him did not feel like a bad thing, and she really needed to talk with a living human at the moment. Leaning closer, she said in a low voice, "And I'm not entirely sure he is my man."

He considered the information. "Well, lass, why isn't he?" Rubbing his chin, he added, "I saw the two of you together. I can tell he wants to be your man by how he looks at you. Why are you uncertain about it?"

"I don't know if I am ready. People have disappointed me a lot in the past." She lowered her head. "Plus, there are complications."

"Such as?"

"Well, I've been taking care of my father ever since my mother died. I am not sure if he could survive without me." She waved her hand. "And, then, there's the practical matter of distance. We live thousands of miles away from each other."

"Will you take some advice from a stranger?"

She nodded.

"I had given up on having a family of my own. For years, I devoted myself to my friend and his family. I put their needs before my own." He shook his head, his blue eyes growing misty. "It was a very lonely existence."

"Then, my sweet wife appeared. Suddenly, all of my dreams were within reach. Though it hurt to leave my friend, I had to follow my heart – and he understood."

He couldn't resist smiling. "She gave me a love that completely transformed my life in ways I never imagined. Perhaps it is time you open your heart, lass."

"What about my father?"

"What about him?" The man shrugged. "If he has any feeling in his heart for you, then he will understand, just as my friend did."

Simone frowned. "I am not sure if the man is capable of caring for anyone but himself."

"Then, that's all the more reason for you to step away."

"Why?"

"Sometimes, you have to take care of yourself first."

She fumbled for another excuse. "Robert lives here, though," she argued. "I live in America."

"Never let distance be a reason," the man said as he stood. "I traveled a very long way to be with my wife. It was the best decision I ever made."

She watched him walk toward the inn. The stranger smiled at Robert as they passed each other.

"Are you ready?" Robert asked when he joined her at the bench.

Simone took one last look at the stranger before answering, "Yes, I think so."

FIFTEEN

SIMONE STOOD BESIDE ROBERT ON THE ROCKY SHORE OF LOCH NESS, THE RUIN OF URQUHART CASTLE AT HER BACK. Waves carved paths in the water and gently lapped the smooth rocks at her feet. A duck with a purple feathered head swam nearby, occasionally squawking its disapproval at their presence. A white boat took tourists on trips around the famous lake. Its name, Nessie Hunter, was emblazoned on the ship's side, leaving little doubt about the stories that were probably being told to its passengers. She shook her head at the silliness.

Robert had been adamant about stopping there instead of traveling straight to Oban. She was secretly grateful. She needed a few moments of peace to collect her thoughts. Everything that happened in Inverness changed the nature of the trip. Completing it no longer centered around collecting a big check upon her return. Now that her situation with Robert suddenly became intimate, she faced new challenges and, worse of all, more decisions to make.

The stranger's words repeated themselves in her head. It was as if her friend Emma had spoken through the man. Opening her heart was dangerous. She had done it many times in the past. Inevitably, lovers and even her father disappointed her. After so many heartbreaks, retreating behind a wall around her heart seemed like the safest option. The environment there was familiar. It was easier to stay in Oak Hill and never take any chances. What would she gain, though, if she let Robert slip away?

The stranger told her his wife brought him love. Emma was gone. Her father would always be a weight around her neck, but should she let it be? The ties that bound Simone to her old life were seemingly unbreakable, but didn't she deserve the chance to break them? Wasn't it time to think about her future? She deserved love and happiness, didn't she?

She glanced at Robert. Her companion stared into the distance, lost in his thoughts. Did he regret what had happened last night? Was he trying to think of a way to tell her?

Please don't be so negative, she thought. The man could be thinking about many other things. She shouldn't automatically believe he wanted to break her heart. The stranger in Inverness was right. Maybe it was time to give love a chance.

Tentatively, Simone reached across the distance that separated them. She placed her hand on Robert's arm. He jumped at her touch and took his eyes away from the rippling waters of the loch. "Is everything okay?"

"I'm scared."

He chuckled and turned his gaze back to the loch. "You need not worry, lass. The stories about Nessie aren't true. She's not going to crawl from the waters and grab you."

Glad for a bit of levity, she smiled. "You know what I mean."

Returning her smile, he said, "Aye, I do. I am scared, too."

She exhaled, not realizing she had been holding her breath. "There are a thousand reasons why this cannot work."

"If it did work, what a story we would have." He caressed her cheek. "I want to know more about you; that's all. We don't have to rush into anything. Will you let me in?"

Simone looked away. He gently turned her face back to him. "Aye, it is terrifying," he said. "I am willing to take the chance if you are."

With her heart beating fast in her chest, she swallowed hard. It was a crucial moment. If she said no, she could return to her old life, and her heart would be safe.

Suddenly, safety seemed less desirable. Giving up a chance to experience the love reflected in his eyes seemed like the most dangerous thing to do.

"Yes," she breathed as she softly kissed his warm lips. Simone suppressed a giggle when his scruffy beard tickled her face. The tender moment was not the right time for laughter, especially at the beginning of a relationship.

Relationship, she thought with a thrill. She never expected to use the word, but the money from the inheritance meant she could use many new words. Of course, what waited for her at home could not be forgotten. Once again, she wondered how Robert would react when she told him about it.

The man in question withdrew from the kiss. "Where are you now? You disappeared on me halfway through the kiss. Was it that bad?" He cupped his hand and breathed into it. Sniffing, he commented, "My breath seems okay."

"It's not you." She eased away from him and handed him her phone. "I just remembered that I haven't sent a picture to the attorney today."

Shaking his head, he took the picture and returned the phone to her. He watched as she sent it.

"So, what's so special about this place?" She took his hand. Holding hands with a beau was a unique experience, something she did not wish to disclose to him. It might make her sound like a lonely spinster.

"In 1509, Clan Grant was given the barony of Urquhart Castle, along with instructions to restore it." He nodded approvingly at the smile of delight on her face. "Aye, I thought that information would get your attention."

As they climbed the short steps from the loch's shore to the walkway leading to the ruin, Robert explained that the castle held a strategic spot on the loch. Its location was a very attractive to any enemy. The gatehouse of Urquhart Castle was destroyed in 1692. British government troops were garrisoned there then and did not want the castle to ever fall into enemy hands, especially if those hands belonged to Jacobites.

"Without going into a rather long, detailed explanation about who the Jacobites were, I'll summarize it for you," he said. "The Jacobites were fighters who did not agree with England about who should rule Scotland."

"Obviously, there is more to the story than that." He grinned sheepishly. "I can prattle on for hours about stuff like this. You would probably be bored to tears."

"Thank you," she said with genuine relief. She wasn't ready for another lecture.

Simone touched the rough stones of the castle's walls. "Why didn't someone restore the castle?"

"Parliament pledged to give the laird money for the restoration. It was never received, so the castle fell into ruin."

Despite his promise not to discuss history's details, Robert then launched into a lesson about the many Jacobite rebellions in Scotland. "Everyone talks about the one in 1745, but there were several rebellions," he explained. He rattled off the years of all the rebellions to thoroughly explain.

She liked the way his eyes shone when he talked about the rebellions. The stories of centuries-old intrigues clearly fascinated him. Listening to his description made her feel she had been transported back in time. *His students must love him,* she thought.

They walked around the ruined castle, climbing broken turrets and admiring the sweeping views of the loch. They peered into the prison cell where a legendary Gaelic bard was rumored to be held.

Robert painted a fascinating picture of how the castle would have looked in its glory days. The crumbled walls and shattered rooms disappeared, replaced with an image of an ancient castle set on the shore of Scotland's famous loch. He talked of the grand banquets that would have been held in the Great Hall and showed her the remains of the Grant Tower. Simone could have stayed there for hours listening to his stories.

Eventually, he guided her up a slight hill to the visitor center and shop. A concrete platform offered a better view of the ruined castle. Standing on a hill to the castle's right, Scotland's Saltire flapped proudly in the breeze. She waited until the flag unfurled in full before snapping a picture. The heavily wooded mountains and rippling waters of the loch were the perfect background for the image, giving her something to treasure in the years to come. Looking up at Robert, she noticed how happy he seemed.

"What is it?"

"I am glad you are finally enjoying the trip." He leaned closer and whispered, "Not just because of last night, of course."

Simone blushed slightly and hurried into the shop. It had been a truly magical evening, but discussing it in the open was embarrassing.

She pretended to be interested in a stack of wool scarves arranged on a table beside the door. "Which one is my clan's tartan again?" she asked as she ran her fingers over the scratchy material.

"There is some debate about whether or not we

truly know the correct tartan patterns for each clan," he said. "But you don't want to hear about that, do you?"

She shook her head.

He pointed to a tartan. "That one." He perused the other scarves on the table. "Don't you want to buy a different pattern for one of your friends?"

She moved to the opposite side of the table. "I don't have any friends."

He put his hands on his hips. "You don't? Why?"

Shrugging, she answered, "Well, writing isn't exactly a social hobby."

"You don't write all the time, do you?"

Simone hesitated. Her lack of social life was not an easy topic. "No," she said. "It's hard to explain."

Robert moved closer to her. "Try me."

"I like this one," she said, plucking a scarf from one of the piles and holding it to her face. "Does it make my complexion look good?"

He took the scarf from her and returned it to the pile. "Please tell me," he said. "Why don't you have any friends?"

"I should pay for the scarf," she mumbled as she retrieved the item and went to the cashier.

He followed her. His lips were close to her ear when he whispered, "This conversation isn't over."

Simone gave the clerk a weak smile. Unfortunately, the transaction was handled with speed. She placed the scarf in her purse and noticed Robert staring expectantly. "Not here," she said in a low voice.

"Fine. Outside then." He turned on his heel and headed for the door, leaving her to trail behind him.

Spotting a bench, she motioned for him to join her. Once they were both seated, she resumed the uncomfortable conversation. "It's not as if I never had friends," she said. "I was very popular in high school."

"High school was a long time ago."

"Yes, it was." Simone fiddled with her purse straps, not wanting to meet his gaze. "After my mom died, things changed. I had to take care of my dad. My friends drifted away. We didn't have anything in common anymore."

"You went to college. Did you have friends there?"

"I worked on school nights and came home to care for my dad on the weekends. I didn't have much spare time."

"And now?"

"People have families to raise or businesses to run. It's hard to make friends as you age, especially when you don't have those things in common."

"This trip can begin a new chapter for you." Robert put his arm around her shoulders. "You deserve to be happy."

The weight of the moment pressed heavily upon her. She felt great trepidation as she considered revealing the second part of the inheritance to him. This was the perfect chance, yet doubt gnawed at her. What would he think of her decision? As uncertainty swirled in her mind, she shifted restlessly in her seat, her fingers tugging on the edges of her jacket.

"Are you cold?" he asked, mistaking her movement for chills.

She chuckled inwardly and shook her head. His comment amused her. The temperature difference between a chilly summer in Scotland and the sweltering heat of the humid American South was quite dramatic. Though jackets were required nearly every day during their road trip, she had difficulty saying she was 'cold.'

The moment to reveal her secret had passed. It was just as well. She was not ready. He would undoubtedly expect her to have a plan because who wouldn't with such a massive sum of money at their fingertips? Unfortunately, she didn't know what she wanted to do. For most of her adult life, preparing for the future seemed impossible. Her motto was to put one foot in front of the other and keep moving.

With that in mind, she offered her hand to him. "Let's head to Oban. I've seen enough, Mr. Tour Guide."

He rose but did not take her hand or follow as she walked away. She turned, confused. "What? Is there some fascinating bit of history I need to know before we leave?"

Robert slowly walked to her side. "Thank you for sharing a small piece of yourself. I know it was hard for you." He kissed her hand. "I hope you will tell me the rest. Something else troubles you."

She looked away. *Busted,* she thought.

He pulled his grandfather's journal from the interior pocket of his jacket and handed it to her.

"When we get to Oban, will you read it?"

She accepted the journal. Releasing his hand, she flipped through the yellowed pages. The unmistakable whiff of an old book reached her nostrils. His grandfather's writing was neat, filling the pages with line after line of words written in tidy cursive. It appeared as if the man offered a very long and detailed account of something, but what?

"He explained why he left and shared a glimpse into the life he led after he left the family," Robert said. "I think he wanted an opportunity to tell his side of the story."

Simone flipped to the last page of the journal. His grandfather apologized for the pain he caused and signed the page. Gasping, she read the signature aloud. "Robert Gordon Sr."

"Aye. My dad was named after the man." He pointed to the page. "Then, I was named after my dad. I never thought about it until I saw my grandfather's signature."

She stared at the signature for a long time. Robert had offered an insight into his life. It seemed only fair that she returned the favor. Removing her phone from her pocket, she tapped the screen several times. "Can you check email on your phone?"

He nodded and gave her his email address.

After a few taps on her phone, she looked up at him. "I sent you a PDF version of one of my novels," she said, tucking the device into her pocket.

"Wow! Thank you. I cannot wait to read it."

"Don't get your hopes up."

He dismissively waved his hand. "I am sure it is fabulous."

"We'll see." She lifted her eyebrows. "Ready to go now?"

Simone felt an overwhelming sense of peace and security as their fingers interlocked. The afternoon sun emerged from the clouds and hovered over them, creating a strange shadow on the black asphalt. It had been too long since she had seen an image of a couple holding hands and had known that she was one part of that couple. The sensation lingered when she hopped into the car.

Was this the beginning of a new chapter, as Robert suggested? Her hometown was a place filled with memories and lost opportunities but now could it transform into a place ripe with new possibilities? She could almost envision the chances ahead, waiting for her to embrace them. But deep down, a question gnawed at her: Would one of those precious opportunities include Robert?

She watched him as he walked around to the driver's side of the car. The way he moved, with an easy confidence and a slight smile tugging at the corners of his lips, drew her attention. Did he genuinely want to be a part of this new life she was crafting?

And more critically, did she want him to share in that journey? The thought lingered in her mind, both exhilarating and terrifying. Simone felt like she stood on the edge of a cliff, contemplating the leap into the unknown.

SIXTEEN

SIMONE NIBBLED ON A PIECE OF FRIED FISH AS SHE PLACED THE JOURNAL ON THE DESK. Despite her invitation, Robert refused to stay with her in her room at their inn in Oban. He told her they both had important reading to do that evening.

He had grabbed a takeaway dinner from what he called "the best fish-and-chips shop in all of Scotland." Presenting her with a blue-and-white food box, he kissed her chastely and bid her goodnight.

So, she found herself alone in the tiny room. There was just enough space for a twin-sized bed, a wardrobe, and the small desk where she sat. The ensuite bathroom was equally petite, with all the necessary fixtures crammed into a space the size of an American closet. She had not inspected the sink for the dreaded two-tap arrangement. Reading the journal intrigued her far more than the modernity of the bathroom.

Placing the takeaway box and journal on the desk, she was ready. She took another bite of fish before opening the journal. Reluctantly, she admitted the food was good. *It's not as good as spending more time with Robert, but it's good nonetheless,* she acknowledged.

Once she began reading, the meal was quickly forgotten. Closing the journal became impossible. His grandfather's tale was riveting. The man possessed a flare for storytelling that she envied. Ruefully, she conceded that if her stories were half as compelling as his, she might have a publishing contract by now.

Robert's grandfather married his grandmother when they were both very young. The woman came from a wealthy family. Despite her parents' hopes, she fell madly in love with the poor man. Though he did not have a steady job and likely would have difficulty providing for her, they married anyway. It was a foolhardy decision based on young love, not common sense.

Children followed, one after another. Robert Sr. struggled to find employment. He bounced from job to job, never able to keep one for more than a few months. The family suffered. According to the words he wrote in the journal, he stayed awake many nights worrying about how to feed his family and keep a roof over their heads.

When his wife became pregnant with their fourth child, he made a difficult decision. Her family maintained strong ties with the woman, giving her money occasionally. He chose to look the other way for the sake of his wife and children. It wounded his pride to admit that the money was badly needed.

If he disappeared, his wife could return to her

family's large mansion in Edinburgh. It was not a guess. The woman's father hinted at it one evening after drinking one too many drams. In time, she might forget him and find another husband to give her and the children the life they deserve.

He loved his family. Knowing his wife and children suffered hurt him deeply. Though the decision felt like his heart was being ripped from his chest, he knew it was for the best. Staying when he could not provide the necessities was selfish.

Late one evening, after everyone was sound asleep, he kissed each child on the forehead. He caressed his wife's cheek. With his heart breaking in two, he walked out the door and never saw any of them again.

Simone wiped the tears streaming down her cheeks. Running to the bathroom, she tore sheets of tissue from the roll and blew her nose. "How could he do it?" she wondered aloud.

She rushed back to the desk. Did the tale have a happy ending? At this point, her dinner had grown cold, the fried food abandoned for a good story. She grabbed the journal and headed for the bed. Wrapping herself in its bedspread, she returned to the tale.

For several years, Robert's grandfather worked at random jobs around Edinburgh. He stayed in small tenement apartments, never finding a real home. He received word about the family's goings-on through friends and found some small measure of comfort in the stories.

As he suspected, his wife returned to the welcoming embrace of her family. The children thrived in a stable environment. They had plenty to eat and a roof over their heads. They had more presents at every Christmas and birthday than he could have ever hoped to give them. During the school year, their clothes were always clean and fashionable, never the rags they often wore when he was the head of the household. The children wanted for nothing.

His wife did not immediately remarry. For several years, she waited for his return, even after the divorce was finalized. However, years of no contact from him made it obvious that he was gone forever. She eventually married an accountant. The man was dull as dishwater, but he had the resources to provide the family with a comfortable life.

Robert Sr. admitted that he was glad to hear it was not a grand love match. All signs pointed to the union being one strictly for the security that the marriage offered. It would have broken his heart to know that his former wife had been able to find love with another man. The nobleness of his sacrifice had limits.

Although his grandfather wished that he could have been the man to give his family all of these things, he was happy to know that they received them in the end. Knowing that his sacrifice had the intended effect gave him a very small measure of peace.

Robert Sr. eventually found steady work on a fishing boat based in Oban. He and a fisherman on the same ship took up lodgings in a neighborhood where fellow fishermen lived. It wasn't the family he left behind, but the community offered him camaraderie and kept him from being too lonely.

Conditions on the sea were dangerous, and many friends died, but he survived and enjoyed the work. It was impossible to think about a family when his attention was focused on daily survival.

The last pages of the journal chronicled his brief retirement years. His body was broken from decades at sea. He lived on a small amount of money that he had managed to save. On his doctor's advice, his grandfather moved from Oban to Inverness, where he shared a cottage with another former fisherman. His living arrangement allowed him to stretch his limited funds and have a companion in his later years. Throughout it all, he never stopped thinking about his family.

He ended the journal with his best wishes for their health and happiness. His sacrifice brought deep regret and pain, but he expressed gratitude if it benefited his family. Nothing was more important to him than leaving his beloved wife and children in safety and comfort. The phrase was repeated several times in the man's chronicle of his life.

Simone closed the journal. Tears poured from her eyes. The tale left an ache in her heart. The man gave up his one true love. Was the sacrifice worth it? That part remained a mystery, for living without love and happiness made for a lonely existence. Sure, the family survived, but did they have the things that money couldn't buy? Only his former wife and children could answer that question.

She also felt a newfound appreciation for Robert. From the first day they started the tour, it was obvious that he didn't want the job. He was overqualified, yet it was an opportunity to do something meaningful for his family. It was the means to an end. In that way, Robert was not different from his grandfather. Both men felt a deep sense of duty to their families.

The same sense of duty lived in her heart, too. She spent many a day cooking and cleaning for her father when he was too drunk to take care of himself. And hadn't she abandoned her dream job when she learned about Emma's cancer diagnosis?

She lied to Emma for three years about sending her work to literary agents and publishers. Landing a publishing contract might have taken her away from her friend when the woman needed her the most. She told Emma no one was interested because the truth would have been too painful.

Sacrifice for a family was ingrained. Her Robert was right. It may be time to start a new chapter. His grandfather did it in the most selfless, gut-wrenching way. His story ended in sorrow, but did it mean hers would, too?

Her Robert. She repeated it. Was he really 'her Robert?' Did she want him to be?

Simone placed the journal on the little table beside the bed and switched off the lamp. The yellow light from the street lamp outside her window illuminated the room, its beams piercing the flimsy curtains. She closed her eyes, but the room was lit just well enough for its light to disturb her. At least, that was her excuse.

Her brain would not switch off. Thoughts of Robert's grandfather swirled. The man's sacrifice was remarkable. Leaving a beloved family took extraordinary courage, and it tormented him for years.

Those thoughts were eventually replaced by worries about her future. The road trip was almost over, and the money and the opportunities the million-dollar inheritance would bring were within reach. Ironically, it was easier when she had no hope of earning so much money. Now, the prospect was overwhelming. She had to do something, but what?

Once again, she asked herself whether she wanted more from Robert. Was he going to be a part of her life as she stepped into the great unknown future before her?

She squeezed her eyes tighter. "Worry about it later," she commanded. "Tomorrow will be a busy day."

Her limbs became heavy, and her breathing slowed. She was almost asleep when one thought screamed in her brain. *He is reading one of your books tonight.*

Simone flung herself upright. "Noooooooooo!!!!!!!!!"

SEVENTEEN

SIMONE WATCHED THE GUILLEMOT FLOAT IN THE WATER OF OBAN BAY. Except for a shock of white on its wing, the bird's feathers were jet black. The bird held a plump fish in its black beak, a prize from its fishing expedition. The animal seemed pleased, as it should be. This morning, at least, it would enjoy a feast.

She spotted ducks and seagulls gliding along the water in front of the massive Cal Mac ferry that entered the bay. As the boat passed, its wake pushed seawater further up the shore. She stumbled back to avoid the splash.

To the left, she spotted little fishing boats packed into the marina so tightly that walking from one boat to another without touching the water would be easy. Rows of stone buildings in various shades of gray and brown lined the neat streets. A hotel made of red sandstone was situated in the center of the harbor area. It promised exceptional views from a convenient location.

Along the Esplanade behind her, Victorian townhouses turned their gray faces toward the bay. Many of them were the former homes of wealthy merchants and were now bed-and-breakfast inns like the one where Robert and she stayed. The blue-green waters of the bay stretched toward the Atlantic Ocean, a sight comfortably enjoyed from any of those same inns.

Oban's seaport was nothing like Oak Hill. Not for the first time, she marveled at the stark difference in the scenery. When she looked out her window at home, she saw a dense forest, deer, turkeys, and mountains, not the rippling waters of the sea.

Bending low, she picked up a conical seashell from the cobbled shore on which she stood. She turned it over in her hand and examined the opalescent whites, grays, and browns of the shell. Its shape looked nothing like the flat shells from the South Carolina beaches her family visited on annual vacations.

She placed the shell in her pocket, a memento of the moment. Traveling to Scotland opened her eyes to the beauty of a new country. She understood why Emma loved to travel. Discovering new places provided a fresh perspective on the situation at home.

It certainly had for Simone. What began as a way to grab an extraordinary inheritance became much more meaningful. What had she done with her life after college? Taking care of others and giving up on her dreams left her over 30, alone, and clueless about what to do next.

Reading Robert Sr.'s journal showed the consequences of sacrifice. The deep ache of leaving his family left a permanent mark on his grandfather's soul. He considered his options and chose to step away so they could have a better life. In doing it, he abandoned all hope of real happiness and love.

Like Robert Sr., she put everyone else first. Her newfound wealth enabled her to do what she wanted, but it presented the most significant problem: What did she want? She never considered it. Each day was something to survive, not really enjoy. The prospect of finding fulfillment seemed like the stuff of fairytales.

Life in Oak Hill would never be the same. Emma was gone. If Simone stayed, it would be easy to fall back into old patterns with her father. Caring for him until he finally died was not a sacrifice she wanted to make. With a shudder, she recalled how hard it was to be around the man. Spending the rest of her life that way held no appeal.

Somewhere deep in her soul, she realized that her father didn't appreciate what she did for him. Emma had; that was the difference. Would she put her life on hold for such a man? If she did, would she wake up one day, filled with regret over a wasted life?

"I'll move," she said aloud as she picked up a small, round stone. "I'll start over some place away from Oak Hill."

To where then? immediately came the next question. Disgusted, she flung the stone into the water. How was she supposed to make a plan when each decision brought a fresh question?

"Good morning!" a voice called from above.

Looking back, she saw Robert walking down the short ramp that led to her spot on the shore. The sight of him made her heart skip a beat. Was it caused by love or an undiagnosed heart condition? Simone pushed aside the very bleak, very negative second option.

Robert scanned the horizon. "It's a fine day, isn't it?"

She scrunched her eyebrows. A layer of fog settled over the bay, blocking all sunlight. The light breeze over the water sent a chill up her spine, making her grateful for the jacket she wore. Nothing about the gloomy weather was fine, in her opinion. She said as much.

"Well, it isn't raining," he reasoned. "It could always be worse."

She could not argue.

"I see the ferry is here," he said, gesturing toward the hulking white ship parked in the harbor. "We will take it to Mull later. From there, it's a bus ride across the island and another ferry to Iona."

"I don't want to go to Iona."

"Oh?" He pointed over her shoulder at a castle on the distant hill. "Do you want to go to Dunollie Castle then?"

"No. I meant I want to see these places." Simone removed the journal from her jacket pocket and handed it to Robert. "Let's find where your grandfather lived. Let's visit his grave."

He shook his head. "The trip is not about me. We

should stick to the itinerary."

"Screw the itinerary!" She tossed her hands into the air. "We are in Oban. Aren't you curious?"

"Aye, I am very curious, but I can return another time. Right now, I have a job to do."

"So, I'm just a task to complete now? Is that what you're telling me?" The old, familiar pain pierced her heart. *It was a bad idea to let down my guard,* she thought. *Why did I do it?*

She shoved past him and headed for the ramp, determined to get as far away from him as possible. Halfway up, she heard him running behind her.

"I read your book." The sentence stopped her. "I stayed up until the wee hours of the morning to finish it."

She folded her arms in front of her as she turned to face him, still not sure if he could be forgiven for what he said. "And?"

"I couldn't put it down. You are an amazing writer."

"Thank you."

"The twist at the end blew me away. I thought the pharmacist did it. I never suspected the janitor."

"I'll tell you a secret." Simone unfolded her arms and drew closer to him, whispering, "For a long time, it *was* the pharmacist. Then, I realized the story would be much better if the janitor did it."

"Well done."

"Thank you again."

"I am sorry about what I said earlier. You are not a

task. It's just...." He paused, looking down at his feet. "I don't want to drag you all over Oban when you are supposed to be enjoying yourself. The trip is your vacation."

"I enjoy myself as long as I am with you." The admission flew out of her mouth before she could stop herself. The answering smile on his face eased her worries.

"Me too. I only want to make you happy, Simone."

Once again, they tread dangerously close to the uncomfortable truth. Once the trip was over, what would they do?

He fell silent and would not meet her eyes. *He knows it, too,* she realized.

She decided to move the conversation toward less serious territory. "Besides, as a writer, I want to see the places your grandfather mentioned. His story was fascinating."

"You finished the journal?"

"I couldn't put it down."

Robert placed a gentle kiss on her lips. "Thank you."

She grabbed her phone. Without comment, she snapped a picture of the bay and sent it to the attorney. "It's settled," she said, returning the phone to her pocket. "The attorney has her daily picture, so I am free to do whatever I want—and I want to explore Oban with you."

"Are you sure you want to do it?"

"Definitely."

"Our first stop is the inn," he said with a grin. "We need a hearty breakfast for our adventure."

"Lead the way," Simone said as she took his hand.

THEY TRAVELLED TO A NEIGHBORHOOD NOT FAR FROM THE HARBOR. Robert said his grandfather rented a cottage there during the long winter when he was not at sea. Based on what he wrote in the journal, the man likely spent those bleak months pining for his lost family. It was a sad thought.

The one- and two-story stone cottages on the treeless street were coated in grimy white harling and crammed so close together that there was little space between each home. Patches of dead grass in front of each property were meant to offer some semblance of domesticity, but they only added to the depressing state of the street. The cracked, uneven sidewalk made matters worse. It was apparent that no one took any pride in the area.

A steady drizzle of rain mixed with the thick fog rolling in from the bay. It seemed like the sun refused to shine in such a bleak environment. The dismal surroundings dampened any enthusiasm the couple had for the discovery.

Simone quickly realized why the neighborhood looked as it did. Each cottage had either a weather-beaten boat or a tangled pile of fishing nets in what was meant to be a front yard. The neighborhood must have belonged solely to fishermen. Their days were spent at sea, not piddling around in their gardens. They had no time for home improvement.

Robert eased the car into an available parking space. Pointing to one of the nondescript cottages, he said, "My grandfather talked about that place in his journal."

She yanked open the car door when he made no move to leave. "Come on," she commanded. "Let's see if we can go inside."

His mouth ajar, he protested. "How rude! We cannot knock on a stranger's door and ask to go inside."

"Why not?" she asked. "I'll do all the talking. They'll think a crazy American tourist is being nosy." She tapped his hand. "Come on! It will be fun."

Reluctantly, Robert accompanied her to the cottage's front door. She knocked several times, but no one answered. Hearing a noise in the back garden, she walked around the side of the house. Her companion pleaded with her to stop, but she refused.

They found an older man standing in the garden, his fingers busy repairing a fishing net. He jumped when he saw them. "Hello," he greeted them warily. "May I help you?"

"Hi! I'm Simone," she drawled. Her Southern accent was incredibly thick when she wanted it to be. Some people heard the accent and enjoyed it. If it disarmed the man, why not give it a try?

"A pleasure to meet you, ma'am. I am Samuel MacLean." His wrinkled face broke into a wide grin when he noticed Robert. "And you are?"

"Robert Gordon III."

"I knew a Robert Gordon once. You look just like

him."

"I do?" Robert glanced at Simone, a glimmer of hope in his eyes. "Was he a fisherman?"

"Aye," He waved a gnarled hand at the couple. "Come inside for a cup of tea. It's nae fit weather to be outside."

Simone raised an eyebrow at Robert as they followed Mr. MacLean into the cottage. "I told you it wasn't fine weather," she whispered.

The man guided them from the back door down a narrow hallway packed with books, old magazines and newspapers, and other mementos from a long life. He motioned for them to enter a small room at the front of the house. He asked them to sit on a green threadbare sofa while he prepared the tea.

"I'm still not sure if this is a good idea," Robert whispered to her. They could hear the man clinking mugs and plates in the kitchen down the hallway.

"It will be fine," she said, patting him on the hand. "Relax."

She scanned the pictures in the room. Sepia-toned photographs in black wooden frames covered nearly every inch of the available space on the walls. The photos varied in size and content, with some showing images of ships. Others captured moments in the lives of children from infancy to what appeared to be university graduations. More recent color photographs showed babies who might have been grandchildren. Those photographs were arranged in golden brass frames on the mantelpiece above a diminutive coal-fueled fireplace that presently did a poor job of chasing away the chill.

The room was packed with memories of Mr. MacLean's life. She wondered if a similar room was in a house somewhere, depicting all the images from Robert's life. The thought intrigued her.

A few moments later, Mr. MacLean returned with a tray containing three mismatched mugs and a plate of ginger biscuits. "I am afraid I don't have any sugar or milk for the tea," he apologized. "My son hasn't returned from the shop yet."

Robert accepted a mug of the steaming liquid. "It's nae bother."

As Simone took a sip, she smiled to herself. Her companion's accent was noticeable around the gentleman. Was it an attempt to disarm the man, as she tried to do? Whatever the reason, she liked the sound. His gentle whispers in Gaelic during their romantic moments still sent shivers of delight all over her body whenever she remembered them.

Ignoring her companion's sexy new trick, she told their host, "My friend's grandfather was named Robert Gordon Sr."

The man wrapped his hands around the mug and seemed to savor its warmth. "I think he is the same man I knew. He talked about a family that he once had." He squinted at Robert. "Until I saw you, I thought his stories were nonsense. You have the look of him, though. His tales must have been true."

"Did you know him well?" Robert eased to the edge of his seat.

"Aye, as well as you can know any man. We shared this cottage until he moved to Inverness."

Simone squeezed Robert's leg. The pair exchanged

a look.

"We worked together on *The Sea Witch*. It was hard work." Mr. MacLean placed the mug on a nearby table. "Eventually, neither your grandfather nor I could keep up. Our bodies were too old."

"He moved to Inverness when his doctor told him the sea air was not good," he continued. "We eventually lost touch. How is your grandfather?"

"He passed away a few months ago."

Mr. MacLean's eyes clouded. "I am sad to hear it," he said. "He was a good man."

"Can you tell us anything about him?" Simone asked. She glanced at Robert. "We know so little."

"I am afraid there's nae much to tell," Mr. MacLean said. "He kept to himself. I never saw him down the pub or visiting with a lady."

The man paused. "He carried around a great sadness." Wagging his finger, he recalled a memory. "Your grandfather told me that, early in his life, he experienced all the joy a man was supposed to have. The rest of his days would be spent in sorrow."

"At the time, I thought it was an awful thing to say. Now, I realize your grandfather may have been right." His eyes swept the room. "I was married long enough to produce a son and a daughter. A fisherman's life is not suited for matrimony. I am old and alone in this cottage. Did I experience all of my joy when I was younger?"

Robert winced. He mouthed the word *help* to Simone.

Placing her mug on the coffee table in front of her,

she stood. "We have taken up too much of your time," she said, tugging Robert's arm. "Thank you so much for your hospitality."

Mr. MacLean struggled to stand. "Would you like to see your grandfather's room?" he asked. "I left it just as it was when he lived here."

At their silent nods, he smiled and motioned for them to follow. He guided them up a creaky staircase, down a dark hallway, and into a small room. Flicking on a light, he said, "I had hoped he might return someday for a visit. I wanted him to be comfortable if he did."

The furnishings in the room were sparse. The black iron bed frame held a twin-sized mattress. Robert stepped into the room and sat on the bed. He ran his hands over the navy wool bedspread. "It's itchy," he mumbled.

Simone walked into the room. A wooden dresser of no real distinction stood in the corner, its brass handles almost black with age. Tattered green curtains covered the only window in the room, which provided a view of the back garden. The beige walls lacked decoration. Except for the dresser and bed, the room did not have other furnishings. Even the oak floors were bare. She shuddered at the thought of spending an extended time in such a depressing room.

"Please wait one moment." Mr. MacLean disappeared from the room. When he returned, he handed Robert a yellowed envelope. "Your grandfather sent me a letter after he moved to Inverness. I want you to have it."

"Thank you." Robert rose from the bed. He stared

at the envelope for a long time but did not open it.

The men shook hands. She followed them down the stairs and out the front door, staying a few paces behind them. Robert promised to drop by the next time he was in Oban. She wondered if he said it to please the man or if he indeed intended to do it. Judging from the look on Mr. MacLean's face, he thought the same thing.

As they gradually pulled away from the curb, Simone turned to look back at the solitary man who stood at the doorway. His eyes appeared wistful. She couldn't help but feel a twinge of sympathy for him, imagining the loneliness that must envelop his days. "I really hope you take the time to visit him," she said, raising her hand to wave.

Robert waved, too. "I promised I would. Why wouldn't I keep my word?"

Her brow furrowed slightly as a flicker of doubt crossed her mind. "Sometimes, people don't keep their promises," she remarked.

With sincerity written across his face, he met her gaze and said earnestly, "I always do." His tone left no room for uncertainty. "Relationships and commitments are always worth honoring, no matter the circumstances."

Simone shifted her attention to the scene out the car's window. Her thoughts drifted to memories of her past. Sighing, she said, "I know some people who don't."

EIGHTEEN

SIMONE HUGGED HER ARMS TO HER CHEST, TRYING TO STAY WARM. The cemetery was on the outskirts of Oban, on the top of a windswept hill. She wasn't sure if the chilly air was due to the geographic location or the somber purpose of the site.

She trudged behind Robert as they scanned the weathered gravestones. Each stone contained the name, dates of birth and death, and occupation of the men buried there. It was a sailors' cemetery that memorialized their vital role in running the ships. One occupation in particular repeated itself so much that she wondered what it involved: donkeyman. All sorts of wild ideas filled her brain.

The grass thinned at the top of the windy hill, replaced by weathered rock and slick, muddy earth. Few gravestones stood there. The wind whipped off the sea below them, stretching its icy fingers over every inch of exposed skin. The rain's steady drizzle made it even more miserable.

Licking her lips, she tasted salt from the rapidly intensifying breeze. She was ready to give up the search and return to the warmth of the car. Fortunately, Robert announced that he had found his grandfather's grave. The task had been problematic since the man lacked a proper gravestone.

They stood over a mound of earth and freshly sown grass. A rectangle of smooth granite with his grandfather's name and dates of birth and death were etched upon it, marking where the man's mortal remains rested. No flowers adorned the grave. No ornamentation of any kind decorated the spot. The marker told nothing about what Robert Sr. did in life.

Robert removed the envelope from his pocket. He told her the return address was that of the cottage his grandfather shared with the man he visited in Inverness. To his surprise, a photo had been included with the letter. He waited to examine it. The letter took higher priority.

His shoulders dropped when he finished it. Shaking his head, he refolded the letter and tucked it inside the envelope. "Nothing important," he said. "He told Mr. MacLean about his new home and invited him to visit."

"But this..." He shielded the photo from the rain. "It is priceless."

Simone took a step closer. The color photo showed an older man standing in front of a two-story stone cottage, presumably the one in Inverness. His stooped frame reflected years spent in hard labor. The plain shirt and pants fit loosely on his body. With gnarled hands, he clutched a black cane.

She noticed the same chocolate brown eyes he shared with his grandson. They had identical jawlines, too, although his grandfather's face was clean-shaven. The man wore a ragged tweed hat that concealed what she assumed was the same dark brown hair. It was like looking at an older version of her companion. The resemblance was uncanny.

"I've never seen a picture of him," Robert said, his voice choked with tears.

"There's no doubt that he is family!" He wiped the tears streaming down his face. "I wish I could have met the man."

He wrapped his arm around her shoulders. "Thank you."

"For what?" Simone was genuinely surprised. Learning more about his long-lost grandfather was essential to Robert, though she did not fully understand why. After all, the man abandoned Robert's father. He may have done it for noble reasons, but his absence left a wound from which the family did not heal. *I know all about wounds like that,* she thought grimly.

"You didn't have to do this," he was saying. "We could have spent the day in Iona. Instead, we are standing in the rain at a cemetery."

She encircled his waist with her arms, stood on her tiptoes, and kissed his cheek. "We are standing in the rain at a *Scottish* cemetery." She giggled. "That makes all the difference to an American tourist."

"Oh, it does?"

"Yes, of course. Everyone knows Scottish cemeteries are dark and mysterious places."

"American cemeteries aren't?"

"Not exactly. The people buried there usually haven't been dead for centuries."

Robert grew serious. "Did it upset you to visit? It has only been a few months since Emma died."

"No, it did not bother me."

"And then there's your mother…."

"I'm fine." She wiggled out of his arms and took a few steps away. Walking toward the hill's edge, she commented, "The view here is amazing."

"Aye, it is." He joined her side but did not look at the sweeping view of Oban Bay. "Simone, how did your mother die?"

"That's a personal question to ask."

He ran his hand through his wet hair. "Aye, it is," he said. "I figured I had permission after what happened in Inverness."

Simone gave him a sideways glance. She couldn't disagree. The moment they shared meant a great deal, but did it entitle him to hear the story?

She understood the significance of the moment. If Robert was going to be a part of her life, the painful story would have to be shared. She allowed another brick to tumble from the wall around her heart. "It's a sad story."

"It usually is."

"Fair point."

"Stop stalling. What happened?"

She scanned the bleak landscape of the cemetery, searching for any form of shelter from the rain. At last, her eyes fell upon a tree standing all alone amidst the weathered gravestones. Its knobby branches reached out like welcoming arms. "Let's get under that tree," she suggested, pointing to it. "We might as well get out of the rain before I share my story."

"In a moment." Robert returned to his grandfather's grave. He produced a flat, black stone from his pocket and placed it on the marker. He stepped away from the grave after whispering something inaudible.

They raced toward the tree as the rain switched from a drizzle to a downpour. The tree's green leaves provided a modicum of shelter in the storm, though fat raindrops still managed to penetrate its canopy.

"You were saying?" Robert said, his eyebrow arched.

Much to her chagrin, she couldn't avoid the conversation. "Fine," she said in exasperation. "I'll tell you."

"My parents went to a party at a friend's house," she began. "They both had a few drinks. Mom didn't think she could drive. Dad thought he could."

Tightly squeezing her eyes shut, she tried to stop the rising pain. "He was wrong. On the way home, he collided head-on with another car. The driver of the other car suffered minor injuries, and my father was badly injured. My mother died instantly."

She opened her eyes, and her gaze hardened. A rush of memories surged forth, sharp and painful, bringing to mind her father's terrible behavior over the years. The angry words from his drunken outbursts haunted her. The outbursts were always followed by half-hearted apologies that felt more like empty gestures than real amends. She could almost hear his slurred words, and the sound of whisky sloshing on the floor when he spoke. He always stumbled over his own excuses for what he said. Each recollection deepened the ache in her heart, reminding her of all that had been lost in the accident.

"He blames himself," she said, a deep sorrow filling her. "He has never been the same since that day."

"Oh, Simone, I am so sorry." He tried to hug her, but she stepped outside his grasp.

"Your grandfather valued the family's happiness above all else. My experience has been very different."

Robert leaned against the tree. "Keep talking."

"I was 16 years old!" The familiar anger rose in her chest. "I was too young to cope with what happened. I needed to grieve too. As soon as my father recovered from the accident, it was unrelenting torment."

Her eyes shimmered with unshed tears. "The man cried almost non-stop. One time, I found him with a loaded gun in one hand and an empty liquor bottle in the other. He had passed out before he could kill himself. Every time I heard a gunshot, I feared he had committed suicide. Do you know how many times guns are fired in the country?" He shook his head and pulled her rigid body close to his.

She trembled as the traumatic story poured out of her. "Well, it happens a lot. I was as jumpy as a long-tailed cat in a room full of rocking chairs."

"He put me through absolute hell." She jerked out of Robert's arms, not wanting comfort. "I had to listen to his moaning about how my mother was gone forever, and it was all his fault. Every holiday, every birthday – it was all about how much *he* suffered. I couldn't grieve for my mother because I was too busy taking care of him."

"Thank goodness Emma saw it and begged me to move in with her. She knew I had lost two parents, not one."

"I am glad you came from a devoted family," she said, wiping her wet cheeks with the sleeve of her jacket. It surprised her that the tears still managed to flow after all these years. "Not all of us have been so lucky."

She pressed her back against the rough bark of the tree. Revealing her deepest pain left her feeling weak and bruised. The sturdy wood supported her. She feared her shaking knees might buckle. "After graduating from college, I returned to Oak Hill and stayed with Emma. I foolishly thought things might be easier if I didn't live under the same roof with him."

"Were they?" Robert asked, his shoulder pressed against hers.

"No. I still cooked and cleaned for him. I never escaped." She laughed mirthlessly. "I decided to work as a waitress until something better came along. I refused to accept anything less than my dream job."

"Then, you got the offer but couldn't take it." He lowered his head. "Oh, Simone, I am so sorry."

She pushed away from the tree. The rain had stopped. "I don't need your pity, Robert. You wanted to know the story. There it is."

Simone took several steps away before turning to face him. "I am ready to go back to Oban when you are. I'll be waiting in the car."

NINETEEN

SIMONE'S PAINFUL REVELATION DRAINED ALL ENERGY FROM HER BODY. The aftermath of exposing her darkest memories and feelings left her raw and vulnerable. She never dared to say those words to anyone, not even Emma. The pain of her father's behavior cut too deeply.

If her friend had known the whole story, she never would have forgiven the man. For some inexplicable reason, Simone didn't want others to feel the same way toward him that she did. She buried her feelings. Ignoring the pain was second nature for her now. When she spilled the ugly truth to Robert, she finally understood how badly she had suffered. Refusing to deal with the trauma had cost her more than she realized.

Upon their return to the inn, she ran up the creaky stairs to her room. Each heavy step was lost in the maelstrom tearing up her brain. When she entered her room, she peeled off her wet clothes and slipped beneath the bedspread. The soft fabric caressed her skin, wrapping her like a cocoon against the painful memories. Soon, sleep wove itself around her and cradled her in its embrace. Thankfully, she did not dream. Reliving the past in slumber would have been too great. She desperately needed the respite that only sleep could provide.

The light rapping on her door woke her. Glancing at the fading light streaming through the window, she guessed it must be very late. "Just a minute," she called as she quickly donned dry clothes.

She slowly opened the door. Robert stood in the hallway, a concerned look on his face.

"Are you ok?"

"Yes," Simone answered. She pushed the door wider. "Do you want to come in?"

"No." He looked very uncomfortable.

Her heart skipped a beat. *I revealed too much*, she fretted. Anytime she shared her true feelings, people immediately withdrew. She should have known better. Folks liked telling her about their problems but never wanted to hear about hers. She worried he was just like everyone else.

Then, Robert surprised her. "If you are up to it, I want to take you somewhere." He pointed to his jacket. "Wear yours. It will be chilly."

THEY FOUND THEMSELVES THE SOLE OCCUPANTS OF A SECLUDED BEACH A SHORT WALK FROM THE INN. Nestled within a cove, the beach was a thin ribbon of sand, nothing like the beaches Simone remembered from her childhood. Smooth pebbles in hues of warm browns, deep reds, and ruddy browns covered the sandy shore.

In the center of the beach, someone had arranged a pile of weathered gray driftwood. Nearby, two precarious towers of stone stood a few feet away from the encroaching waves, their surfaces slick from the salty kiss of the sea. She would have never discovered the charming scene if Robert hadn't led her to this hidden gem.

He took her hand and guided her to the pile of driftwood. Within moments, he set the wood alight, creating a comfortable blaze to warm them against the chill of the approaching night's air.

She rubbed her hands together and held them in front of the fire. "Did you do all of this?" she asked, pointing to the driftwood and the stone piles.

"Aye." He shrugged off the straps of his backpack and tossed the bag onto the ground. He withdrew a blanket from the bag, spreading it before the fire.

Curious, Simone peeked inside the bag. She spotted sandwiches wrapped in thick brown paper. The revelation may not have spooked him after all. Instead, he seemed to have planned a romantic fireside picnic. It was not the act of a man who wanted to run away from a bad situation. Perhaps she had misjudged him.

Robert plopped onto the blanket and beckoned her to join him. She accepted, grateful that he had brought the blanket. Its thickness cushioned their bottoms against the lumpy stones on the shore.

He handed her a sandwich and said, "It is not a fancy dinner, but I hope you will like it all the same."

She took a bite of the ham sandwich. It crunched in her mouth from the spray of sand and salt in the air. She didn't care. After the emotional discussion at the cemetery, the moment's serenity by a warm fire soothed her soul. It was the balm she needed.

"You are probably wondering why I brought you here," he said after he finished his sandwich. He drank from a silver flask and then handed it to her. "You are carrying a lot of weight on your shoulders. I can help you…if you will let me."

"What do you have planned?" she asked, taking a long drink and trying not to cough from the fiery liquid that scorched her throat. "Getting me drunk on Scottish whisky?"

Chuckling, he took the flask from her and screwed on the lid. He tossed it into the bag. "Tempting, but no. I had something else in mind."

He pointed to the piles of stones. "Do you know what those are?" At the shake of her head, he explained, "They are memorial cairns, one for Emma and one for your mother."

The sea's waves crept closer to the stones. Within minutes, the tug of the sea would unsettle the rocks and send them tumbling onto the sand. His hard work assembling the cairns would be for naught. Simone mentioned it.

"That's the point." He rose and offered his hand to her. "When the cairns fall, I want you to release their souls. Let them rest in peace, as you should, too."

"You have carried a heavy burden for years, Simone," he continued. "Let it go. You deserve happiness."

She slipped her hand into his and held it tight. The next wave crashed into the cairns, covering them with frothy sea foam. Another wave came on its heels. The towers quivered but held firm. Wave after relentless wave pounded the stones until each cairn eventually tumbled onto the sand. The rocks now looked like the others strewn across the beach. Their significance only lived in her memory.

Tears trickled down her cheeks. Each drop was a testament to her unrelenting and, until that moment in the cemetery, silent suffering. Grief suffocated her spirit. It seeped into every moment and cast a shadow that dimmed even the happiest of her memories. She always felt trapped, unable to think about tomorrow, next week, or even next year. There was only today, and it was overwhelming.

With the inheritance, she could explore so many possibilities that previously seemed like unachievable dreams. She couldn't let the echoes of the past drown out the hopeful message of the future. For far too long, the needs of others came before her own. Maybe Robert was right. It was time to begin a new chapter in her life, one focused on her dreams, not those of her father's.

Simone gazed up at him. She revealed the deepest part of her soul and shared her private pain with him. He even read a book that no one else had read. To her complete shock, the man did not run from her. She dared to think that he might be different.

"Thank you," she said as she wrapped her arms around him. "Thank you so much."

"Are you ready to move on with your life?" he asked, his voice low. He held her close. "Will you?"

She felt as if she took her first breath when she inhaled. "Yes."

He kissed her, lingering in the moment. The feeling of that slow, deep kiss seemed to suspend time. Her thoughts and worries melted away, leaving the warmth of their connection.

The crackling fire sent sparks soaring high into the indigo night sky. The gentle hiss of the wood and the whisper of the waves created a serene melody for their intimate embrace. They tumbled onto the blanket and wordlessly undressed each other, stopping long enough to exchange passionate kisses.

Under the moon's pale light, they made love. Their bodies moved in time to the rise and fall of the sea. Their passion had no urgency, only the affirmative answer to a tender question. Just as the sea washed over the rocks, waves of passion crashed over them. Their bodies became one as they clung to each other amid the stormy sea of love that had led them to the moment.

As he kissed away the tears flowing down her face, she felt her heart swell. How long had she waited for someone who would stand beside her, unafraid of the worst parts of her past and ready to experience everything a new life could offer? She wanted to be a lover, not a caregiver. With him, the dream could be realized.

Their two souls were joined in that moment. They

were bound by an unbreakable connection that neither had anticipated. As she felt the last brick crumble away from the fortress she had built around her heart, a sense of peace washed over her. Though it was both terrifying and exhilarating to welcome Robert into her life, it felt right.

Simone could feel love seeping into the guarded corners of her being. This moment marked the beginning of a new chapter, one that would be filled with love, hope, and possibilities.

TWENTY

SIMONE LOOKED AT HER PHONE FOR WHAT SEEMED LIKE THE HUNDREDTH TIME. It was early afternoon in Scotland but morning back in Oak Hill. She wanted to call the attorney as soon as Robert asked. Instead, she sent a text message, realizing the time difference worked against her. Waiting for so many hours was frustrating. She needed an answer.

After sleeping in very late, the couple missed breakfast at the inn. They strolled to a restaurant nearby and enjoyed a leisurely brunch. He asked if she could extend her trip for a few more days. His next tour did not begin right away, so they could enjoy time together before her return to America.

The conversation was tense at first. Neither Robert nor she wanted to talk about what would happen when she returned to Oak Hill, at least not yet. Old insecurities crept into her mind. Simone feared he might forget the time they shared once he began his next road trip across Scotland. She shared her concern and was stunned at his response.

"I'm not taking overnight trips with anyone else," he informed her. "You were an exception. Tabby – she owns the touring company – offered me a lot of money to take you. From now on, I'll do day trips around Edinburgh."

She wanted to squeal with delight every time she recalled his words. Others had let her down in the past, so she expected an entirely different response. His revelation affirmed her decision to start a relationship with the man. It was a new day indeed.

Zipping shut her suitcase, she glanced at the phone again. No missed calls or texts. She huffed in frustration as she rolled the bag to the doorway. "Shouldn't the attorney have responded by now?" she grumbled.

Deciding to stay busy, she headed for the bathroom. She scanned the countertop for any item she might have missed. Seeing none of her items there, she moved into the bedroom and opened the door to the wardrobe—nothing there either.

After they returned from their romantic encounter on the beach, they had decided to share Robert's room for their last night in Oban. The bed would accommodate two people. His room was, of course, nicer than hers, something that no longer surprised her.

Her cell phone buzzed.

"I suppose I should say 'good afternoon.' How are you?" the attorney asked when Simone answered.

"I am fine. How are you, Ms. Whitmire?"

"Fine, just fine." Her voice echoed over the speakerphone. "And, please call me 'Joanna.' You know I don't like 'Ms. Whitmire.' It sounds so stodgy."

"Very well, Joanna." She wondered if cutting the chit-chat and getting to business was appropriate. Of course, there is only one way to find out. "As I said in the text, I want to extend my trip."

"Emma hoped you might."

"Really?"

"She wanted you to catch the travel bug. What are your plans?"

Simone sat on the edge of the bed and picked at its wool bedspread. "I just want to stay in Edinburgh for a few more days. There's more to see, I think."

The silence was so long that she feared the call had dropped. Pulling the phone away from her face, she glanced at the screen. The call was still active.

"Interesting." Joanna paused. Was the woman waiting for details? When Simone did not provide them, she continued, "Well, I already asked my assistant to book you on another flight. It leaves in four days. Will that be enough time?"

She hurriedly calculated how much time Robert had until the start of his next tour. Thinking about what happened afterward was too bleak. It was best to focus on the precious moments they could enjoy until her departure. "Yes, it will. I appreciate your help."

"My pleasure. I cannot wait to hear all about your

trip."

"I have one more question." She hesitated. The last thing she wanted to do was sound like the money was her only concern, but she had to know the answer. "Do I still need to send pictures to you?"

The attorney lifted the receiver and spoke directly into the telephone, "Simone, let me tell you a little secret. Emma set that condition for the beginning of your trip. If it was obvious that you made it to Scotland and were having a good time, you could stop." She chuckled. "I enjoyed seeing the pictures so much that I didn't ask you to stop sending them. I probably should have. Sorry about that."

"I understand. So, what does that mean for the rest of my trip?"

"You wouldn't ask to extend it if you weren't having fun. No, you don't have to send me pictures." She laughed and added, "Unless you want to. I love seeing the sights."

"Thank you, Joanna," Simone replied with relief. It might be hard to send pictures from Leith that did not include Robert.

"Relax. Enjoy your vacation. We'll take care of the inheritance when you return." She shuffled papers in the background. "Now, is there anything else I can do for you?"

"No. Thank you so much for your help."

"You are most welcome. Watch your email. My assistant will send you the new flight information." Giggling, she added, "Give your guy a kiss for me." Before Simone could protest, the attorney ended the call.

She stared at the dark screen of the phone. *Four more days.* The extra time would be fantastic. They planned to head straight for his apartment in Leith. It would be fun to see where his neighborhood was and get a taste of his daily life.

Of course, another thought teased her brain. She must tell him about the inheritance. During the trip, they revealed the deepest parts of their souls and forged a delicate bond. It felt wrong to withhold one final secret. If she did, what did it say about their burgeoning relationship?

She tucked her phone into her pocket and headed for the door. What would he say?

"I'll worry about that later," Simone said as she left the room.

TWENTY ONE

Four glorious days later

SIMONE AWOKE TO THE SOUND OF VOICES. Listening carefully, she realized Robert had spoken to a woman downstairs in the kitchen. What the hell? She never considered herself a jealous person, but the sound of the woman's voice stirred that side of her personality. The relationship was too new for competition.

She flung aside the covers and dashed into the bathroom. Hurriedly, she splashed water on her face and pulled her hair into a ponytail. She slipped into the first clothes she found, hoping the outfit looked good enough for whatever awaited her. Unfortunately, there was not enough time to do more to her appearance. She dashed down the metal stairs, eager to see who the mysterious woman was.

Robert's apartment was in a former biscuit factory

that had been converted into hipster living spaces. The high ceilings allowed for a stylish loft space where his bedroom and bathroom were located. The kitchen and living area were downstairs. The open nature of the apartment allowed sound to carry. As Simone rounded the stairs and headed into the kitchen, she hoped that quality would favor him. It was impossible to be discreet.

"Oh, there she is!" Robert exclaimed as she entered the kitchen. "I had hoped the two of you could meet."

A woman sat on one of the swivel barstools at the kitchen's island, nibbling a muffin. Her jet-black hair cascaded in lovely curls down her back. Little ringlets of blue framed her face, adding just the right pop of color. Her brown eyes looked like two perfect almonds set into flawless skin that resembled rich caramel. The woman could have been a supermodel.

Dammit, Simone thought. Silently, she wished she had taken more time with her outfit selection. Her basic gray sweatshirt, loose-fitting pants, and bare feet were no match for the cool look of her competition. The woman's ripped black jeans and black t-shirt paired well with leather boots that stretched above her knees, making her slender legs look miles long. Simone felt like a country mouse beside someone who looked so chic.

"I'm Tabby Simpson," she said, extending her hand. "I own the Castles and Cairns Touring Company."

Simone's eyes slid to the front of the t-shirt the woman wore. The company's logo was emblazoned across it. Recognition dawned—Tabby was Robert's boss.

With a quick inhale, she gathered her thoughts and accepted the woman's handshake. The embarrassment of her earlier jealousy washed over her. As she circled the polished concrete island, she ignored Robert's low snickers. "I hope you didn't come here to scold Robert about Oban," she said. "Changing the itinerary was my idea, not his."

Winking, Tabby said, "I dropped by to find out how the trip went. Since you're here, I guess it was good." She dapped her mouth with a napkin. "Whatever happened in Oban is between the two of you. I don't know anything about it."

Her eyes twinkled with amusement. Simone would have bet money the woman lied. Tabby knew everything that happened in Oban. *Everything.*

"Cuppa?" Robert lifted the whistling kettle from the stovetop and poured the boiling water into a teapot.

Tabby shoved her empty mug toward him. "I also wanted to talk to both of you about my newsletter."

Simone glanced at him. He seemed equally confused. "Why?"

"Robert told me you are a great writer."

She briefly thought about the pile of rejection letters on her desk in Oak Hill. Evidence might prove otherwise. Shaking her head, she banished the negative thoughts.

"I need help with the copy. He knows history, but he sucks at translating it to the page." The woman waved her hand at him. "Don't look offended. You know it's true."

"Aye, it is," he said with a sigh of resignation as he poured hot tea into Tabby's mug. "My students say it all the time."

"Have you tried using A.I.?" Simone grabbed a mug from the cabinet and helped herself to a hot cup of tea.

"I don't like it. The tone just isn't right. Besides, I like the idea of a human writing the words, not a robot."

"What do you want from us?" Robert asked, sipping his own mug of tea.

"You provide the historical information. Simone will give the material all the pizzazz it needs."

"You haven't read my writing, have you?" She shifted her gaze to Robert. "Did you show Tabby my book?"

He held up his hands. "Absolutely not. I know better."

Simone tapped the side of her mug. It was an interesting opportunity.

Tabby reached into a tote bag resting on the stool beside her. She fished out a notebook and pen. Scribbling on a piece of paper, she said, "Here's my contact information."

She placed the paper on the countertop and locked eyes with Simone. "We can try it for one newsletter. We don't need to make a long-term commitment."

Grabbing the bag and easing off the stool, she said, "It was a pleasure meeting you." She turned to Robert. "Good luck with the tour tomorrow."

Simone stared at the paper while Robert followed Tabby to the door. At the bottom of the page, the woman had written, "Girl, you've got this!"

Emma used to say the same thing to her whenever she was frustrated about her writing progress. Was it a sign?

THEY HAD AVOIDED TALKING ABOUT THE FUTURE. For the last four days, they immersed themselves in Leith's lively atmosphere. The neighborhood seemed a bit more residential than the touristy side of Edinburgh that Simone had visited. Some of the streets were a bit gritty and decorated with graffiti in sections, but the overall sense of community was evident. She loved it.

They meandered along the lovely waterfront nearly every evening. On nights when neither Robert nor she felt like cooking, they enjoyed delicious dishes at one of the many fine restaurants outside their doorstep. Afterwards, they headed to his favorite pub and laughed for hours while exchanging stories over drinks.

Each evening, they lost themselves in each other's arms. The sweetness of their connection made the world around them fade away. In those moments, it was easy to deny what lay ahead. They had only the present moment.

However, Simone's imminent departure for America approached no matter how desperately they wished against it. Each day spent together was filled with joy yet overshadowed by the unspoken truth. As their time together dwindled, confronting what happened next was inevitable. Finally, on their last day together, it was time to sit down and have the serious talk they had both been avoiding.

Tabby's offer opened the door for the dreaded conversation. If they worked together on her newsletter, they would have a natural opportunity to stay connected. The collaboration allowed them to share ideas and offered a new excuse to keep in touch. All that remained was whether or not they both wanted to do it. Simone knew her feelings on the subject but was terrified of what Robert's might be.

Of course, she knew there was another opportunity, too, that would make it a lot easier to see each other on a regular basis. She was extremely apprehensive about what his reaction might be.

"There's something I need to tell you," she said when Robert returned to the kitchen after walking with Tabby to the door.

"Me first." He hastily added, "Please."

At her nod, he said, "I've been trying to figure out how to afford a plane ticket to America."

"You have?"

"I have some time between my last tour in August and the start of the school term. Maybe I could visit you." He took her hand. "I can pick up more tours, and Tabby's offer might bring in some extra money too."

He stared expectantly at her.

Simone swallowed hard. "We need to sit down for this discussion." She remained silent until they were comfortably seated on the sofa. "You don't have to worry about coming up with the money for the ticket. I can buy it for you."

"No, no, no," he protested, waving his hands in front of him. "You cannot afford it on a waitress' salary."

"Yeah, that's the thing." She cleared her throat. Her heart pounded in her ears, and it suddenly felt very hot in the apartment. "This trip wasn't the only inheritance I received."

Her mouth felt as dry as the desert. She briefly considered dashing to the kitchen for a glass of water but decided against it. The confession could no longer be delayed. Before she could chicken out, she blurted, "I'm rich now."

Robert's mouth dropped open as his eyes widened in shock. "Excuse me?"

"I didn't just get a free trip to Scotland. I'll receive one million dollars for completing it. That's the other reason why I've been sending pictures to the attorney."

He stood abruptly and took several steps away from her. Running his hands through his hair, he paced and muttered something inaudible under his breath. Finally, he returned to the sofa. "Please be honest," he said. "Was it a fling, just something to forget when you return to America?"

"No!" Simone exclaimed, her eyes darting away. He had asked her to be honest, and honesty was proving to be a struggle.

Taking a deep breath, she turned back to him. "I admit, when we first set off on this trip, all I cared about was the money. I saw it as a job to complete. But then, as I got to know you, I discovered what an incredible person you really are. I...I..." Her voice faltered, caught between the truth she wanted to express and the vulnerability it required. She was scared to say the words. What if he didn't feel the same way? Deep in her heart, she knew he did, but what if?

Just say it! Emma's voice screamed in her head.

"I fell in love with you." She exhaled, not realizing she had been holding her breath. A weight lifted from her shoulders at the admission. "I love you, Robert."

"I love you, too." Wiping away the tears that trickled down his cheeks, he lowered his head and took a jagged breath. "I love you so much that I must let you go."

Simone gasped. She hadn't expected *that* response. "What?"

"My grandfather left his family so they could thrive. Now, I understand why he did it." He caressed her cheek. "The money is your salvation. You should pursue your dreams. Don't worry about me."

"I want to pursue those dreams _with_ you."

"I live in Scotland. You live in America." He shook his head. "What are you going to do? Spend your fortune jetting back and forth across the Atlantic?"

"Don't be like your grandfather. He gave up everything and lived a miserable life." She clasped his hand. "His sacrifice wasn't as noble as you think. Sure, the family had material things, but did they have love? Did they have laughter? Your grandfather surrendered everything, for nothing."

In a whisper, she added, "Don't be like him."

Robert's gaze remained fixed on her, his inner turmoil etched deeply on his face. Simone knew each word had bruised his heart and stirred up conflicting emotions. She wanted to be indifferent to their impact. It hurt deeply to watch him struggle, but she had to be strong. The future of their relationship depended upon his realization that she spoke the truth.

They discovered a precious love together. After enduring the relentless hardships of the past few years, she clung fiercely to the joy she had found. Letting it slip away from her grasp because of the inheritance was a price too dear to pay.

His shoulders dropped as he exhaled. "I cannot allow you to buy my ticket." Shaking his head, he admitted defeat. "When I visit, I do it with my own money."

She nodded but remained silent, lest her words change his mind.

"And, I don't want you jetting over here every time you get a fancy," he said, pulling her into his arms. "Use that money to do everything you always wanted to do. Write your books. Travel. Move to a bigger city. Find a publisher. Whatever you want, ok?"

Tears sprang into her eyes, threatening to spill down her cheeks. "Right now, all I want to do is be with you," she whispered.

"I want the same thing." He lightly pushed her out of the embrace so their eyes could meet. "I am willing to try this long-distance thing, but only if you are happy."

She allowed the tears to cascade down her cheeks. Her heart overflowed with love as he tenderly kissed them away. She felt joy at the possibilities before her for the first time in a really, really long time. Her life was her own to live again.

As the kisses deepened, Simone shoved aside all worries. Yes, a long-distance relationship would be challenging. Robert's stubbornness to take money from her would prevent them from seeing each other as often as they wanted. None of that mattered now. They were together at this moment. It was enough.

It had to be enough.

TWENTY TWO

SIMONE NEVER COUNTED HER CHICKENS BEFORE THEY HATCHED, AS THE SAYING WENT. Before she left for Scotland, she told no one about the possible windfall that waited upon her return. The million-dollar inheritance seemed like a dream. Fearing it could turn into a nightmare, she waited for the money to be in her hands. Something could go wrong. A big windfall just didn't happen to people like her. It was wiser to wait until the money was actually in her account before making any hasty moves.

Of course, the trip was successfully completed. The money was now officially hers, ready to be used in any way she wanted. When she viewed the account's balance for the first time, the sight should have filled her with glee. Instead, a wave of anxiety washed over her as she asked herself, "What now?"

The only move she had made in advance was to

quit her job. It would have been wrong to expect the folks at the restaurant to hold the job for her, so she did it before leaving. They had been so gracious during Emma's last days. Giving them plenty of notice was the least she could do. She reasoned that, if the inheritance was lost, finding another job as a waitress would be easy.

But she had not changed her living situation. The prospect of finding somewhere else to live was overwhelming, so she delayed the search. Instead, she stayed in Emma's old house, remaining in her familiar bedroom. It seemed like a good idea, except she hadn't realized how eerily quiet and desolate the house would be. The silence was haunting. Pictures of Emma were everywhere, showing her in various places all over the world. Odd objects like an unfinished journal held memories, too, of a life interrupted. Emma's presence could not be avoided.

Each morning, as she woke up in her well-worn bed, Simone found herself questioning the reality of it all. She wondered if the adventure had truly happened or if it was merely a beautiful dream she had yet to awaken from. In quiet moments of reflection, she found herself confronted with a daunting question: *what's next?*

The whirlwind of the last few weeks stripped her of certainty, leaving her to ponder her place in a world that felt both familiar and foreign. Her feelings for Robert awakened a part of her soul that she thought had died long ago. Suddenly, she saw new possibilities for her life, yet she remained trapped between the excitement of new romance and the fear of the unknown.

Connection with him was a soothing balm to her troubled soul and a reminder that the whole thing really had happened. Random texts always brought squeals of delight. The mere sound of her phone's chime caused little flutters of happiness in the pit of her stomach. Their video chats were special moments, adding thrills to her day. Seeing his smile and hearing his voice filled her with joy. Just thinking of him brought a genuine smile to her face.

Unfortunately, concerns for her father overshadowed the happiness she felt with Robert. The man had not responded to her repeated texts. She drove by her childhood home several times. Each time she visited, he was not there. On several occasions, she used her key to go inside. The house was always clean and tidy, as if no one had been there. The meals she placed in the refrigerator were untouched. It was bizarre.

Inquiries around town yielded no information. Something about the look in people's eyes hinted there was a bigger story, but no one wanted to tell it to her. Simone felt helpless, angry, and frustrated, all at the same time.

Deep in her bones, she knew that she stood at a crossroads. Falling back into the old routines of life in Oak Hill would be so easy. She could spend her days in the small-town comfort of the place, never taking any risks to see the outside world or publish her novels. Days could pass in the safety of the well-known world around her. Caring for her father could resume, though his strange absence might make the task harder. Prior to the windfall, it was exactly how her life might have been lived.

Something had shifted in her mind, making her unwilling to accept a mundane existence. She didn't want to survive; she wanted to thrive. Yet, she remained paralyzed with indecision. She often spent most days at home, wandering rooms that once echoed with laughter.

The attorney's visit today might put an end to her stay there, though. Simone took a deep breath as she glanced at her phone, noting the time. She had to stop fretting about everything that had happened since her return and focus on the present. Today would be challenging.

Sitting on the front porch, she scanned the driveway for any sign of Joanna's car. The woman was supposed to arrive at any minute. During their last meeting, she had hinted they might need to discuss more matters in the coming days. The vague statement sent a chill through Simone. It could only mean one thing.

Just thinking about it made her break into a cold sweat. The inevitability of the house's sale hung over her like a dark cloud. Whether or not she was ready, it seemed that her living situation was about to change. Taking time to make a decision was no longer a luxury.

Simone's mind was tangled in an exhausting cycle of *what-ifs*. Joanna's visit offered hope for a temporary pause, or it could force her to do the one thing she had not been able to do – make a decision.

SIMONE PACED BACK AND FORTH. The well-worn wooden boards creaked under her feet. She hardly noticed the sound as her anxious eyes flicked repeatedly to her phone. She searched for missed calls or texts, tapping the screen with growing frustration. A knot of worry tightened in her stomach. The woman was late.

Looking at her phone again, she noticed the time and clenched her fists in frustration. "Where the hell are you?" It wasn't that she was eager to hear bad news, but the unknown hovered over her shoulder like a specter. Knowing what the woman would tell her seemed less frightening than conjuring all sorts of frightful possibilities.

The crunch of gravel on the driveway alerted her to the car's slow approach. "Finally!" she exclaimed as she bounded down the steps.

A second car followed behind the green Mercedes sedan. Squinting, she stared at the other car until she finally recognized the blue Mini-Cooper. "You have got to be kidding me," she said, irritated by the sight. "Why is she here?"

The Mercedes rolled to a stop in front of her. Joanna Whitmire climbed out of the car and walked over to Simone. "I am so sorry that I am late," she said. "I had some last-minute things that required my attention."

Simone glanced at the Mini-Cooper as the car stopped behind Joanna's vehicle. "Why is Sylvie here?" she asked, leaning closer to the attorney. Emma's sister was the last person she wanted to see today.

"You know how she is. She insisted on coming when she found out where I was headed."

"Besides, she needs to go through the contents too," Joanna added before the woman drew close enough to hear the conversation.

"She does?" Simone asked. Her stomach dropped at the woman's next words.

"We have to clean out the house before the sale is finalized," the attorney said loudly enough for Sylvie to hear.

Sylvie Jenkins was a force of nature. The woman's bold manner would have been off-putting if a heart of gold did not beat in her chest. She had zero tolerance for the word 'no' at her age. Though she refused to disclose her real age, most people knew it was around 70. Age had not slowed her, though. She moved at a breakneck pace and expected everyone else to keep up.

Telling her that she could not do something was impossible. It was no surprise that she was there, but it didn't mean that her presence was wanted. The whirlwind was about to descend.

Simone forced a smile as the women exchanged hugs. "It is nice to see you."

"How was your trip?" Sylvie asked.

"It was wonderful. Anything exciting happen while I was gone?"

Sylvie smirked. "Nothing exciting ever happens in Oak Hill, sweetie." She removed her tortoiseshell sunglasses and popped them on top of her head. Pointing to Joanna, she said, "Y'all do your business. I'm heading inside to look around."

They watched Sylvie as she tucked a fine designer

handbag under her arm. The woman nodded to them before climbing the steps, flinging open the front door, and disappearing inside the house. Cocking an eyebrow, Joanna said, "Well, I guess we have our orders."

She withdrew a piece of paper from her bag. "My assistant emailed you all the important documents. I wanted to go over a few things in person, though." Motioning to the rocking chairs on the front porch, she suggested, "Why don't we go up there and talk things over?"

The paper contained the name and contact information of a good accountant. The attorney urged her to contact the lady. It was sound advice, given the amount of money involved.

Joanna also explained that the house had been sold to a couple from Florida. They paid for the sale in cash and technically could have moved into the house as soon as the sale was finalized, but she talked them into waiting thirty days. "I figured you needed a little time to sort out where to go," she said, her voice filled with sympathy.

The attorney took a moment to admire the view from the porch. Emma's house sat at the top of a mountain. It was her family's old two-story farmhouse, though no farming had been done on the property for decades. The wide front porch ran the length of the house and offered an excellent place for relaxing on hot summer evenings.

A lush, green valley of rolling hills stretched before them. As with most mountain properties, the nearest neighbors were miles away. A graveled, tree-lined driveway extended from the state-maintained road at the bottom to the top of the property, creating a buffer against civilization. The area's quiet offered a peaceful escape where one could think clearly. It was one of the reasons why Simone liked it so much.

"Why didn't you use some of the money to buy this house?" Joanna asked. "Frankly, I was surprised you didn't ask when you returned from your trip."

"If Emma isn't here, it is not home anymore."

"I understand." Extending her hand, she said, "Thanks for all of the great pictures from Scotland. Good luck."

Simone shook her hand and followed her down the steps. As she watched the dust swirl behind the woman's departing car, she briefly regretted that they did not chat longer. Joanna Whitmire was the closest thing she had to a friend in Oak Hill now that Emma was gone.

Sighing, she mentally braced herself for what awaited her inside. Sylvie would probably quiz her about her plans. With no answers to give, she did not want the inevitable interrogation. She climbed the stairs and slowly opened the door.

Sylvie stood in the living room, tapping her foot impatiently. The physical resemblance was uncanny. Of course, Emma and she were sisters, so it was only natural that the women would look alike.

The women shared the same blond, perfectly straight bob hairstyle. They both had little lines around their mouths from laughing. While Emma's complexion dulled from rounds of chemotherapy, Sylvie's skin was as radiant as ever. The twinkle in her eyes exuded the same vibrancy and lust for life that

Emma once had. Though Simone tried to brace herself for it, the shock of seeing Sylvie alive and standing in Emma's living room hit like a blow to the stomach. She took several deep breaths to calm her nerves.

"Y'all done?" the woman asked. "We have a lot of work to do."

Simone folded the paper in half and stuck it in her pocket. She was in no mood for a fight. "Take whatever you like. I only plan to bring my things."

Sylvie jerked her head back. "You don't want the furniture?" She pointed a well-manicured finger toward the kitchen. "What about the dishes? You'll need them in your new place."

Simone plopped onto the sofa and put her face into her hands. "I don't know where I am going or what I will do."

The sofa sank as Sylvie sat beside her. She felt the woman drape an arm around her shoulders. "I miss her too, sweetheart," she said.

Simone wrapped her arms around Sylvie. She inhaled the woman's sweet cologne, a big contrast to the scent of plastic IV bags, rubber tubing, and acrid medicine that eventually became Emma's signature smell. In a sick, bitter way, she found it funny how a scent triggered memories.

Yet, tears did not come. Perhaps her eyes were dry at this point. Enough tears had been shed over the last few months to last a lifetime.

Though tears did not flow, she found comfort in the woman's arms. Fighting against the feeling was pointless. Snuggling closer, she closed her eyes and allowed herself to relax.

"You don't need to make rash decisions," Sylvie said as she smoothed Simone's hair. "Your life has been hectic lately. You need time to catch your breath. I told Emma the trip was too soon."

Simone pushed away. "What?"

"There were no secrets between us sisters."

"Did you know about the million-dollar inheritance, too?"

"Whose idea do you think it was?"

"I don't understand."

"Well, I told her that she couldn't take the money with her. It could change your life. Why not give it to you?"

"Whose idea was it to attach the trip to the money?"

"Oh, that was Emma's." Sylvie smiled. "She knew you wouldn't go unless she added a little sweetener."

"She was right."

"Of course she was! We Wyatt girls always are."

Despite the grim discussion, Simone laughed. "We talked about the trip all the time."

"I know," Sylvie said, squeezing her shoulder. "She appreciated everything you did for her. It wasn't easy, especially in those final months. Emma wanted you to have a vacation."

Simone rose from the sofa and walked to a nearby window, her back to Sylvie. She could not deny that the money changed her life. Without realizing it, she chuckled out loud. The conversation between the two sisters would have been something to hear. The two sisters probably argued over the timing of the trip, the inheritance, the house – everything would have been discussed until one person capitulated to the other's argument.

Turning, she looked at the petite woman sitting on the sofa. She would have sworn that Emma sat there if she did not know better. The realization should have brought sorrow, but it did not. Since her dear friend was gone, Sylvie was ready to take her sister's place. This acid-tongued lady had ensured her future security and would, without a doubt, be ready to help in any way she could. To paraphrase the woman, the Wyatt girls always did.

"Thank you for everything," Simone said, returning to the sofa.

Sylvie playfully slapped her arm. "Oh, don't mention it. After what you did for my sister, you deserved it." Tilting her head to the side, she asked, "How *was* your trip? Did you meet a handsome Highlander?"

Blushing, Simone averted her eyes.

Sylvie clapped her hands. "Oh, I knew it!"

Resistance was futile. One way or the other, the woman would know every detail before leaving. Simone told Sylvie about Robert and the trip. Removing her phone from her pocket, she showed the pictures she had taken. The smile on her face was so broad that her cheeks hurt. It was impossible to disguise how happy he made her feel.

When she recalled how difficult it was to leave, the woman gave her a harsh look. "Then, why the hell did you come back? You should have stayed in Scotland."

Simone picked at an imaginary piece of lint on her pants. "Well, he didn't ask me to stay."

Sylvie rolled her eyes. "Some people are too busy getting in their own way. You have to take charge sometimes." She slapped her hand against the sofa and stood. "That settles it."

"What?"

She hurried across the room and plunged her hand into the handbag. After digging for several seconds, she found her cell phone. "Your salvation is at hand," she said, waving the pink phone at Simone.

Sylvie stepped into the kitchen to make a call. Simone could not hear the short conversation. She wasn't sure precisely what the woman had planned but suspected it might not be good. For all she knew, the woman was on the phone with King Charles, demanding that he travel to Edinburgh and drag Robert out of his apartment so the man could catch the next flight to America. The image made her snicker despite her anxiety.

Grinning widely, Sylvie returned to the living room. "I've got it all taken care of," she announced. "Let's pack up your things. You're moving today."

"Wait a second. What did you do?"

"I called a friend." She wagged a finger at Simone. "Don't spend the rest of your life in Oak Hill. That's why Emma gave you the money. You can stay at John's old place until you figure out where you are moving."

Sylvie picked up a cardboard box and headed for

Simone's bedroom. "Come on," she commanded. "We've got work to do."

TWENTY THREE

"JOHN'S OLD PLACE" WAS A ONE-BEDROOM APARTMENT SITUATED ABOVE CADENCE AND THE WOOLLY BOOKWORM SHOP. Both businesses were located in a two-story building in the middle of Oak Hill's downtown. The area offered Simone the unique experience of being surrounded by businesses instead of trees. Being in an urban environment reminded her of the sweet days she spent with Robert in bustling Leith, even though Oak Hill's quiet streets hardly classified as busy.

She was familiar with John Sweeney's story. As she knew all too well, Oak Hill was a small community. Everyone knew everyone else's business.

When his Aunt Cora passed away, John inherited the building. Eager to revitalize the property, he started with the second-floor apartment where his aunt and uncle had lived for years. The apartment's vintage charm featured the original hardwood floors that were well-worn but full of character. The floor-length windows offered a view of the quiet street below.

According to the stories that Simone heard, the decor had remained untouched for decades. The floral wallpaper plastered on some of the walls echoed the style of an earlier time, and the furniture had seen better days. To John, the challenge must have been not just to renovate but to honor the legacy of his relatives while creating a fresh, modern living space. Fortunately, he succeeded in his efforts.

The new space had open, airy rooms filled with natural light. Each carefully designed room blended contemporary comfort with the warmth of the apartment's rich history. To her relief, the floral wallpaper was gone, yet the original silvery tin that had been attached to the soaring ceiling remained. It would have been a disaster if he removed the interesting feature.

He had gutted the bathroom and installed slick, modern fixtures. He had added a dishwasher in the kitchen but left the cabinets his Uncle Floyd built decades ago. He kept an ancient, single-door refrigerator, too. The fancy stove was a recent gift to his Aunt Cora, so it stayed.

Simone loved the apartment's cozy, vintage vibe. Its comfortable feeling allowed her to relax while she tried to figure out her next move. Begrudgingly, she admitted that Sylvie had been right.

The location was a huge plus. The rural area of Emma's farmhouse gave her no opportunity to escape the restless thoughts in her head. Everywhere she looked, there was a reminder of her former life.

Falling back into her old ways was too easy there.

Unfortunately, downtown Oak Hill was not free from distractions. If she wanted to – and she usually did – it was easy to avoid making decisions. The two biggest distractions were conveniently located one floor below the apartment.

On the ground floor of the building, the old feed-and-seed store had been beautifully transformed into a badly needed entertainment venue, Cadence. The place was a hub for live music, community events, and artistic performances. She often dashed down the stairs and enjoyed an evening's entertainment.

Next door to Cadence, the Woolly Bookworm Shop offered another escape. The shop's updated décor, more inviting layout, and expanded selection of books gave her plenty of options for distraction. The bookstore was nothing like she remembered from her youth. In its new format, spending hours exploring every nook and cranny was easy.

She often noticed that Peg Sweeney worked downstairs beside her husband, John. Simone covertly watched them. The tale of the couple's romance was well-known around town. It always made her smile whenever she thought about it. No one was surprised when the couple married and decided to live in Peg's farmhouse on the outskirts of town.

The couple used the apartment as guest quarters for out-of-town friends who didn't want to stay at the farmhouse, so it was mostly vacant. With Sylvie's phone call, it became Simone's new temporary residence.

It only took an afternoon for Sylvie and her to

pack up her few belongings and bring the boxes to the apartment. All the necessary items – from furniture to plates – were already there. Settling into the new place was easy.

Simone used the dining table as her workspace. A laptop, printer, and office supplies were strewn across its surface. A pile of manuscripts for the novels and short stories she had written threatened to topple at any moment. Beside it, a smaller stack of bills, legal papers, and related memoranda awaited her attention. Since she usually ate meals in front of the television, the table's new purpose suited her.

The bed was more comfortable than her old one. Its huge size meant she could sleep diagonally if she wanted and still have plenty of space. When Robert came for a visit, they would have plenty of room.

The bathroom was absolutely divine. She couldn't wait to show Robert the shower and, most importantly of all, single tap on the faucet. Every time she used the faucet, the sight of the single tap made her giggle. Yes, she was a bit spoiled to be annoyed by the double tap configuration often found in the inns where they stayed in Scotland, but she felt no remorse about it. A line had to be drawn somewhere. Apparently, hers was at the bathroom sink.

Creating a new routine was easy. Though Oak Hill's downtown district lacked the bustle of the big city, she enjoyed watching the patrons at the Shaky Hillbilly Coffee Shop every morning, browsing the books at the bookstore below her apartment, and listening to good music at Cadence. With few commitments, she could tackle life on her own schedule, a new feeling. The relaxing lifestyle suited her.

The best part of her new life was the occasions when she and Robert could video chat, as they planned to do today. All thoughts about her new life fled her mind. She excitedly clicked the buttons on the mouse. The window for the video chat app was displayed on her screen. After a few more clicks, it showed a welcome sight.

"Hello, gorgeous!" Robert exclaimed with a smile and a wave. "How are you?"

She blew him a kiss. "Better now," she said. "How was your day?"

The time difference between Edinburgh and Oak Hill meant that his day was done. Hers was just getting started. Robert recounted his experience with two older women who wanted a guided trip to Rosslyn Chapel. They were big fans of *The DaVinci Code* and insisted he explain the meaning behind each carving in the chapel.

"It was exhausting," he said. "They were determined to find a hidden meaning in everything. We were there all day."

He shook his head. "Enough about me," he said. "What have you done so far today?"

"Well, I found a place for these." She spun the laptop so he could see the beautiful floral arrangement in a crystal vase on the coffee table. "Thank you so much!"

He ducked his head, grinning bashfully. "I wanted to brighten your day. I am glad you like them." He pointed to the daisies in the arrangement. "I asked the florist to use wildflowers. Do you like those better than roses?"

"Yes, I prefer them." She placed the laptop on the dining table and leaned closer to the screen. Not for the first time, she was amazed at how happy seeing him made her feel.

He lifted an empty tin to the web cam and waved it in the air. "The cookies you sent were fabulous," he said. "I'm afraid they are already gone."

"Well, I guess I'll have to send you more."

He smiled at the thought. "So, what else have you done today?"

"I unpacked the last box of my stuff." She lifted a stack of papers. "I found a bunch of stuff for the Castles and Cairns website that I need to review. Tabby and I are going to chat about it. She has some ideas to discuss with me."

"Tabby is really excited." Robert took a sip from a glass half full of amber liquid. "Are you doing anything with your own work?"

Simone's gaze drifted to the rejection letters, which she left in a pile all to themselves. The last box contained them, too, along with several manuscripts. "No," she answered guiltily.

Robert leaned forward, his chocolatey eyes close to the screen. "And, why not?"

She twirled a pen on the table's wooden surface. "I've been busy," she lied. "A lot is going on here."

"You just told me that you unpacked *one* box. That does not sound very busy to me."

"Well, it was a big box."

He leaned back in the chair and stared at the

screen for several seconds. She was just about to ask if the app froze when he folded his arms over his chest. "You aren't being honest with me. What's the matter?"

Simone struggled to put into words everything she felt. "For half of my life, I cared for my father and then Emma, too, when she got sick. I had a daily schedule – doctor's appointments, cooking, cleaning. When I wasn't taking care of them, I had to work. Everything was planned. Everything was familiar." She buried her hands in her hair. "Now, I don't know what to do. I thought the lack of choice was bad. It turns out that having lots of opportunities to do anything I want can be just as bad!"

She briefly looked down. "My father isn't answering any of my texts. He knows that I am back."

"Do you want him to respond because you genuinely want to see him? Or is it because you need to take care of someone?"

She shifted her eyes away from the screen.

"Simone, look at me," Robert commanded. When he had her attention, he said, "You were given a second chance to live your life. It is time you cut the cord."

Laughing mirthlessly, she said, "That's easier said than done."

"The relationship is toxic. You don't need it in your life anymore."

Robert spoke the truth, yet she struggled to explain the task's difficulty. Ignoring her father felt like abandonment. As terrible as things were between them, he was still her father. Children were supposed to care for their parents, weren't they? Wasn't that the natural order of things?

As if sensing the depressed mood, he changed the subject. "Do you like your new place?"

She lifted the laptop from the table. "Yes," she said. "I *have* to show you this shower. It is incredible."

Flicking on the light in the bathroom, she stopped briefly at the sink. "Check this out," she said, pointing to the single tap on the faucet. "Modern plumbing technology."

"Oh, ha, ha," he mocked her. "Privileged American."

She tilted the laptop so the webcam offered a good view of the shower. With its many knobs and showerheads, it looked like the inside of Doctor Who's Tardis. "If I cannot have you, at least I have this thing."

Robert laughed. "I should be offended, but how can I be? That shower looks amazing."

She exited the bathroom and spun the laptop to show the open kitchen and living area. "They left all the furniture." Pointing to the bookcases lining the walls, she said, "They have a few books about Oak Hill's history and an assortment of novels. I added a few of my own books, too."

"Why? You aren't planning to stay long-term, are you?"

Simone avoided the question. The topic of leaving Oak Hill always made her uncomfortable. Everyone expected her to leave. She wished someone would tell her where to go. The question was well meant, so she tried to ignore the annoyance it brought.

"Let me show you the bedroom," she said. The afternoon sun illuminated the room. The gray comforter on the king-sized bed was rumbled. Despite Emma's repeated entreaties, she never made her bed. Why start now? "It's a lot nicer than my old bed. I didn't bring my old furniture from Emma's house. I guess the new owners will donate it to charity."

"When will they move in?"

"They get the keys next week. I'm thinking about driving by the place one last time before they move in. What do you think?"

"It's a good idea. Say your goodbyes." He grinned broadly. "Like on the beach in Oban."

She blushed at the memory. More than a night of passion, it represented the true beginning of their relationship. They wouldn't even be on the call right now if she had not allowed space for him in her heart. She brushed her fingers against the cold glass of the laptop's screen, wishing he was there.

Simone heard the chime of her phone. She carried the laptop into the living room and retrieved her phone from the coffee table. The smile on her face quickly vanished.

"What is it?" Robert asked, concerned.

"My dad sent me a text. He wants me to drop by sometime. He needs to discuss something."

"Does he say what?"

Snorting in derision, she answered, "Of course not. He never does." She flopped onto the sofa and flung the phone across it. "I texted him for weeks, and he never responded. Now that he wants something, he decided to text."

She shook her head. "He always does this. He acts as if it is urgent. When I rush over, I'll find out it is nothing serious."

"This is the opportunity you need."

"What do you mean?"

"Visit him. See what he wants. Tell him that he is on his own."

"You make it sound so easy." She hunched her shoulders, looking away. "Don't you think I want him to take care of himself?"

"Aye, on some level."

"What's that supposed to mean?"

"It is getting late, lass. I have a tour first thing in the morning. Shall I call you tomorrow afternoon, as always?"

"No! Tell me what you meant first."

"I don't want to start a fight."

"Well, too bad. Tell me."

"You told me you were used to being his caretaker. You might believe you would be lost if you weren't."

She felt her face flush, anticipating what he might say next.

"With Emma gone, maybe you want your father to need you again, so you have an excuse for not doing something that makes you happy."

Simone gasped. "I'll talk with you tomorrow," she

said as she slammed shut the lid on the laptop.

Her phone played a cheerful tune. She took a deep breath before answering the call.

"We don't end conversations like that," Robert chided.

"I am sorry," she said, sweeping her hand through her hair. "I shouldn't have done that."

"I struck a nerve. If you don't want to discuss it anymore, say so."

"Ok." She paused. "I don't want to talk about it right now."

"Fine." He exhaled. "We have to discuss it eventually. You know that, don't you?"

"Yes." She sank deeper into the sofa, resting her aching head against its cushions. "I am overwhelmed. Everyone expects me to make all of these big decisions."

"Hey, lass, you don't have to do anything right away, okay?" She could hear the sadness in his voice. "I am so sorry you are going through this without me."

"I wish you were here," Simone said. It was a common refrain during their conversations.

"I have some good news then."

"Oh?"

"I found a great deal on a plane ticket. If you are open to it, I have enough saved for a visit."

"Yes!" Then, she immediately regretted her quick answer. A thought popped into her head. "You aren't using some of the money you set aside for your grandfather's gravestone, are you?"

"Between receiving good tips and picking up extra tours, I should have enough money for both."

"I wish you would let me buy your ticket."

"I appreciate your offer, but – "

"I know, I know," Simone said, exasperated. The man's pride was frustrating. "When can you come?"

"August 1. Is it too soon?"

She mentally calculated how long it would be. "Two weeks," she said aloud. "It cannot come fast enough."

"Aye. I miss you so much, Simone."

She closed her eyes and imagined his arms wrapped around her. "I miss you too."

"I hate to end the call, but I must."

"Sleep well. I love you, Robert."

"I love you, too."

As the call concluded, Simone felt the all-too-familiar pang of emptiness settle in her chest. Her days had become a game of waiting for random texts and scheduled calls with Robert. Opening her heart to someone took immense courage, and the physical distance between them compounded the challenge.

Traveling to Scotland lingered at the edge of her thoughts. It was a tempting possibility that was always within her reach. Almost daily, she found herself on the cusp of booking a ticket. Yet, the memory of their last conversation echoed in her mind, holding her back. Robert had asked her not to make the trip, and, out of respect for his wishes, she had kept her promise.

A sudden knock on the door broke through her melancholic thoughts. She hurried to answer it. When she swung the door open, a smiling woman stood before her.

"Hello," the woman said, extending her hand. "I'm Peg Sweeney."

Simone shook her hand. "Yes, I know who you are." She invited the woman into the apartment. "Thank you for letting me stay here."

"My husband and I are glad that someone gets some use of it." Peg glanced at the stacks of papers on the dining table. "I see you've unpacked."

Embarrassed by the mess, Simone raced to the table and tried to arrange the loose papers into neat stacks. "Yeah, sorry. I wasn't expecting company."

"Oh, don't you fret, sweetie. I didn't come here to criticize your housekeeping."

"Please have a seat." Simone pointed to the sofa. "Do you want something to drink?"

"No, thank you." The woman smoothed the skirt of her soft pink cotton dress as she primly sat on the sofa. She looked around the room and smiled, "I am thrilled you are here. The apartment goes to waste most of the time."

"Sylvie said you have friends who stay here sometimes. I hope I didn't disrupt anyone's plans."

Peg waved a surprisingly well-manicured hand. "You did not."

Simone knew enough about Peg to realize the woman would never admit if plans were impacted. It would have been bad manners. "Well, I've been looking for another place to rent around here," she lied. She still had no clue but didn't want to admit it.

The woman's green eyes widened. "Why on Earth would you want to do that?"

"Excuse me?"

Peg lowered her voice, though no one was around to hear the conversation. "Sylvie told me you got a lot of money from Emma's estate. Why don't you use it to get out of here?"

"Sure, I came back, but my circumstances were different," she added. "You are young. You have so much potential."

"Everyone keeps telling me that, but no one tells me what I should do."

"Honey, never let someone tell you what to do." Peg patted her hand. "I spent too many years listening to other people's opinions. You will figure it out."

The woman flipped her long, golden-brown hair over her shoulder and lifted herself from the sofa. "While I enjoy chatting with you, I need to get back to the shop. We are short-handed today, so John needs my help."

Simone followed Peg as they headed for the door. "I came up here to invite you to dinner tomorrow," the woman said. "Sylvie is coming over, too. We are going to have a cookout."

"Thank you for the invitation, but I am not sure if I can come."

"Nonsense," Peg said, already in the hallway and headed for the stairs. "Sylvie said you can. She will pick you up at 6:30."

She watched as the woman descended the stairs. Shaking her head, she returned to the apartment and closed the door. Why did Peg even bother inviting her if Sylvie told her they would be there?

And how did Sylvie know that she wasn't busy?

TWENTY FOUR

SYLVIE DIDN'T BOTHER TO KNOCK; INSTEAD, SHE FLUNG OPEN THE UNLOCKED DOOR TO THE APARTMENT. She strode confidently across the kitchen, eyes scanning the countertops cluttered with spice jars and dirty utensils. With a shake of her head, she continued her quest and said nothing, much to Simone's relief. The last thing anyone needed was a lecture.

Telling Sylvie to make herself at home was pointless. Simone watched as the woman headed for the fridge, a gallon jug of sweet tea in her hand.

"I'm gonna put my contribution in the fridge," the woman yelled from the kitchen. She placed a jug of sweet tea inside it and hovered in front of the fridge's open door for a few seconds. Her eyes closed, she savored the blast of cool air. "Girl, it is hotter than a sinner in church out there! Wear something light, or you are gonna burn up."

Sylvie wasn't the only person who knew about the hot and humid weather. Simone's sleeveless sundress was nothing fancy, just a simple yellow cotton frock. She wanted a light, casual look for the cookout. Based on Sylvie's basic outfit of white cropped pants, a pastel pink blouse, and straw sandals, it was a good decision. As she spun in a circle, the hem of the dress exposed her bare legs. "Does this meet with your approval?" she asked.

Sylvie scanned Simone from head to toe. "Not bad," she finally said.

The woman spotted the loose bundle of dainty daisies, light blue delphinium, yellow sunflowers, orange tea roses, and greenery wrapped in brown paper and idly tossed onto the dining table. Turning to the kitchen cabinets, she asked, "Do you know where Peg keeps the vases?"

Simone pointed to the cabinet underneath the sink. "I wasn't sure if I should put them in a vase or bring them like that."

Sylvie found a suitable vase and popped the flowers inside it. "Well, if Peg doesn't like the vase, she can change it," she said as she filled the vase with water. "She will appreciate the effort."

Simone chewed her lower lip. "You know, I haven't spent much time with them."

"You'll love them."

The Sweeneys were well known in Oak Hill, thanks to the popular bookstore and adjacent music venue they owned downstairs. The story of Peg and John's romance offered hope to everyone who wished for a later-in-life romance. Simone felt old, although she was still in her 30s. Now that Robert was in her life, the Sweeneys' love affair gave her inspiration that maybe it wasn't too late for her.

Sylvie snapped her fingers. "Are you listening to me?"

"Sorry."

"Let's get a move on. We don't want to be late."

Simone rushed to the bedroom to retrieve her shoes. "Yes, ma'am."

WHEN THE COUPLE MARRIED, PEG AND JOHN SETTLED INTO HER RENOVATED FARMHOUSE ON THE OUTSKIRTS OF OAK HILL. The move was fortuitous for Simone since his apartment above the Woolly Bookworm Shop was vacant. His improvements, especially the fancy shower, modernized the space. The overall look suited his masculine sensibility.

Peg's farmhouse was the opposite. Its cozy décor felt like a warm hug. Simone immediately relaxed when she walked through the front door and into a generously-sized space that opened into the kitchen, living room, and dining room. Soothing shades of white, beige, green, and blue spread throughout the area. The straw rugs on the hardwood floor and seashells scattered on the fireplace's mantel reminded her of the beach. Hadn't she heard a rumor that John used to own houses on Kiawah Island, off the South Carolina coast? Were the seashells a souvenir from there?

Peg motioned for them to follow her into the

kitchen. She took the jug of tea from Sylvie, arching an eyebrow. Shaking her head and smiling, she placed the jug on the kitchen's island. "You still haven't learned to cook?"

"At my age, why start now?" Sylvie asked.

"Oh, the flowers are beautiful." Peg smiled with delight as she accepted the arrangement from Simone. She leaned forward and smelled the delicate roses before placing the vase in the center of the dining room table.

Sylvie looked through the cabinets for glasses. She found what she wanted and quickly filled them with ice. Peg pulled one to the side as her friend placed four glasses on the countertop. "John wants water, not tea."

"Why?" Sylvie asked as she poured tea into three of the glasses.

"He's got a physical tomorrow. He has been drinking water with meals for the past two weeks." Peg added in a whisper. "He packed on a few extra pounds. He is afraid the doctor will fuss."

"There's nothing wrong with having a few extra pounds when you age," Sylvie said, sipping from her glass. "It helps you when you get sick."

She hurriedly cast a guilty look at Simone. "I'm sorry."

With a wave of her hand, Simone said, "Don't worry about it." She turned to Peg. "How has your garden been this year? The heat is brutal."

Peg groaned. "Not as good as previous years, but I guess I cannot complain." She placed her glass on the island and motioned for Simone to follow her. "Let's go to the canning room. I put up a bunch of goodies last season. You might find something you need."

"No, I couldn't." Simone protested as she followed the woman down a hallway and into a room that had shelves stocked with jars of jewel-toned jellies, thick jams, green beans, peppery relishes, and other delights.

Peg grinned mischievously. She plucked a jar of strawberry jam from one of the shelves and handed it to her. "Oh, don't be shy. You'll need something tasty when your man comes to visit."

Simone's mouth dropped open. How did Peg know about Robert's impending visit? Shaking her head, she muttered, "Dammit, Sylvie." She told the woman to keep it a secret. The last thing she wanted was for her father to show up unexpectedly.

"Oh, don't fuss," Peg said. "She only told me and the girls."

Yeah, right, Simone thought. Sylvie was a social butterfly. She was friends with half of Oak Hill and related to the other half. If Peg had learned about the visit, the odds were high that others would have known about it, too.

Peg sobered when she saw Simone's face. "Hey, I was only teasing."

"It's not you – or Sylvie."

"It's your father, isn't it?"

Simone nodded. She focused on the jar of jam in her hands. Its rich ruby color was lovely. Robert would probably love it. She avoided addressing her real concern.

Peg lifted her chin. "You don't have to worry about him," she said. "He will be too busy to bother you."

Frowning, she was about to ask what Peg meant when the woman's husband opened the door to the canning room. He held a platter of chicken that he cooked outside on the grill.

"Oh, hello," he said when he noticed her standing beside Peg. He deposited the platter onto the long table in the room and extended his hand. "I'm John. You must be Simone."

Nodding, she accepted his warm hand and took a moment to study him. He was completely bald. His skin was tan, likely from time spent outdoors gardening and tackling other chores. Though he appeared to have packed on a few extra pounds, the man still seemed fit. His biceps strained against the fabric of his short-sleeved shirt, revealing a hint of a tattoo on one arm. His dazzling white teeth, broad smile, and twinkling eyes drew attention to his handsome face. She totally understood how the man caught Peg's eye.

She glanced at the woman, who was blushing. Would Simone have the same moon-eyed look when Robert walked into a room? Embarrassed, she realized the whole town would buzz if she did.

He grabbed the platter and headed for the kitchen. Simone caught a whiff of his spicy cologne mixed with smoke from the grill as he passed the ladies. Memories of Robert's heady scent flooded her brain. Her cheeks reddened as other scenes came to mind, too.

Peg handed her a jar of blueberry jam, bringing her attention to the present moment. "Have you thought about what you will make?" she asked as she scanned the shelves.

"Honestly, not at all." Menu planning was the last thing on her mind. When she counted the days until his visit, her thoughts always turned to how great it would feel to hold him in her arms. The food they would eat was unimportant, especially with the Constellation Café just down the street from her apartment. Great meals were a short walk away.

"Well, when you do, let me know." Peg pointed to several jars of vegetables. "I can give you some of those, or maybe something will be ready in the garden. Don't buy the stuff at the grocery store. Nothing tastes as good as homegrown."

They walked back to the kitchen, where Sylvie and John chatted. He drank from a tall glass filled with ice and water. She doubted watching his diet for a few days would impact his upcoming physical exam results. Simone chuckled at the sight but said nothing.

She placed the jars of jam on the island and retrieved her glass. "What are y'all talking about?"

"A fabulous bluegrass band will be playing at Cadence while your man is in town," Sylvie said, referring to the music venue beside the Woolly Bookworm Shop. "Y'all should come."

She ignored the casual reference to *your man*. Since she told Sylvie about Robert, the woman desperately tried to extract information. The comment was an apparent attempt to goad her into revealing a tantalizing detail. "We'll see," she said noncommittally.

"Ladies, I'm starving." John grabbed a plate from a stack placed on the kitchen's island. "Let's dig in."

Everyone attacked the buffet assembled on the kitchen's island. Vibrant green beans, steaming oven-roasted potatoes, grilled chicken, and hot biscuits made Simone's mouth water. After Emma's passing, the community provided casseroles and fried chicken. Nothing could top piping hot, fresh food, though. Everyone talked about what an amazing cook Peg was. She was giddy as she dropped a heaping helping of potatoes onto her plate. She was in for a treat.

They took their plates and drinks to the dining table and ate the delicious food. Conversation ceased, aside from idle comments about the tastiness of the food.

John's portions were smaller, so he finished the meal first. He leaned back in his chair and patted his stomach. "Another fabulous meal, as always, Peg." He clutched her hand. "I will tell the doctor that the extra pounds are all your fault."

"You needed fattening up," she said, a slight blush on her cheeks. It deepened when he kissed her hand.

Sylvie wiped her mouth with a linen napkin. "If anyone can do it, Peg will," she said. "Her food is fantastic."

"I agree," Simone said, looking down at her empty plate.

"I hope y'all saved room for dessert," Peg said as she rose from the table and collected everyone's plates. Sylvie followed her into the kitchen to help.

"I heard your guest will be here soon," John said to Simone when the women were out of earshot.

"Yes. Is it okay if he stays with me?" She wasn't sure how concerned John and Peg might be with the impropriety of the situation. After all, some townspeople might frown upon an unmarried couple sharing an apartment and, more specifically, a bed.

He relieved her anxiety by dismissively waving his hand. "Of course it is! Peg and I aren't prudes."

"Well, some people around here are very conservative."

"Yes, they are." He lovingly looked at his wife. "We didn't exactly follow all the pre-marital rules if you catch my drift. I don't expect the same from you and your fella."

Peg and Sylvie returned to the table with plates of chocolate cake. When Peg placed a large slice in front of John, she clucked, "Eat it. One piece of cake isn't going to matter."

He obediently picked up a fork and took a bite. Moaning with pleasure, he said, "Your cakes are the reason I gained ten pounds."

"Nobody told you to eat half of the cake every time I make one!"

John dropped his head and grinned like a little boy caught with his hand in the cookie jar.

Peg turned to Simone. "When is your fella gonna be here?" she asked in between bites of cake.

"August 1."

"Well, I'll make y'all a cake. Does he like chocolate?"

Simone considered the question. During their trek through Scotland, their only dessert had been the sticky toffee pudding in Maiseach. They never ordered dessert at any restaurants during the rest of the road trip or in Leith. "I really don't know."

Sylvie gave her a sideways glance. "They were too busy to bother with dessert." She nudged John's hand. "You know how that is."

Peg cast a sympathetic look at Simone. Sylvie's bluntness could be embarrassing. "If y'all are finished with your cake, why don't we sit on the porch and watch the sunset?"

She silently thanked the woman. While John and Sylvie headed for the porch, she helped Peg gather the dirty dishes.

Before they joined John and Sylvie on the porch, Peg put her hand on Simone's arm. "Don't let Sylvie get under your skin," she said as she slammed shut the dishwasher door.

"Yes, ma'am."

AS SOON AS SIMONE STEPPED THROUGH THE DOOR OF THE APARTMENT, SHE PEELED OFF HER WEDGE SANDALS AND TOSSED THEM ASIDE. Her feet ached with every step she took up the staircase. The shoes were stylish and coordinated with her sundress, but they were not forgiving. Each wedge dug into her skin, a reminder that fashion often comes at a cost.

She sank onto the sofa. Its cushions enveloped her like a warm hug. Groaning, she stretched out her legs, letting them rest on the throw pillows scattered across the couch. "Beauty is pain," she muttered under her breath.

Rubbing her sore arches with her fingers, she glanced around her messy apartment. The state of the place was downright shameful. She promised herself that she would tackle housekeeping chores tomorrow. In her new living situation, keeping a tidy living space was no longer important.

Her cell phone chimed, the familiar sound when a text arrived. It was too late for Robert to text her. It had to be in the early hours of the morning in Edinburgh.

Reluctantly, she left her comfortable spot and retrieved her purse from the dining table. After digging through it, she located her phone. She tapped the screen several times.

"Son of a bitch." She shook her head as she read the text. It was just like her father to ruin a perfectly good evening.

I haven't heard from you yet. I still need to talk with you. Come by when you can, it read. She mumbled a stronger expletive under her breath. The man didn't ask how her trip went or say why he had not responded to her texts. He didn't even consider that she might be too busy. Whatever her schedule or personal feelings might be, they were irrelevant. He wanted something. She was expected to comply immediately, as always.

She returned to the sofa and collapsed face down onto its cozy cushions. "I'm too old for his nonsense," she said, her voice muffled. "Why?"

As silence settled over the apartment, Simone

pulled herself upright and folded her legs underneath her body. She hugged a pillow as she stared blankly at the yellow rays from the street lamp's light. Dust motes danced lazily in the light, another reminder of the necessity for better housekeeping.

The stillness around her did not settle her restless mind. Robert's words still echoed in her heart. She could almost feel his presence as he urged her to acknowledge the change that must come. It was time to shed the layers of doubt and fear that had accumulated over the years. The past no longer served her.

Simone acknowledged she was on the brink of a new journey, one that could bring opportunities and adventures for someone brave enough to experience them. Before she could take that journey, though, she needed to deal with her father. It was time to cut the cord.

TWENTY FIVE

SIMONE TOOK TWO DAYS TO GATHER HER THOUGHTS AND SUMMON THE EMOTIONAL STRENGTH NEEDED FOR HER VISIT TO THE HOME WHERE SHE HAD GROWN UP. Filled with anxiety and dread, she mentally prepared herself for the visit. This time, taking charge of the situation right away was imperative. Otherwise, falling into the familiar trap of caring for the man would be too easy. She must remain firm in the ultimate goal of closing the door on him forever. They could keep in touch, but he needed to take care of himself.

Her father still occupied the family home, steadfastly refusing to leave. In truth, the man had no choice. The modest home was all they could afford.

Though he may have wanted to leave, it was not an option. Without steady employment, her father had no means to pay for another home in Oak Hill or anywhere else, for that matter.

Visiting her father was never easy. Between the flood of joyful memories about her mother and bitter ones over her father's inconsiderate behavior, she often felt emotionally drained whenever she entered her former home. Some families had fond memories of their childhood homes. Regretfully, hers were tarnished by the man who lived there now.

As she steered her car up the short, paved driveway, Simone took a steadying breath. The house loomed ahead. Her stomach was twisted into knots.

Clenching the steering wheel tighter, she stared at the house. "You can do this," she murmured under her breath, the words tumbling out over and over again. "You can do this."

She parked her car beside a green Dumpster that took up most of the driveway's space. The receptacle was filled with assorted papers, furniture, and other items. It was not there the last time she came by the house, which was only a few days ago.

Hesitantly, she stepped out of her car, pausing to stare at the house. The presence of the Dumpster perplexed her. Her father had shown no interest in home improvement for the last several years. What sparked the sudden desire to fix up the house?

Her family's home had never been fancy. It was a simple three-bedroom, two-bathroom brick house. Her father worked in construction, which was a nice way of explaining why he was frequently unemployed.

The family survived on her mother's salary as a librarian. They were not flush with cash by any stretch of the imagination. It never bothered Simone, though, because her mother made sure they felt wealthy. The woman turned something as trivial as a visit to the park into a grand adventure.

When her mother died, the world turned gray. The home reflected the somber mood. The flowers planted along the concrete walkway leading to the front door had died years ago. The shrubs underneath the windows became wild. The branches of the trees in the yard stretched too close to the house. No one in the family bothered to make the place look as tidy as when her mother was alive. Simone always considered it an absolute shame. Her mother's memory deserved better.

In exasperation, she admitted everything fell on her shoulders. It was impossible to care for her father and keep the house looking like the cheerful family home that her mother had created. The sight of the Dumpster brought back all of the memories. Was it possible that her father had finally decided to be interested in something other than himself?

It was a foolish idea to indulge in such optimistic thoughts. Her father had failed her far too many times to remember, each disappointment carving a deeper mark on their relationship. With a heavy heart, she realized it was wiser to guard herself and keep her hopes low to avoid the sting of inevitable letdowns.

She heaved a cooler out of her car's trunk. Though she fully intended to set new boundaries with the man, making sure he was fed was something she couldn't resist doing. The cooler was packed with cold dishes meant to sustain her father for a few days. No one wanted to eat hearty dishes in the summer's heat, so she made him a big tub of chicken salad for sandwiches, gazpacho that could be eaten cold, and fruit salad for dessert. The food could fill his stomach until he learned how to cook his own meals.

Taking another deep breath, she walked toward the house. The front door was unlocked. She entered the living room and discovered that most of the furniture was gone. Several of the family pictures that hung on the wall were missing, too. Confused, she called out to her father.

He summoned her to the kitchen, where he was busy going through the refrigerator. An open trash can in the center of the room was half-filled with miscellaneous food and plastic storage bowls. "Good, you're finally here," he said as he tossed a bowl into the trash can. "Do you want anything in here?"

Simone sighed heavily. Typical. She hadn't seen the man since she got back from Scotland. He didn't bother to ask her how she was doing, how her trip went, et cetera. Unless it involved him, he was not interested. Some things never changed.

She dropped the cooler in the middle of the kitchen floor. Taking a closer look at the man, she was shocked at the transformation. His white hair was usually a wild mess plastered to his face, wet from tears or sweat. She couldn't decide which. Today, it was neatly trimmed and freshly washed. He had shaved, too. His clothes were tidy, not wrinkled or haphazardly tossed onto his body. And – wait – was that a new shirt?

Her father noticed her scrutiny of the garment.

"Do you like it?" he asked. "Susan bought it for me."

"Susan?"

"Yeah, you know her." He dropped another container into the trash can. It looked like the chicken casserole she made before she left for her adventure in Scotland. "She is Bob Cutshaw's widow. He had a heart attack about a year ago. Poor guy didn't make it."

"The man you used to go fishing with? That Bob Cutshaw?"

"Yep, that's the one." Her father scanned the refrigerator's shelves, missing the angry look on her face. "Real shame. He was a good man."

Simone clenched her fists. "Why did Susan Cutshaw buy you a shirt?" she asked, her frustration growing.

He emerged from the fridge with a bottle of salad dressing. "She wanted me to look nice," he said as he spun the bottle. "Geez, this expired a year ago." He shook his head and tossed it into the trash can.

She wanted to grab him and shake the story out of him but refrained. "Dad, that's an awfully personal thing to do," she said.

"Well, we've been dating for a few weeks," he said matter-of-factly. "Susan decided our wardrobes needed an update."

Simone stared at his back while he continued going through the fridge. The man just dropped major news and acted as if he gave her the latest weather forecast. *Unbelievable*, she thought.

Shaking her head, she peeked into the trash can. It

was filled with contents from the freezer – all the soups, stews, and casseroles she had made over the last six months. Her hard work to keep the man fed was now a massive pile of trash. That's what it all meant to him.

"Hon, I found another box in the closet," a voice called from the back of the house.

"Bring it to the kitchen," her father yelled. "Simone's here."

A tall woman strolled down the hallway and into the kitchen. Her brittle, thinning hair was bleached so blond that it was almost white. Simone guessed the woman probably used a can of hairspray every day to keep the coiffure so high on her head. Deep wrinkles creased the skin around her brown eyes. Judging from the expression on her face, they got there from constant squinting. Did the woman think glasses to correct an obvious vision impairment made her look old?

The turquoise pants that she wore clung to her body so tightly they threatened to split if she bent too deeply. Paired with her low-cut shirt's garish fuchsia hibiscus flowers, the overall look screamed for attention. Simone watched her father gape at the woman. The man was mesmerized, so the outfit's intention was achieved.

"What do you want me to do with this?" the woman asked, dropping a clear plastic storage tote at his feet. "There's three more of them in the closet."

"Let Simone have a look through." Turning to his daughter, he said, "You remember Susan Cutshaw, don't you?"

"I remember your husband Bob very well," she said, taking the woman's cold hand.

"*Late* husband," Susan corrected.

"Yes, of course," Simone replied with an insincere smile. "I am sorry for your loss."

Her father interrupted the ladies' conversation, oblivious to the tension in the air. "Take whatever you want, Simone." He pointed to the tote and waved his hand. "There or anywhere else in the house, for that matter. Your mother saved a lot of stuff. I don't need any of it."

Susan smiled, the thick makeup on her face nearly cracking from the effort. "It was nice to see you again, Simone."

She watched the woman sashay down the hallway into her parents' bedroom. "What is going on, Dad?" Simone hissed when the woman was out of earshot.

"We are moving to Cabo San Lucas, Mexico," he announced, tossing another container into the trash. He grinned from ear to ear. "Bob and I used to go there all the time for deep-sea fishing. It's a beautiful place."

He stuck his head into the refrigerator again. "I sold the house while you were galivanting all over Scotland." He retrieved a bottle of ketchup. "I need to clear out of here by next week."

Simone's mouth dropped open. "You sold the house??"

"Yeah, Carla Jenkins-Rigsby helped. We were both surprised that it sold so fast." His eyes swept the kitchen. "What do they call it on those home improvement shows? A 'fixer-upper?' I figured the condition of the place would put people off, but someone wanted it anyway."

She squeezed her eyes shut and pinched the bridge of her nose. "Let me see if I get this straight. You sold the family home so that you could move to Mexico with a woman you have been dating for only a few weeks."

Her father gave her a sympathetic look. "Sweetheart, I am not a young man. I don't have time to waste on months of dating or years to decide about moving."

"I understand that, but come on! Dad, this is a big deal. You are going too fast."

He looked at the bottle of ketchup. "Susan might want this. It's still good." He placed the bottle on the kitchen countertop.

"Dad! Focus!" She snapped her fingers. "For years, you have skulked around this house, unable to take care of yourself. Now, suddenly, you are selling the house and moving to a foreign country. I don't understand what happened to you."

"I found a good woman and wanted to enjoy what little time I have left. That's what happened." He folded his arms in front of his chest. "Frankly, I don't appreciate your tone, Simone. I thought you would be happy that your father found some peace."

"Oh, you found a piece, alright!" She shook her tingling hands. "What the hell are you thinking? Bob is barely cold in the grave, and you are running off with his widow."

"That's enough!" her father exclaimed. "You have

no idea what it is like to live alone after you have been married for so many years. It broke my heart when your mother died." His voice cracked as he looked away. "I'm so glad Susan didn't wait as long as I did. The grief can destroy you."

"Yes, I know!" Simone roared, no longer caring if the woman heard the argument. "Did you stop for one second to think about my feelings? I lost my mother. I never had a chance to grieve. I was too busy taking care of your sorry ass!"

"Do you have any idea what that was like?" She didn't wait for a response. "I was 16, Dad! When I got home from high school, I had to cook and clean while my friends were having fun."

Her heartbeat thundered in her ears. "Oh, and forget about enjoying college! I worked after classes to make enough money to eat. I hurried home every weekend, not because I wanted to see family. Oh, no, I spent it cooking enough meals to keep you fed for the week and doing all the laundry and all the cleaning – and – "

"I never asked you to do any of that," he interrupted.

"No, you didn't." The realization hit her like a punch to the face. He hadn't.

She wanted to explain the reasons behind her actions, but the words would not come. What she did was part of the silent, unspoken sacrifices that children made for their parents, a ritual woven into the very fabric of family life. To Simone, it seemed like the natural order of things. Parents nurtured their little ones, and when those children blossomed into adulthood, they would, in turn, care for their aging parents. That was the way the world worked, wasn't it?

As she thought back, she realized that he hadn't truly taken care of her. Her mother was the constant presence in her life. The woman gently tucked her daughter into bed each night. She read books to her, her soothing voice weaving tales that transported Simone to faraway lands.

When she had a cold or the flu, it was her mother who prepared steaming bowls of chicken noodle soup. When her stomach was upset, her mother plied her with crackers and ginger ale. After she had recovered, her mother always put freshly laundered sheets on her bed. It was as if the woman swept away the germs and transformed her bed into a safe place.

Her mother always cheered from the front row of every school play and recital, the pride shining in her eyes. Whenever Simone faced challenging homework, it was her mother who patiently guided her through the complexities. The woman fostered a love for storytelling and never pressured her to go outside. Instead, she nurtured Simone's creativity. It was always her mother, steadfast and unwavering, who stood by her side. Her father remained a remote figure in the shadows of her childhood.

"You used my college fund to pay bills and buy liquor." Simone shook her head. "I took on a mountain of debt to pay for college."

She pointed to the discarded containers in the trash can. "I cooked all of that food," she said in disbelief at the growing stack of containers. "For fifteen years, I watched out for you."

"I appreciate it." He stepped forward and attempted to hug her.

She pushed him away. Simone gave the tote's lid a little shove to reveal the contents. Bending low, she sorted through the items inside. A child's drawing of the ocean. A head with hair made of yellowed, dried macaroni, some pieces of which fell off long ago. A red felt Christmas stocking with her name written in gold glitter. Her mother saved each item as a precious memory of moments long past.

Her eyes drifted over the once-familiar surroundings of a house that felt oddly foreign to her now. Everything was dull and lifeless. Her gaze eventually landed on her father. The chasm between them was wider than it had ever been. He was even more of a stranger to her.

Perhaps her father was right, in his own callous way. Time was indeed fleeting. Wasting it in sorrow felt like a betrayal to the memories of those Simone had loved so dearly – her mother and Emma. She recalled the years spent devoted to his care and the countless hours she dedicated to easing his grief while she swallowed her own pain and suffered in silence.

It was a painful realization. All her sacrifices amounted to nothing more than a pile of old mementos and wasted food that he didn't want, all destined for a large green Dumpster. She shakily rose to her feet, grabbing the cooler and not bothering to empty it. The man would probably toss its contents into the trash anyway. She worked too hard preparing the food to let that happen. "Have a nice life, Dad," she said, surprised at how easy it was to say the words.

"Don't you want to look through the boxes? Don't you want to take anything from the house?" He followed her to the front door. "Your mother saved a lot. You might find something you want to keep."

"No," Simone said as she walked out the door. "I'm done here."

TWENTY SIX

SIMONE RACED TO ANSWER THE KNOCKING AT HER APARTMENT'S DOOR. The news that her father sold the family home and planned to move to Mexico was stunning. One person who might know the details was a phone call away: Sylvie. As Simone headed back to her apartment, she called the woman. If anyone knew all the dirty details, it would be her.

It surprised her to hear the knocking so soon after her own arrival. Sylvie promised to come over but wanted to make a stop at the Shaky Hillbilly first. Simone didn't say anything but knew that the stop could easily take an hour if Sylvie bumped into someone she knew – and she knew nearly everybody in town.

Still, when she opened the door, the last person she expected to see was Peg Sweeney. She quickly masked her disappointment and put on a welcoming smile. "Hello," she said as she ushered the woman into her apartment.

"I promised you a cake," Peg said, brandishing a carrier that concealed the sweet treat.

"Oh, thanks. I completely forgot." She hurriedly shoved a stack of papers to the other side of the dining table. "You can put it here."

Peg opened the carrier, releasing the decadent scent of chocolate into the air. She removed the cake and placed it in the cleared spot. "You never told me whether or not he likes chocolate," she said, a slight reproach in her voice. "If he doesn't like it, bring it downstairs. John will devour it in seconds."

"He isn't on a diet anymore?"

"Oh, that was just for the physical." She winked. "Now that the exam is done, he's back to eating sugar and fat."

Peg's eyes wandered around the cluttered apartment, taking in the messy surroundings. Simone was deeply embarrassed and mentally acknowledged that the space appeared even more disorderly now than the last time the woman visited. The surface of the dining table was littered with stacks of papers. Some piles were neat. Others threatened to tumble over. The crumbled papers revealed her long to-do lists and unfinished projects.

In the sink, a mountain of dishes waited to be washed. The unsightly collection of pots, pans, and plates bore the evidence of recent cooking. Greasy smudges marked the surfaces, and dried remnants of meals clung stubbornly to the sides of the dishes. Several mugs were stained from tea and coffee.

Almost all of the silverware was dirty and haphazardly scattered in the basin.

Near the sofa, a few pairs of shoes lay abandoned, including the wedge sandals she had worn to the cookout at Peg's house. The flowers in the arrangement Robert sent had died several days ago. Their dried petals were strewn across the dusty surface of the coffee table. The dead stems hung limply in the vase, no longer drinking from the puddle of green water inside it. The scene felt like a good summary of Simone's life at the moment: a cluttered mess.

"Sorry about the state of the place," she said as she picked up the sandals. "I promise that I am usually a better housekeeper than this. I've just had a hard time getting motivated lately."

Peg rolled up the sleeves of her shirt. "Well, you know what they say." She removed the dishes from the sink and began placing them in the dishwasher. "Many hands make light work. Let's get this place ready for your fella's visit."

"Oh, please don't. I'll do it."

Peg smiled. "Sweetheart, let people help you when they offer, especially if it involves cleaning." She shook her head and added, "During my first marriage, I thought I had to take care of everything. I never asked for help. Well, let me tell you something. You need it! There's no shame in admitting it."

Simone tossed her hands into the air. "Fine," she said. "You work in the kitchen while I attack this mess on the dining table."

AS MUCH AS SIMONE HATED TO ADMIT IT, PEG WAS RIGHT. The two of them cleaned the apartment in less than an hour. It would have taken her all day if she did it by herself. The dishwasher churned quietly in the background, scrubbing all the dirty dishes. A load of sheets stripped from the bed spun in the washer. The scent of pine from the cleaning solution drifted from the sparkly, fresh bathroom. All the papers, office equipment, and supplies had been scooped up and tucked into the closet. The dining and coffee tables smelled of lemon polish, their surfaces gleaming in the sunlight. The dead flowers from the arrangement found their way into the trash, with the vase thoroughly cleaned and added to the collection in the cabinet.

Their work done, it was time for a much-deserved break. Simone handed Peg a tall glass of icy water. The women sat on the sofa, sipping the cold beverage. The cleaning chores may not have taken a lot of time, but they were both sweaty and exhausted. It was hot work on a sweltering day.

"When you opened the door, you expected someone else, didn't you?" Peg asked as she wiped the condensation from the glass with a napkin and dabbed her flushed cheeks.

"Sylvie was supposed to be here an hour ago. She said she would stop by the Shaky Hillbilly and pick up something for us."

"If she stopped at the coffee shop, it's no wonder she is late. I bet she ran into someone she knows." Peg rolled her eyes. "She's probably getting an earful of gossip."

"Sylvie knows everyone and *everything*." It was one

of the reasons Simone liked her. Emma's sister distracted the dying woman with the latest rumors and juiciest local scandals during the worst days of her illness.

Rather than wait for Sylvie to arrive, she wondered if Peg could help. After all, she was Sylvie's close friend. Casting her hesitation aside, Simone said, "At the cookout, you told me my dad would be too busy to bother me. Did you know he had sold the house and planned to move to Mexico with Susan Cutshaw?"

"Yes."

"Does *everyone* know?"

"Sweetheart, the whole town knows whenever anything happens in Oak Hill."

She groaned. "What's the consensus then? Do they all think it is a crazy plan?"

"Who cares what anyone else thinks?" Peg patted her hand. "I am gonna offer you a piece of advice."

"When my ex-husband Harold and I were married, I paid too much attention to other people's opinions." She shook her head. "I was so worried about embarrassing Harold or our son, Four. I stopped doing everything I loved because they didn't think those things were appropriate."

"Do you know what it got me in the end?" She paused but didn't wait for an answer. "A divorce. It didn't matter one bit what I did. I gave up everything that made me happy, for nothing in return. I was never going to please that man or our son."

She slid a coaster across the coffee table and

placed the empty glass on top of it. "It took me a long time to realize what I did. Don't make the same mistake. It doesn't matter what other people think." For emphasis, she pressed her finger against Simone's arm. "What do *you* think about it?"

"I am angry...and maybe a little envious." She ran her finger along the rim of the glass. "I am mad that I spent all those years taking care of him and worrying about what *he* needed. I never considered my own needs or wants – and I'm angry that he didn't seem to care about that either. Aren't parents supposed to care about those things?"

"Parents make mistakes like everyone else." Peg took her hand. "Of course, in your father's case, he is a narcissistic ass, so…"

"Peg!"

"It is terrible to say, but you know it is true."

"What did he do to you?"

"I have had the misfortune to be around him a couple of times." She frowned at the memories. "Plus, Sylvie was good friends with your mother. She knows how things were in the marriage and how he treated you all these years. He's an ass, and I don't mind calling him one, even though it is very un-Christian of me to do it."

Simone laughed despite the woman's comments. "Well, I cannot argue with you."

"No, you cannot." She squeezed Simone's hand. "Now, what about the envious part?"

"I guess it's because he is walking away from our family and our life in Oak Hill. He thinks he can find happiness by starting over with Susan." She shook her head. "I envy that freedom."

Peg tilted her head to the side. "I don't understand."

"Well, he is moving to Mexico...."

"No, I heard that part." She sighed. "I don't understand why you envy it. No one said you couldn't do the same thing."

"What?"

Peg lowered her voice even though no one else was in the room. "Sylvie didn't tell me how much money you inherited, but I'm sure it was quite a bit. Emma was always good with her money."

"Yes, Emma was very generous." There was no point in disagreeing. As Peg said, the whole town knew everything.

"You are still young. Take that money and get out of here." She swept her hand around the room. "Don't spend your life in a one-bedroom apartment over a bookstore."

Peg scooted closer, taking both of her hands. "I want you to close your eyes." She waited until Simone complied. "Take a deep breath. Now, I want you to describe a scene that makes you happy."

"I am sitting in front of my laptop. The cursor races across the screen as the words flow from my fingertips. Robert brings me a cup of tea and kisses me on the cheek."

"Are you in Oak Hill?"

Simone opened her eyes, gasping in shock. She realized precisely where she was. "No. I am in

Robert's flat, in Leith."

Peg released her hands and leaned back in satisfaction. "See there," she said. "You didn't picture yourself in Oak Hill."

"No, I didn't. How strange."

"Not really." At Simone's stunned expression, she explained, "When Emma gave you that trip to Scotland, she opened your eyes to a world outside the borders of our little town. Staying here will hold you back."

"But you went out into the world, so to speak, and ultimately came back here."

"Yes, I did. I built a little fortress where I could hide. I thought I was protected from anything the world might do to hurt me." Peg idly touched the heart-shaped pendant on the necklace she wore. "My friends helped me to see how much I had given up on myself. Then, my husband showed me that it was not too late for me to find more happiness than I ever imagined possible."

Simone envied the wistful expression on the woman's face. All the anxiety and fears about her situation weighed so heavily upon her soul. It appeared that Peg had found peace. "Is it too late for me, too?" she whispered.

Peg abruptly stood. "No, it's not too late for you either. You already know what makes you happy. If you've been waiting for an answer, sweetheart, I think you just got it."

She grabbed the empty cake carrier. "Tell Sylvie I said hello."

Simone didn't get up to accompany Peg to the door. Instead, she sat frozen on the sofa, the woman's words echoing in her mind.

TWENTY SEVEN

SYLVIE FINALLY ARRIVED AN HOUR LATER, AS PREDICTED. She had been ensnared in a conversation at the Shaky Hillbilly. The woman Sylvie spoke to seemed to be a source of constant melodrama and had meticulously recounted her many trials and tribulations in great detail. Though it had been only a week since the two women last saw each other, the lady's existence appeared to be a never-ending series of afflictions and setbacks.

Simone sat there, clenching her fists and gritting her teeth as she listened to the stories of misfortune. While she felt a twinge of sympathy for the woman's plight, her mind was preoccupied with more pressing matters like her father's surprise move to Mexico with a woman he barely knew. Interrupting would have been bad manners, no matter how desperately she wanted to do it.

After what felt like an eternity, Sylvie concluded the story by saying, "Well, bless that poor woman's heart."

It was finally Simone's turn to speak. She shared the details of her recent encounter with her father and described in detail Susan's presence at the house. When she finished, she asked, "Did you know he was seeing her?"

"I did." Sylvie shook her head. "Before her husband was barely cold, he started sniffing around. I was surprised that they waited so long to officially start dating. The whole thing was disgraceful."

"I couldn't believe it when she sashayed down the hallway, carrying a box of my mother's belongings."

"From what I hear, he stays at her house all the time. The two are inseparable."

"It's not like Mom died a few months ago." Simone shook her head in disbelief. "She's been gone for years. Why does he suddenly want a companion?"

"It doesn't matter how long they have been gone," Sylvie said, her eyes glistening. "You miss some people forever."

Sylvie's tender revelation touched Simone, but she remained unmoved in her opinion of her father. "I am not ready to be that understanding of my father's feelings," she said, her voice steely. "He is the kind of person who needs someone caring for him 24/7."

"Yes, he is," Sylvie said. "Well, it looks like he got his wish."

"I still cannot believe he is moving to Mexico. If

you gave me a million guesses, that wouldn't have been one of them."

"Maybe they both want a fresh start. They won't have any memories down there. Let's face it—everywhere you turn in Oak Hill, you remember the other person."

"True." Simone recalled the countless memories made in her small town. Each place meant something, both good and bad, in every year of her life. It was especially hard to go anywhere that didn't have some random memory of time spent with her mother.

Simone realized that her father, too, may have felt a profound connection to Oak Hill, shaped by his own experiences and memories. The daily reminders of his past life could have been overwhelming. Starting anew in Mexico allowed him to escape those memories and create new ones – with someone else.

As she pondered these thoughts, she decided against sharing them with Sylvie. It felt too raw, almost like exposing a piece of her soul. She was not ready to forgive the man, and her thoughts would have given the impression that she was.

The touch of Sylvie's hand roused her. "Simone, sweetheart," Sylvie said. "You can carry those memories with you wherever you go."

"What are you saying?"

"You know exactly what I'm saying."

"We are talking about my father, not me."

"Should we be?"

Simone frowned. "What do you mean?"

"It's obvious he let go of you a long time ago. It's

time for you to do the same."

She told Sylvie about the conversation with Peg. The revelation that her dream scene happened in Leith, not Oak Hill, was fascinating. "What do you think? Am I standing in my own way?"

"Yes," Sylvie replied, her gaze steady and unyielding.

"Geez, don't sugarcoat it," Simone shot back, but a hint of a smile crept onto her face.

Sylvie chuckled lightly. "You already knew the answer to that question," she said, reaching across the sofa to take Simone's hand. "Why are you so afraid?"

Simone felt the full weight of her insecurities. "I've focused on everyone else for so long that it's become a habit," she confessed, her voice barely above a whisper. "I don't know how to think about myself. I never did. I only focused on surviving the present."

With an exaggerated roll of her eyes, Sylvie replied, "You need a new tune."

Sylvie's bluntness sometimes grated on Simone's nerves, yet there was truth to the woman's words. "What am I supposed to do?" Simone asked.

"Honey, my sister gave you a lot of money. Are you really planning to spend the rest of your life in a one-bedroom apartment above a bookstore?" Sylvie asked, exasperated.

"Peg told me the same thing."

"Listen to her." Sylvie stood. "She knows how terrifying it is to take a big chance, but Peg would also tell you how rewarding it can be."

Simone followed Sylvie to the door. Leaning on

the door frame, she said, "In your usual subtle way, you're telling me to fish or cut bait, right?"

Sylvie patted her on the shoulder as she walked out the door. "Stop asking people what you should do. Jump off the cliff, girl."

She closed the door and returned to the sofa. Was it finally time to redirect her attention from people like her father to herself? The man's actions clearly showed that he didn't give nearly as much thought to her feelings as she did his. Why was she so afraid? Maybe Sylvie was right – it was time to jump off the cliff.

She glanced at her phone and realized it was actually time for something else. She and Robert had a video chat scheduled in five minutes. "What an excellent diversion!" Simone exclaimed. She couldn't wait to tell him everything that had happened and, more importantly, find out exactly what time she could expect him the following day. Squealing with delight, she grabbed her laptop.

TWENTY EIGHT

SIMONE HADN'T SLEPT WELL. Her mind replayed the conversations she had had with Peg and Sylvie. When she wasn't fretting about their advice, her thoughts drifted to anticipation of Robert's forthcoming arrival. His plane was scheduled to arrive later that evening. Finally, after what seemed like forever, she could hold him in her arms and kiss his lips.

The combination of excitement and anxiety made it impossible for her to find any peace. Frustrated with her restless tossing and turning, she decided to rise when the soft yellow rays of dawn spilled into her bedroom. Lingering in bed was futile.

Checking the time on her phone for what felt like the hundredth time wasn't helping her either. She needed a change of scenery and a distraction, so she slipped out of her pajamas and dressed quickly before heading to the Shaky Hillbilly.

The familiar scent of freshly brewed coffee greeted her as she stepped inside the shop, and she felt a wave of comfort wash over her. As she settled into her favorite corner, she savored the heat of her coffee and the tastiness of the blueberry muffin she had bought for breakfast. She began to tune in to the lively chatter around her. The snippets of conversations from other patrons piqued her interest. One particular tale, told animatedly by a customer at the next table, sparked a brilliant idea for a novel. She grabbed a paper napkin and hastily scribbled down her thoughts, eager to capture the idea before it vanished.

She finished the coffee and muffin before glancing at her phone. "Another eight hours," she groaned.

Simone decided that she had spent enough time in the coffee shop. Stuffing the napkin into her pocket, she grabbed her purse and walked down Oak Hill's Main Street.

John Sweeney's music venue, Cadence, and the refreshed Woolly Bookworm Shop next door sparked a downtown revitalization. Still, the area was not expansive. She walked to the end of the street in less than ten minutes, passing old buildings slowly being repurposed into studio spaces for artists or occupied by various small businesses. Once a desolate space, the town buzzed with the excitement of new possibilities.

The familiar two- and three-story wooden structures, all built within the last hundred years at most, looked so different from the ancient stone buildings in Scotland. Once, she considered Oak Hill's downtown area to be old. Now, her travels showed her what *old* really was.

The buildings faded into the background as she walked the street, completely lost in thought. Peg and Sylvie joined an ever-growing chorus of folks who urged her to leave, yet she felt shackled to the place. Oak Hill was her home, the only one she had ever really known. All of her memories were made there. Who would she be if she lived somewhere else?

As she climbed the stairs to the apartment, she overheard Peg and John talking in the bookstore below. Their conversation was unintelligible, but the subject was inconsequential. Hearing the woman's voice reminded Simone of the courage it took to start a new life.

Squaring her shoulders, she whipped out her phone and furiously typed the text. She hit 'send' before she could change her mind. To her surprise, she received an immediate reply.

She jammed the key into the apartment's lock and pushed open the door. Dashing to her laptop, she opened the video chat app. It did not take long to make the connection.

Within seconds, Tabby's face popped up in the window on the screen. The woman's hair was a tousled tangle piled high onto her head, with loose strands of blue ringlets framing her face. An oversized, paint-splattered sweatshirt and well-worn leggings replaced her typically polished outfit. Simone realized why Tabby was so disheveled when the woman abruptly moved away from the computer and ran to the door of the room she used as a home office.

"Oy! Shut it for five minutes, will you?" Tabby screamed as she yanked open the door. "I'm on a call!"

She slammed the door and returned to her chair in front of the computer. "Sorry about that," she said. "The bloody bastards are on my last nerve today."

Biting her lip, Simone held back the laughter. The 'bloody bastards' were Tabby and her husband Jayson's two boys, aged five and seven. The children seemed to be a perpetual source of frustration since they interrupted nearly every call the women had. Today, the consternation level seemed to be at eleven. "Don't worry about it," she said. "I thought they were staying with Jayson's parents."

Tabby brushed aside a curl that tumbled onto her face. "They were until the boys fought over a penalty kick at the football match. George thought it should have been given. Reggie disagreed." She flung her hands into the air. "Or maybe it was the other way around – anyway - it got physical."

She tucked wayward strands of hair into the loose bun on her head as if ready for business. Tabby lifted her phone and re-read Simone's text. "Let's discuss your big idea."

"Well, if you're too busy with your kids, we can talk later."

Tabby shook her head as she took a sip from a mug. "It's nae bother as long as the call is short. I won't have a house left if we talk too long. The little bastards are in destruction mode." She grabbed a pen and a notepad, ready to take notes. "Now, what's your idea?"

"I've looked at your statistics for tours this season. Americans booked the majority of the tours."

"That's not a surprise, is it?"

"No, but it got me thinking. What if an American led a tour?" She leaned closer to the webcam. "The work I do for you hardly constitutes a full-time job. If I live there, though, we could expand it to something close to full time. I could maybe do two or three tours a week during the high season. Work on copy at other times. You wouldn't have to pay me much. The job could give me plenty of time to write my books."

"And, most importantly, it gives you an excuse to move to Edinburgh." Tabby winked. "We'd need a few weeks to go through the visa process. A friend of mine is an immigration attorney. I am sure she could help to speed things along."

Simone chewed her lip. "Moving to Scotland would be a big step."

Tabby grinned widely. "Aye, it would." A loud crash outside her door drew her attention. Turning, she yelled, "You have five seconds to pick up whatever you just dropped!"

She took a deep breath before returning her attention to Simone. "Robert misses you. He won't admit it, but I can tell. This whole long-distance romance thing is tough. If you lived here, it would be a little easier." She paused. "Give it some thought. I'd be thrilled to have you here, but you must decide *why* you are moving. It should be for you, not for him."

"Tabby, are you a secret feminist?"

The woman chuckled. "I have had some experience in moving for a relationship. Sometimes, it works out. A lot of times, it doesn't. You would be moving to a new country. Make sure it's for the right reason."

"What reason is that?"

"Because you have a better chance to try something new here than you do there." Her attention was drawn away again to another crash outside her door. "The job sounds like a grand idea. It is yours if you want it. I better go before the bastards tear down the bloody house."

Simone stared at the blank screen for several moments before closing the laptop lid. "Did I do the right thing?" she asked aloud.

In the stillness of the apartment, the ghost of her departed friend whispered in her ear. *You know the answer to that question, honey.*

TWENTY NINE

DESPITE SIMONE'S PREFERENCE FOR THE QUIET SOLITUDE OF HER APARTMENT, ROBERT INSISTED ON SEEING OAK HILL. He wanted to immerse himself in the area that formed who she became. He told her that she saw his homeland. Now, it was time to experience hers.

They set off on long, meandering drives along country roads that were flanked by trees and fields. The area's gentle mountains looked nothing like the rough, rocky peaks they saw when traveling in Scotland. The county's remote hollows were a far cry from the bustle of Leith's city life, as were the farms that spread across North Carolina's hills and valleys. Unlike the scraggy sheep that scaled craggy peaks in his homeland, the livestock in Oak Hill tended to be of the bovine variety. Cows in colors of ruddy brown, dirty white, and inky black lazily munched in the grassy fields.

Like their journey through Scotland, the drives allowed the couple to learn more about each other. Simone shared long-forgotten memories of the places they visited. She told him the area's history, or at least what she recalled. To her shame, her skills as a tour guide were not equal to his.

Robert talked about his upbringing. He was the middle child, with an older brother and a younger sister. He grew up outside Edinburgh in a sleepy village similar to Oak Hill. The family home butted against a forest where he and his siblings spent most of their time. He shared tales of their adventures, laughing many times at the wild stories they concocted about the fey who probably lived in the trees.

The stories made Simone smile. Growing up as an only child, she always envied people who had big families. It would have been nice to have playmates.

During one outing, they discovered a hidden spot along a trail on the Blue Ridge Parkway. The peaceful setting made it an excellent place for a picnic. They unfurled a plaid blanket upon the lush green grass. Wildflowers swayed gently in the breeze. The sweeping views of mountains painted in hues of blue and green created the perfect backdrop for multiple usies.

The food had been as delicious as the view. Their picnic was a tasty spread of artisanal sandwiches, juicy ripe fruit, and decadent homemade pastries, all courtesy of the Shaky Hillbilly.

Their exploration of the area included downtown Oak Hill. The coffee shop was a favorite spot for breakfast every morning. The couple sipped coffee or tea and watched Oak Hill's residents from the restaurant's large windows. Overhead conversations from its patrons provided lots of amusement.

Dining at the Constellation Café became a highlight of their evenings. Since they were her former employer, Simone was friends with the owners and staff. They treated the couple with special care, preparing dishes just for them. The food was wonderful and gave Robert a taste of the local ingredients.

Every night, they strolled through the streets of Oak Hill, hand in hand. The quaint shops lining the sidewalks beckoned to them with windows that displayed the handcrafted items and unique treasures inside each shop. Though Robert was not a shopper, he enjoyed looking at the crafts and even purchased a hand-carved wooden bowl for Tabby.

On evenings when Cadence featured concerts, they enjoyed live music from the region's artists. Songs played on fiddles, guitars, and mandolins always made him smile. On more than one occasion, he recognized some of the ballads as aged tunes from Ireland and Scotland that were still played there today.

Their attendance at the concerts also allowed Simone to introduce him to Peg, John, and Sylvie. Everyone loved Robert's soft Scottish accent and was delighted at his appreciation of the town, the music, and, most importantly of all, the food.

John was especially amused to hear the man's complaints about the late summer heat. "If you think this is bad, go to Southeast Asia," he had remarked. During his days in the Navy, the man must have explored every corner of the globe.

Unfortunately, time seemed to slip away like sand through their fingers. Before either of them realized it, two weeks had passed. Robert felt a deep longing to extend his stay. However, he had promised to take his father to Oban, and now that time had come. The gravestone was ready, waiting to be unveiled at his grandfather's grave after its installation.

As a reason for leaving, it was a good one. He had taken the tour guide position over the summer solely to earn the funds necessary to create the gravestone. Finding love with her had been an unexpected bonus. Their adventure through Scotland's picturesque hills and iconic lochs had filled their days with newfound love. Their discovery of his grandfather's story solved a painful family mystery.

His trip to Oban with his father symbolized the culmination of a long and often painful journey for the family. Simone wished he could linger just a little longer in Oak Hill. Yet, she understood that it would be selfish to ask him to stay. With a heavy heart, she swallowed her disappointment and offered him a sincere wish for safe travels.

THEIR ONLY CONFLICT HAPPENED ON THE FINAL DAY OF HIS VISIT. Robert asked to see the home where she grew up. Simone flatly refused. The last thing she wanted was to introduce him to her father. She had had zero contact with the man and wanted to keep it that way. He accepted her refusal without comment.

Each moment that day tasted sweeter, even though his impending departure hung over them like a dark cloud. It threatened to overshadow their time together. Despite their efforts to remain upbeat and cheerful, an air of melancholy lingered around them, making their attempts seem hollow.

That evening, their words dwindled to mere whispers. The seriousness of the moment eventually silenced their voices. When they came together, it was a slow and deliberate dance. Each movement was filled with tenderness as they savored every kiss and every touch. They lingered in this shared intimacy, unwilling to face the new day that would bring separation. The simple joy of being together for a few precious moments was all that mattered. Concerns of the outside world disappeared.

Wrapped in each other's arms all night, they expressed undying love and dedicated themselves to their relationship. The road ahead would be difficult. They had navigated it thus far. It could be done. It *must* be done, Robert repeatedly told her. Living on opposite sides of the sea couldn't impede the rare gift of their love.

For days, Simone had wanted to discuss the possibility of moving to Scotland. Something always stopped her. Was it fear she might offer false hope when she wasn't sure if she could do it? After all, Tabby had advised her against making a rash decision of moving simply for a relationship.

That last night together, it felt right to finally broach the subject. She gathered the courage and said, "Tabby and I were talking about me moving to Leith. How do you feel about it?"

He slipped out of her arms, leaned over to the bedside table, and switched on the lamp. "Whoa, that's a big deal!" he exclaimed, propping his pillow against the headboard. "What prompted this?"

Simone lifted herself, arranging her pillows so that she could face him. She took her time, shy about discussing something that seemed more like a dream than something she could really do. "My father is moving to Mexico," she replied. "I don't really have a reason to stay here."

"There is nothing I would love more than for you to live in Leith." He lifted his hand. "But, your father's move to Mexico is not a good reason."

She lowered her head. When she played the scene in her mind, he was thrilled. She hadn't expected a negative reaction. "Why?" she asked. "There's nothing here for me anymore."

"Don't you mean there's no one here to take care of? Moving to Scotland just so you can take care of me is not a good reason. Eventually, you will resent me, just like you do your father."

Simone pulled the bedcovers closer to her body. She couldn't look him in the eyes.

"Happiness is something you must find in yourself before you can find it in others," he said, stroking her hand.

She lifted her eyes to his. "I am happy when we are together."

He shook his head. "What about when I am not here? You must be happy then, too."

"I thought you would be thrilled if I moved." Disappointment was a bitter pill to swallow, but the truth of his words could not be denied.

She shook her head. She hadn't planned on having yet another discussion about what she wanted from life. "I get what you are saying, though," she said, her voice filled with resignation. "I promise that I won't move unless I can say it is for me, not you. Fair enough?"

He slid closer and wrapped his arms around her. "Yes," he said. "You know that I only want the best for you, don't you?"

"I do."

"Good." He adjusted the pillow. "Now, we have to leave for the airport in a couple of hours. Let's try to get some rest. It's going to be a long day."

"You get settled," Simone said as she flung away the covers. "I'll be right back."

She headed for the bathroom and closed the door. The conversation had not gone as planned. After splashing water on her face, she stared into the mirror. "Now what?" she whispered.

She wiped the water from her face. His words rang in her ears. In her heart, she knew her happiness should come first, but ever since she was 16, taking care of others had been her priority. Dreams of doing something fulfilling were just that – dreams. The opportunity to make them into reality was possible. Was she ready to try?

"What if I fail?" she asked the mirror.

So what? Emma's ghost whispered into her ear. *I gave you enough money to at least try, sweetheart.*

Her departed friend's words were the truth. Returning to Oak Hill was always an option if she moved to Scotland and hated it. She could afford it.

She saw the fear in her eyes. The path before her was one on which she had never trod. It could lead to heartbreak. Or, it could lead to happiness beyond anything she ever could have imagined for herself. However, the journey could not begin until she took the first step.

When she mentioned moving to Robert, she thought it represented taking that first step. His words popped that balloon, yet he was right. She needed to figure out what brought her joy.

Simone briefly closed her eyes and thought about the moment with Peg, when she described a scene that made her happy. She knew what to do. It was the 'doing' that terrified her.

"You must make the jump," she said to herself. She switched off the bathroom light and headed back to bed.

It could be months before she shared a bed with Robert again, if she didn't move to Scotland. She snuggled close to him and reveled in the feel of his warm, soft skin. He breathed slowly and deeply in his sleep, untroubled by the doubts and fears that plagued her. As it had been since her return to Oak Hill, big decisions needed to be made.

But not right now. Simone's eyes grew heavy. Soon, her frenzied brain quieted. Her breathing slowed to match that of her companion's as sleep finally offered sweet release.

THE DRIVE TO THE AIRPORT FELT

ALARMINGLY SWIFT, ALMOST AS IF TIME ITSELF CONSPIRED TO HASTEN ROBERT'S DEPARTURE. Both he and Simone wished time would stop. They could not speak during the drive or while they unloaded his luggage. The pain of their impending separation was too great.

Once inside the busy terminal, the sad reminder of the distance that would soon separate them could no longer be avoided. They stood amidst the crush of travelers and exchanged promises to put in the necessary work on their long-distance relationship. They reaffirmed that Simone would visit in just a few months, as if the promise lessened the pain. "I cannot wait for you to meet my family," he told her. "They are going to love you as much as I do."

Simone smiled nervously, not wanting to mention what might happen *after* her visit. The unspoken future hung heavily in the air. It was too daunting to discuss at the moment.

The final boarding call echoed through the terminal, a voice cutting through air filled with emotion. With lingering reluctance, she loosened her grip on his waist. He kissed her one last time before walking toward the security line that would lead him away from her.

She stood rooted in place. Her eyes strained to catch another glimpse of him long after he vanished. Maybe he would turn back and rush into her arms. It was a desperate wish. The moments eventually passed, and he did not return.

With a deep sigh, she turned away. The familiar heaviness settled on her shoulders. The brief reprieve from her worries was over, and the old ache of uncertainty crept in.

As Simone made her way to her car, two questions burned in her brain: Would her life continue in the comforting familiarity of Oak Hill, or would she embark on an adventure into the unknown that waited for her in Leith?

THIRTY

SIMONE SAT ON THE STEPS OF THE HOME SHE ONCE SHARED WITH EMMA. The lazy summer sun slowly sank over purple mountains, its rays streaking across the sky in soft shades of orange, pink, and blue. The yard's green grass, taller than usual, waved in the light breeze that offered a balm to the August heat. Even at the late hour of the day, the air was so hot that it wrapped around her and squeezed out all of the moisture from her body. Tiny beads of sweat trickled down her back. A glass of icy water would have been a blessing.

Her discomfort over the weather was the least of her worries. Robert had been gone for nearly a week. She was adrift in his absence. When he was there, it gave her an excuse to think of anything besides her life. Now, making up her mind was unavoidable.

Sylvie was right. She needed a new tune. Her old excuses about postponing her life so that she could care for her father or Emma were no longer valid. Taking the big leap to find new passions in life was frightening.

Emma's generous inheritance ensured she had plenty of money, even if she stayed in Oak Hill. She could sit in the apartment and daydream all day long. She could travel to Scotland to see Robert whenever she liked, for as long as the relationship survived. Her life would be comfortable and familiar.

A long-distance relationship would only work for so long. Someone eventually had to make the big jump – either move to be nearer to the other person or call it off. At some point, a significant decision would be required. Would she move? Would Robert? Or would they separate?

Simone dropped her head into her hands. Visiting her former home seemed like a good idea. She had returned to where she last felt certainty about her life. Everything had changed, though. The new owners had not yet moved into the house. The person she wanted there – Emma – was gone forever.

Months of analysis finally yielded a surprising result. For the first time, she realized that her old life was a mess, too. Nothing was sure back then. Every day was lived without any thought given to the future. It was all a slow shuffle to get from one day to the next. Life just felt easier because she could always blame her inaction on others. Caring for someone else rather than herself was her default move. The problem was, all those people were gone. There was no one else to blame but herself. What was she supposed to do with her life?

It's time, Emma's voice whispered in the breeze

that lifted the hair at her neck and offered soothing comfort from the August heat.

"I had hoped you would come," she said aloud as she lifted her head.

I will always be there for you.

"Thank you for the gifts you gave me – the trip, the money." She looked at the house. "A home."

Home isn't a place, sweetie, the ghost whispered in the wind. *It's the feeling you have in your heart.*

"I don't know where home is anymore."

Simone told her about the opportunity in Leith. Offering tours to other Americans and spending days off exploring the city and writing novels were things she would have never imagined doing. The opportunity to be closer to Robert was a bonus. Yet, the thought of leaving behind the familiar life in Oak Hill terrified her. What if she hated the job? What if she couldn't think of ideas for novels? What if Robert and she broke up? What if….

Here's a 'what if' for you…What if you are happy? Emma's ghost pointed out.

The inner monologue of negativity halted as the words pierced her brain. All of her adult life, she had lived in fear. Invariably, something bad always happened. It was wiser to tamp down any expectation that hopes or dreams might be realized. But the inheritance changed all of that. With the money, she had the power to make those dreams a reality.

The crunch of gravel on the driveway interrupted her musings. Lifting her hand to her face, she shielded her eyes from the sun. She recognized the blue Mini

Cooper that eased to a stop in front of her. Sylvie hopped out of the car.

"I thought you might be here," she said as she climbed the steps and sat beside Simone.

"I wanted to talk with Emma." She gave Sylvie a sideways glance. "You don't think that's kooky, do you?"

"No, I talk to her all the time," Sylvie nudged her shoulder. "Did she answer you?"

"Basically, she said I should stop whining. I might be happy if I left Oak Hill."

"Good advice."

"I know, but…."

"Oh, not one more 'but' from you," Sylvie said, clearly exasperated. "I've been married three times. The last one damn near killed me. When Ted died, my heart broke into a million pieces. I wasn't sure if I wanted to go through that heartache again."

"Then, I had a good cry and picked myself up off the floor. I'm still young." At Simone's snort of derision, she added defensively, "Hey, it ain't over 'til it's over!"

A hint of a smile teased the corners of her mouth as she continued, "I wouldn't mind finding another fella and still have time to do it. I cannot let a heartache keep me from the thrill of new love."

"I'm not as strong as you, Sylvie."

"Are you kidding?" She rolled her eyes. "You are one of the strongest people I know."

"Why do you think that?"

"Honey, after your mom died, you took care of that sorry excuse of a father," Sylvie said, an angry look on her face. Like Emma, she witnessed firsthand how poorly the man treated his only child. "And, when my sister got sick, you cared for her, too. You never complained. You never walked away, even when things were bad."

"Moving to another country is a huge step."

"Yes, it is." Sylvie took her hand. "You are too busy thinking about everything that could go wrong to see how great it will be when everything goes right."

"You are an eternal optimist."

"Is there any other way to live?" They laughed at her remark. "What do you have to lose?"

"Well, I could be miserable and decide it was all a big mistake."

"So?"

"So? That's a pretty big deal!"

"No, it isn't." Sylvie shrugged. "If you aren't happy there, then move back. I don't see what the big deal is."

Simone stared at the woman, hating how much Sylvie was right. Moving back *was* financially possible. It hadn't taken much of the inheritance to pay off her student loans. She had plenty of money left. Still, she hesitated.

"What about my father?" She grasped for any impediment at this point. The woman's logic was too sound. "He might need me."

The intense look on Sylvie's face sent a chill

creeping up her spine. An uneasy feeling settled in the pit of her stomach. She had never witnessed the woman's fury before. It was a startling transformation.

"You haven't been by the house lately." Sylvie's expression softened slightly as she explained, "The sale of the house was barely finalized before Susan and he had packed their bags and vanished. That man is long gone, honey."

The revelation pierced her heart more deeply than she had anticipated. The realization that her father hadn't even had the decency to inform her of his departure stung. The abruptness of the exit was brutal. Yet, in her heart, she knew the man would drift away from her life only to reappear when he needed something again. That is, if she stayed in Oak Hill.

With her head bowed, she whispered softly, "I see." The conflict raging inside her was impossible to express. Abandonment from her father was hard to accept, but it could make her decision to leave so much easier. After all, she could vanish, too.

Sylvie tried to be kind. "There's nothing to keep you in Oak Hill anymore."

Deep in her heart, Simone understood. "What about Robert?" she asked. "It might be too much for him."

Sylvie squeezed her hand, a grip surprisingly firm for a woman in her 70s. "Moving to Scotland should be about the opportunities it will bring you, not just a chance to see your fella. Take some advice from an old lady: never let how someone else feels about you determine your happiness."

"I have a job waiting for me if I want it."

"I hope you aren't going to be a waitress. You can stay here and do that."

Simone chuckled. "No, I met the owner of the company who organized my tour. I've been helping her with some copy. I could also lead a few tours for the Americans who book with her company. I would still have time to write my own stuff."

Sylvie released her hand and descended the steps. "It sounds like you have it figured out," she said as she walked around her car. "What are you waiting for? Make the jump."

As she watched Sylvie drive away, the once-gentle breeze shifted to a full gust. The wind nearly shoved her from the steps. Rising, she asked, "You too?"

No answer came from Emma's ghost. Simone didn't need one.

THIRTY ONE

THE ELECTRIC KETTLE BUBBLED LOUDLY, THE SOUND ECHOING AGAINST THE TILED KITCHEN WALLS. Simone carefully lifted the kettle from its base and poured the hot liquid into a ceramic teapot. The tea leaves danced and twirled in the diffuser, releasing a pleasant aroma. With care, she popped the lid onto the pot. Grabbing her phone, she set a timer for four minutes. Letting the tea steep too long would yield a bitter brew, and she was determined to get it just right.

Her new friend Tabby Simpson watched from one of the kitchen stools. "I have trained you well," she said with a playful smile.

Simone returned the smile as she retrieved two mugs from the cabinet. "If I'm going to live here, I better learn how to make it right," she replied, placing the mugs on the smooth countertop. "Besides, after everything you did for me, I can at least offer you a good cup of tea."

Tabby waved her hand dismissively, a twinkle in her eyes. "Are you kidding? I had an absolute blast." She leaned back, surveying the apartment. "It was fun browsing for places to live and shopping for everything you needed. I hope you like what I found."

"Without your help, it would have been so hard," she admitted. It was true. The apartment...or 'flat,' as they were called there...was a little gem tucked away in Leith. Like Robert's place, it was in a former factory that had been converted into flats. Each one featured elevated loft spaces for the bedrooms and bathrooms and petite kitchens below. The kitchens were especially nice with their small islands and accompanying wooden stools.

Each flat had soaring ceilings, held aloft by the original steel beams, that created an airy atmosphere. The small flat looked much bigger than it was as a result. Exposed ductwork snaked along the ceiling, a reminder of the building's industrial past. A wall of tall windows flooded the interior with bright sunlight whenever the clouds parted.

When Simone had called Tabby to share her decision to move, she was astounded by how quickly the woman had found the flat, furnished it with all the essentials, and even secured the necessary work visa. All she had to do was buy a plane ticket, which should have been easy.

Completing the task proved more daunting than anticipated. It was one thing to fantasize about moving to Leith, but another to leap into the unknown.

Sylvie was her ally in Oak Hill. She had been over the moon about Simone's decision. She helped manage the details and packed a few belongings into boxes that would be shipped later.

"Honey, you better stay in touch," she said, her eyes shimmering with excitement and sadness as they hugged goodbye at the airport.

The soft chime of her phone jolted Simone from her thoughts. She poured the fragrant tea into the mugs. The steam curled around her hand as she handed a mug to Tabby.

"Have you seen Robert yet?" Tabby asked, taking a delicate sip of the tea.

"No."

"I thought you guys had video calls every day."

"We do. I've blurred my background so he doesn't know I'm here."

"Clever," Tabby acknowledged before taking another sip. "How have you managed to avoid bumping into him? He lives just around the corner."

"I only venture out when I know he's at work."

"Damn, that's dull," Tabby teased.

"You spend your evenings watching the same cartoons on an endless loop." Simone frowned. "That sounds pretty dull to me."

"Hey, those cartoons are very entertaining. You should babysit sometime and see for yourself," the woman retorted with a wink.

She remembered the chaos caused by Tabby's children during every video call. The idea of being alone with them was overwhelming. "No, thank you," she quickly said.

"You've been here for a week." Tabby placed her empty mug in the sink. "Why are you waiting?"

Simone nervously traced her finger along the rim of her mug. "I don't know," she finally answered.

"Yes, you do. Say it."

"I'm afraid."

Tabby shook her head as she slipped into her jacket. "You are ridiculous."

"Excuse me?" Simone asked, taken aback by the candor of the remark.

"You dared to move here. Now you're afraid to tell your boyfriend. What's wrong with you?" Her friend's words were firm but laced with affection.

She averted her eyes. "Geez, that's harsh, Tabby."

"Just tell him!" Her friend insisted, yanking open the door and slamming it shut as she exited the flat.

Shaking her head, Simone picked up her mug and wandered towards one of the large windows. She spotted Tabby on the street below. When their eyes met, she raised her middle finger and laughed. Her friend grinned broadly and returned the gesture.

She moved away from the window and settled onto the plush sofa. Leaving everything behind in Oak Hill and starting anew in Scotland had taken immense courage. For perhaps the first time in her life, the uncertainty of her future no longer terrified her. The possibilities ahead filled her with a sense of exhilaration.

Unfortunately, her confidence about her new life did not extend to her relationship with Robert.

Anxiety gnawed her stomach. How would he react when he discovered she was here? Would he misconstrue her decision as a demand for swift progress in their relationship? Would he think she expected marriage? It was the last thing she wanted at the moment. She needed more time with him, not a ring.

Regretfully, she realized there was only one way to discover his feelings. The move was intended to mark the beginning of a new adventure. She didn't travel across the ocean to spend her days hiding in a flat while ruminating on what Robert may or may not think about it. The days of mental torture were behind her. As part of the move, she vowed never again to fret about things that may or may not happen.

Time to take the jump, Simone told herself as she placed the mug on the table and headed for the door.

SIMONE DREW A SHAKY BREATH. It was Saturday, so Robert would be home. They were supposed to have a video chat in ten minutes. He was probably inside his flat, preparing a cup of tea before setting up the laptop on the dining table. His hair might be wet from a shower, tousled from a rough rub against the bathroom towel.

He looked so sexy after a shower, with his hair in a wild tangle on his head. She remembered how water formed little beads on his muscular chest and glided down his stomach. Closing her eyes, she recalled one lovely, after-shower moment they shared when he visited her.

Opening her eyes, she mentally shook herself. It was silly to stand outside his door, thinking about those moments, when he was literally within reach. She swallowed hard as she extended her hand and knocked on the door with more confidence than she felt.

When he opened the door and saw her standing there, he gasped in surprise.

"My guide was supposed to take me to Iona but didn't," she said, trying to sound witty. "Would you take me instead?"

"What are you doing here?"

"Aren't you going to invite me inside?"

"I'm sorry," he mumbled. He swung the door wider and motioned for her to come inside the flat.

Simone was surprised her wobbly legs still worked. She followed him as he headed for the living room. They sat on the sofa, a little distance between them. He continued to stare at her in disbelief.

"Video chats can never replace face-to-face time," she said, still trying to keep the mood light. "Don't you agree?"

"Aye." He rubbed his hands against his pants and averted his eyes. "So…."

Like a bolt of lightning, a terrible thought hit her. Maybe he wasn't alone. Perhaps another woman was there, and Robert wanted her to leave. She jumped to her feet. "Oh, I am sorry. I shouldn't be here."

She raced for the door, mentally chastising herself. What the hell had she been thinking? Robert was a handsome man. He had probably found someone else and hadn't told her yet.

He grabbed her hand and pleaded, "Simone, wait."

"No, I'll leave," she whispered, avoiding his gaze. "Just pretend I am not here."

Her hand was on the doorknob. He knocked it away. "You just surprised me; that's all." He hugged her, adding, "I am thrilled to see you."

"If someone else is here…."

"No one else is here." He pointed to the laptop on the dining table. "We were going to chat soon, remember?"

"Come back to the sofa," he urged. "Let's talk."

Although she dreaded the conversation that would follow, she accompanied him to the sofa. It had not occurred to her that he might have found someone else. Robert once told her his last relationship ended because he wanted to settle down and have a family, which would be impossible in a long-distance relationship. Perhaps their situation was more than he could bear. When she planned to visit over the holidays, he probably intended to break up with her. He was the kind of man who would want to do that sort of thing in person, not over a video chat. *You are such a fool,* she chastised herself.

He grinned widely. "When did you arrive?" Looking back to the door, he said, "You don't have any luggage. I hope you aren't staying at a hotel. I'd love to have you stay with me."

"I moved here."

"Ok," he said, taking a deep breath and swallowing hard. "When I visited, you told me that you were considering it. What finally prompted you to do it?"

"There's nothing for me in Oak Hill – and everything for me here, in Leith."

"Wow, that's…." Robert struggled for words. "If you can be happy here, then that's great news."

She suppressed the urge to smack him. His current reaction was underwhelming. "You understand that I moved across an ocean to be here, right?" she said, her voice rising. "I didn't just come here on a whim."

"When we discussed this, I told you that I didn't want you to move only because you wanted to be with me." He searched her eyes. "Please tell me why you moved here."

"Tabby gave me a job. I'm going to take Americans on tours around Edinburgh. I will continue to help her with the copy, too. This is a great compromise. I can work for her and still have time to write my own books."

"I didn't realize you wanted to be a tour guide."

"I worked as a waitress for a long time. I am used to dealing with the public." She shrugged. "I decided it might be fun to try something new. Besides, it's not as if I'll always be doing tours. I will be writing, too."

She shook her head. "Look, Robert, I realize this whole thing is unexpected." She eased to the edge of the sofa. "I just wanted you to know that I am here. Maybe we can get together sometime."

"What are you saying?" He leaned closer to her. "Did you come all this way to break up with me?"

She couldn't resist laughing as she answered, "No!"

He heaved a sigh of what sounded like relief. He fell back onto the sofa. Was it possible she had misread the situation?

"Robert, are you seeing someone else?" She decided to stop beating around the bush and ask the burning question.

"Absolutely not! I apologize if I wasn't as enthusiastic as you had hoped." He pointed to the laptop. "I thought we'd be using that infernal device to chat today. I never expected you to show up at my door. Forgive me, but I just need to hear the words. Are you finally happy with yourself?"

Simone stared deeply into his eyes. "I am a work in progress," she said. "It will take a while for me to sort out my feelings about my past and create a new life for myself. I decided that I should do it here, not in Oak Hill. I have lots of opportunities to do all of those things in Leith. I really believe that I can find happiness here. I'm ready for a big adventure."

She leaned closer. "And I would like to take the adventure with you."

He kissed her, slowly and thoroughly. The kiss left no doubt that he was glad to see her. How often had she wanted to feel his soft, warm lips pressed against hers and have his strong arms wrapped around her?

When Simone withdrew, somewhat reluctantly, from the kiss, she gazed into his eyes. They burned with love and passion, not disappointment.

Still, she hesitated. Uncertainty suddenly cast a fresh doubt into her mind. For so long, the decision to move to Scotland revolved around her dreams and aspirations. She now recognized that another person's life was intertwined with her own. It would be selfish to ignore his feelings. After all, hadn't she spent years angry at her father for ignoring hers?

Out of respect for him, she had to consider the impact of her decision on his life. Her voice trembled slightly as she said, "If my living here is a problem, please tell me. I don't want you to feel trapped or obligated to stay in this relationship if it's not what you truly want."

"I moved here because I needed a fresh start." When the words tumbled out of her mouth, she discovered that she really meant them. The new challenges were exciting, not terrifying. "We can end it now. I will cherish what we had for the rest of my life."

"I do not understand what you are saying to me." His voice was shaky. "I love you. I want to be a part of your life."

Months ago, on the beach in Oban, she had felt the carefully constructed wall around her heart tumble like the cairns swallowed by the relentless waves of the sea. As she sat across from him now, she realized that a few stubborn stones still clung to the fragile barrier. They prevented her from fully embracing the possibility of love.

Life had taught her hard lessons. Whenever she allowed someone to slip past her defenses, they either let her down like her father had or were taken from her too soon like her beloved friend Emma. Should she close off her heart forever? With tears welling in his eyes, she finally believed that Robert wanted to be with her.

Although she did not realize it at the time, her decision to move to Leith had been deeply interwoven with her feelings for him. The love they shared was rare and beautiful. She would lose an extraordinary chance to experience that love if she turned him away. Could she forgive herself if she did?

She knew there was only one answer. "I love you too," Simone whispered. She let the wall around her heart disintegrate as she melted into his waiting arms.

EPILOGUE

One year later

SIMONE SEALED THE LAST CARDBOARD BOX AND ADDED IT TO THE PILE BESIDE THE DOOR. She looked around the flat. Its furniture was covered with white sheets to protect it from dust. All of her things had been packed in boxes. The movers would arrive later that afternoon to take the items to the cottage Robert and she bought in the country. The property had a large shed in the back garden where he could make furniture and a sunny conservatory where she could write.

The years since her mother's death had become a faded memory of a different, sadder part of her life. Time spent caring for her father and then enduring Emma's cancer battle taught her how to survive. In Leith, she learned to thrive.

Emma's inheritance allowed her to create a life

beyond anything she could have imagined. Working as a tour guide in Edinburgh during the summer was an absolute delight. Exploring hidden parts of the city that were away from the typical tourist haunts gave her an appreciation of its centuries of history. Dealing with sightseers certainly had challenges, but the positives outweighed the negatives. After all, her "office" was a beautiful city steeped in history.

Another opportunity had presented itself, too. Simone invested some of the inheritance in the Castles and Cairns Touring Company. With the infusion of cash, Tabby hired another tour guide and offered longer, multi-day trips around Scotland. She also hired a marketing consultant to broaden the company's outreach efforts. Owning a share in a business was never something Simone imagined happening, but it offered an undeniable sense of empowerment.

Although she had not found a publisher or literary agent yet, she had not given up. On days when she wasn't guiding tourists around town or working with Tabby on the latest marketing campaign, she passed hours writing her own stories. Time spent walking the cobbled streets or sitting in secluded corners at coffee shops gave her fresh ideas that stimulated her imagination.

Would she have tried any of these things without the money she inherited to support her? Ruefully, she doubted it.

Of course, venturing to Scotland on the road trip was the impetus for everything. Without the trip, she would never have met Tabby or seen the possibilities of a new career far from Oak Hill.

And she wouldn't have met Robert.

She didn't try to stop the broad smile that spread across her face. *Robert.* The man had taken the road trip solely for the money, a shared purpose. After all, she wouldn't have taken the trip if the million-dollar inheritance hadn't required it. They both had ulterior motives, yet ended up discovering a profound love.

Simone was so lost in happy thoughts that she did not hear Tabby enter the flat. She jumped when the woman cleared her throat.

"I dropped by to offer sustenance," Tabby said, waving a brown bag in one hand and a beverage carrier holding two cups in the other.

"And here I thought you came by to help with packing."

Tabby cackled as she unloaded the goodies on the kitchen's island.

They settled onto the stools in front of the kitchen's island. Tabby had picked up warm blueberry scones and hot tea from a nearby bakery. The ladies devoured the delicious treats in seconds.

She pointed to Simone's hand and said, "Let me see it."

Simone extended her left hand. "It was his grandmother's ring." The small diamond in the engagement ring's center sparkled in the sunlight. The sides of the white gold ring were accented with three channel-set round diamonds. The ring may have been simple, but its significance was not. Every time she looked at it, she became a little misty-eyed.

"It's lovely," Tabby said. "When's the wedding?"

"We are in no rush," Simone answered. "We want to get the cottage ready before the wedding. Some of my friends from Oak Hill will need a place to stay."

"Who's coming?"

"Well, Peg and John Sweeney will probably come. I am certain Sylvie will be here, too."

"Sylvie?" Tabby tapped the side of her cup, her nose crinkled as she struggled to recall a fact. "Is she Emma's sister?"

"Yes."

"It will be fun to meet her in person."

Simone cocked an eyebrow. "What?"

"She didn't tell you?" At the shake of Simone's head, she explained, "Emma and Sylvie were deeply involved in planning the tour. When your friend couldn't take the trip, I thought Sylvie would come instead."

"I never expected they would send you." She patted Simone's hand. "Don't worry. I am really glad that they did."

"Anyway…they were very curious about who the tour guide would be. They wanted to see a picture." Tabby took a sip of tea. "So, I snapped a photo of Robert and sent it along with a summary of his qualifications. They must have liked what they saw because they insisted that he provide the tour. They even paid extra to make sure he did it.

Simone's mouth fell open in disbelief as she gazed at the sparkling ring adorning her finger. The diamonds' brilliance caught the light and cast a kaleidoscope of colors on the floor. The cool metal still felt strange against her warm skin. How could Emma have known that she would meet the love of her life?

"What about your father? Is he coming?" Tabby had no idea that a simple question like that would infuriate Simone. It wasn't the woman's fault. How could she have known about the father and daughter's long and painful history? The topic was never discussed.

"Doubtful. I don't even know where he lives, so I cannot send him a wedding invitation," Simone replied, her voice tinged with sadness. Ever since that last afternoon at her childhood home, they hadn't seen or spoken to each other. He had vanished entirely, not just from her life but from the lives of everyone in Oak Hill. Her father had ghosted those who genuinely cared for him, the friends and family who had reached out over the years and watched over him when she went on the trip to Scotland.

Simone could almost imagine the hushed whispers among the townspeople as they tried to piece together what had happened. She knew him too well. There was no doubt in her mind that he would resurface one day when he needed something. To him, it was as if their past ties mattered only in moments of desperation.

Now, in Scotland, she felt like she had turned a new page in her life. She had begun a chapter full of possibilities. The pain of her past was a distant memory. Here, the landscapes were breathtaking, the air crisp, and her heart was beginning to heal. She had created a life where no ghosts from her previous life could haunt her. For the first time in years, she felt free.

"Well, that's his loss," Tabby said and did not probe further, letting the painful topic pass. Instead, she collected their empty cups and stuffed them into the bag. She scanned the flat and commented, "It looks like you have packed everything. Are you ready to go?"

"Yes," Simone replied as she slid off the stool. "I'll walk out with you."

Tabby approached the door, chatting about her sons' latest football matches. Her voice became a steady hum in the background as Simone took another look around the flat.

She felt a surge of nostalgia. If Robert wasn't at her flat, then she stayed at his. They enjoyed many takeaway dinners at the kitchen's island or movie nights curled together on the sofa. Her first year in Scotland was spent there. Leaving the place felt sad, just as it had when she left Oak Hill.

Lifting her left hand, she smiled at the sight of the ring. In one final gesture, her friend had guided her there and set the stage for the amazing life ahead. Emma's push propelled her into a career she loved and into the arms of a man who treated her with tenderness and respect.

"Thank you," Simone whispered as she closed the door to the flat.

A Fortune to Claim

LIKE THE WRITER?

Search for more novels from *C. Renee Freeman* on Amazon. Available in both e-book and paperback versions.

For historical fiction, check out the *Through the Mist* series:

> *Through the Mist: Restoration*
>
> *Through the Mist: Adrift (a novella)*
>
> *Through the Mist: Reunion*
>
> *Through the Mist: Reflection*
>
> *Through the Mist: Redemption*
>
> *Through the Mist: Christmas Eve*

For contemporary romance, check out these books:

> *Love at the Woolly Bookworm Shop*
>
> *A Fortune to Claim*

Expect more novels in the future. Happy reading!

A Fortune to Claim

ACKNOWLEDGMENTS

Writers often find themselves deep in their own thoughts, and I can certainly relate. I sometimes get lost in my own world. Fortunately, I have wonderful people in my life who remind me when it's time to step out and connect with others.

To H. - I can't thank you enough for always being there to listen. Whether I'm sharing ideas about my books, chatting about family, or rambling about my dog and my latest obsessions, you always listen and never tell me to hush. Your support means the world to me. You give me the confidence to chase my dreams.

To Sir Chewie of Bacca - I tend to be a little absorbed in writing. Ignoring you for five minutes is horrible. Let's head out for a walkie and, of course, enjoy some well-deserved belly rubs and treats.

A special shout-out to my Aunt Lib and my sister Amanda - I'm so grateful for your encouragement!

Lastly, I want to extend my heartfelt thanks to everyone who picked up this book. Your time and continued interest in my books mean everything to me. I hope you thoroughly enjoy the stories.

A Fortune to Claim

ABOUT THE WRITER

C. Renee Freeman lives in a small town located in the mountains of Western North Carolina. So far, she has written eight books, six in the *Through the Mist* series and two contemporary novels.

Writing gives her an opportunity to escape into another time and place. When she is not writing, she enjoys cooking, reading, spending time with her dog, and researching topics for her next book.

She begins each book by asking questions. What drives people to do the things they do? What would it be like to live that person's life?

You can learn more about the goings-on in the writer's life by checking out her website, *creneefreeman.com*, or visiting her on Facebook.